DATE DUE

The

The Gospel According to Sydney Welles

A Novel

Susi Rajah

BLOOMSBURY

Published by Bloomsbury USA, New York
Distributed to the trade by Holtzbrinck Publishers

All papers used by Bloomsbury USA are natural, recyclable products made from wood grown in well-managed forests. The manufacturing processes conform to the environmental regulations of the country of origin.

LIBRARY OF CONGRESS CATALOGING-IN-PUBLICATION DATA HAS BEEN APPLIED FOR.

ISBN-10: 1-59691-347-9
ISBN-13: 978-1-59691-347-9

First U.S. Edition 2007

10 9 8 7 6 5 4 3 2 1

Typeset by Westchester Book Group
Printed in the United States of America by Quebecor World Fairfield

For Corey

It's a typical LA story. Girl meets actor. They keep meeting. Relationship summits are held. But before they can walk, hand in hand, toward a scenic solar event, another girl-meets-actor story begins. Another girl. Same actor.

She turns out to be the dreaded triple threat—large breasts, small vocabulary, no visible panty line. He turns out to be looking for exactly those traits in a partner. And I, it turned out, got dumped with a weak improvisation on the "it's not you, it's me" speech. So weak, it confirmed what I'd suspected all along. He wasn't a very good actor.

Days passed before I found someone else—a writer. Now I get to enjoy being with someone with even higher levels of self-obsession and insecurity than an actor, only without the hindrance of nice pecs and a cute butt.

Charles is the perpetrator of a newspaper column. A day or so after I was dumped, and still sore at men in general, I read his column and knew he was the last man on earth I wanted to be involved with. It followed that a relationship was in the cards.

The column went on and on about how girls are doing better in school than boys due, I suspect, to girls now being allowed to attend school. What annoyed me—along with the pie charts—was the way the column ended, with the recommendation that something must be done to help the poor boys.

I found it so annoying, I wrote a letter to the newspaper suggesting alternative uses for the column and its author. Knowing how these things work, I doubted the letter would get read. I certainly didn't expect Charles to answer me with a letter of his own.

He didn't expect it either. He has a policy of only answering letters from readers publicly, within the safety of his column. There are, apparently, sick people out there who, given the encouragement of two-way communication, will stalk anyone possessing a modicum of fame, even a newspaper columnist. Charles said he knew he was making a mistake answering a letter written by someone so clearly disturbed, but he couldn't help himself. I'd pissed him off in fewer words than anyone ever had before.

He wanted to know if I was one of those bitter career women without a life, who sat home nights writing letters to newspapers and talking back to the television because there was no possible way I could get a date. He asked if my take-out menus were arranged in alphabetical order and how many cats I owned, or would I prefer that he called them my familiars?

My take-out menus aren't arranged alphabetically. They're sorted by cuisine.

I replied: I wrote that letter at work, hence the letterhead, idiot, and I have a fabulous life because I have a career and the good fortune never to have dated a newspaper columnist. If I'm at all bitter, it'd be a result of dealing with misogynists like you, and no, I don't own any cats, but if you don't like them, I'll go out and get one immediately.

He wrote back with the guess that I last had sex a decade ago. In return, I sent him a note suggesting his penis was small. From there we started to correspond regularly.

He wrote: You wouldn't know a penis if you sat on one. Besides, I've never had any complaints, and, unlike you, I've had sex this century. My girlfriend is extremely happy, thank you.

I wrote: I admit it. Women aren't as penis-fixated as men fantasize we are. I can't name a woman who wouldn't trade one for its weight in chocolate cake. That said, I know enough to sense you don't measure up. By the way, it must be a dreadful inconvenience to have to inflate your girlfriend every night.

He wrote: An inflatable doll would be preferable to someone as cynical as you, depending, of course, on what you look like. What do you look like?

I wrote: I agree. The doll would be the better intellectual match. Women with IQs this side of 75 would have men like you scratching your heads, that is if you could tear yourself away from scratching your balls. I can't believe you asked me what I look like. How would your girlfriend feel if she found out? It'd take the wind out of her and then where would you be? You're very lucky she can't read.

He wrote: I take it from your answer you're not even remotely attractive. Munchkins must run screaming whenever you appear. Do you like scaring the little guys? Or do you force them to date you? No doubt your last boyfriend was chopped up into pieces and buried in your backyard when he tried to escape. And please, tell me, what makes you think my girlfriend can't read? Is literacy not a trait you demand of your partners? You can't afford to be that picky?

I wrote: If she could read, she'd read your column and wouldn't be able to bring herself to sleep with you, even if she thought as much of your penis as you do. However, I agree with you on one point. Literacy is an overrated ability. Men only misuse it. You're a shining example of this. And, for your information, I'm extraordinarily good-looking from certain angles, I'm kind to munchkins, and no, my ex-boyfriend isn't fertilizer in my backyard, but that's an excellent suggestion, thank you.

Our relationship blossomed from there. We may have started out disliking each other, but over time we found we liked disliking each other more than we liked disliking anyone else. We've been involved for a little more than a year now. Of course, Charles and I have never had sex. For that to happen we'd have to actually meet.

I've never suggested to Charles that we meet up, mostly because he's never suggested it either. He writes to me every week without fail, but I don't know if he's ever considered taking it further.

Anyway, if we did meet, the relationship would be over. I'm pretty sure of that. Charles is too conservative for me and I have it on good authority—his—that he thinks I'm impossible. Also, there's the girlfriend to consider. He hasn't mentioned her for months but if I had to guess, I'd say she's still around. I'll even go so far as to concede she's not inflatable, is probably capable of reading, and doesn't require the lobotomies I've recommended for her on several occasions.

So apart from the time it takes every week to write a short letter, fold that page into an envelope, and place the envelope on top of the outgoing mail, my love life is no great burden on the rest of my life—which is less fabulous than I make it out to be in my letters. Charles is right. My descent into crazy cat-lady-hood is only a kitten away.

In any romantic film, the more two people hate each other at the start, the more probable it is they'll be together by the time the credits roll. Following this logic, I think Charles is the person I'm destined to be with. I also think he'll marry his girlfriend. They'll have two or three little misogynists, and he'll be too busy indoctrinating them to write to me. Our correspondence will dwindle to the occasional Christmas card, which, if I become more sentimental as I get older, I'll keep in an old shoebox—so the cats can't shred them—and we'll lose touch.

If that was the worst my future held, I was content. Who really ends up with the person they're meant to be with anyway? The idea that you can live in harmony with someone for a lifetime is frighteningly optimistic. Most relationships are mistakes. Successful relationships happen when the two people concerned both stubbornly refuse to admit they made a mistake. Yet this doesn't prevent most women from actively searching for their next mistake.

Not me. I know better. Kiss a frog and he doesn't morph into a guy in a Gap ad. He stays a frog. Or becomes something slimier. I think that going senile in the company of cats is more desirable than living life with a rat.

If I get bored, this is LA; there are always plenty more rats to go out with. Los Angeles is a rodent Mecca. Once here, the rats are all willing to date Woman With Steady Income until fame or fortune allows them to move up the food chain to date the girls who ignored them in high school. Of course, rats don't date the women who personally ignored them in high school. After all these years those women are too hard to track down. So, symbolically, rats date the girls who would ignore them now if they weren't rich rats. Only by sheer coincidence are the majority of these girls still in high school.

I wasn't unhappy with my life. There were actually some aspects of it I was pleased with. When you stop believing in things that don't exist, life becomes a lot less complicated. I had no desire to change a thing. That was when something happened to change everything.

I found God.

To be precise, He found me. I don't think He was looking

for me. I was just in the wrong place at the wrong time. There was no shaft of light, no angel chorus, no trumpet herald. Nothing. He just showed up one day at work and ruined everything.

From: Sydney Welles <s.welles@fbmm.com>
To: God ourfatherwho@inheaven.org
Date: Monday, May 16, 2005 7:40 PM PDT
Subject: Hi

Dear God (And not just any old god. I want The God. The one everyone prays to: the one in charge of the California Lottery.),

You haven't heard from me before. There's reason for that. To simplify my life, I made a decision not to become involved with you or your affiliated organizations. Up until now, my soul has been Switzerland. Not much has changed in that respect. I'm not writing to you because I've suffered a conversion to faith. I'm writing to you because if we're going to have an effective working relationship, you should know where I stand.

I don't believe in you. Let me clarify that. I'm not talking about whether or not you exist. That's beside the point. Even if you burned my bushes, shouted from the sky in a booming voice, or glowed before me as a gigantic, disembodied head, I still wouldn't believe in you. I don't think you're worth believing in.

You are, after all, the greatest warmonger of all time. Presidents, generals, dictators, all claim you put them up to it. Furthermore, once you get a good battle going, you confuse the issue by fighting on both sides.

People, even very good people--who if left to their own devices would do nothing wrong--will murder, steal, and commit horrific crimes in your name. Your religions and representatives on earth have a dirty, bloody history of being sexist, racist, oppressive, hypocritical, corrupt, and power mad.

By the way, just what are you doing with yourself these days? Judging from the number of people who thank you personally at music award ceremonies, you seem to be spending the majority of your time overseeing the production of rap music. Perhaps if you spent a little less time on your recording projects, the world wouldn't be in the mess it's in.

You and I have managed to get this far without getting personally involved. That suited me fine. Suited you too, I think--one less soul to worry about, when you've got billions on your plate who aren't doing so well.

However, you've seen fit to change the status of our relationship. So from now on, I'm going to be in your face like the rest of your flock. I expect the basic package. You have to micromanage my days, look out for me, supply the stuff I want, and accept blame for whatever goes wrong in my life. It's only fair. If you take up my time, I'll take up yours.

Yours--if not faithfully then at least--sincerely,

Sydney Welles (When you look down at Sunset Avenue, Venice, California, I'm the ant who lives in the cottage with the blue roof.)

The only problem with the perpetual sunshine in Southern California is you can never rely on the weather to be ominous, even on the day you find out the world is going to end.

Monday had started like any other day. The sun was shining, the sky was blue, the smog was in the valley, and I was in bed well after I should've been up. It didn't become apparent the end was nigh until I was well out my front door.

Californian bungalows and Hockneyesque swimming pools abound in Venice, just not on my street. Here, high concrete walls are the order of the day. The affluent people who live here choose to reside near drug dealers, gang members, and the homeless to show the world they are real in spite of being rich. But they're not so real as to want these people to visit, so security prevails. It's the same architectural style used to great effect by the U.S. government overseas. Nothing says "fuck off" quite as effectively as a U.S. embassy in a third world country.

My home is out of place and style. A tiny, demilitarized cottage in a yuppie combat zone.

Keeping within the under-siege theme, all my neighbors drive cars originally designed to transport troops into battle. The fortified street is lined with these tanks, making it impossible for me to park anywhere near my front door.

Not that I minded much that particular Monday morning. That morning, with the bounty of vitamin D from above and the birds twitting rather than shitting in the trees, I didn't mind much of anything at all.

It was one of those days when you feel, if you believe in

that kind of thing, that the world has a babysitter: an old guy with a long, white beard, watching over us from his invisible house in the sky. And for once he wasn't as pissed at us as he normally is, and might be persuaded to give us all cookies.

I was willing to believe this was the case even after I noticed the rabbit in my front yard. Easter was only a month ago. A spontaneous bunny, while a few weeks late, was in keeping with the season.

People never recognize life's most significant moments at the time they occur—at least people like me never do. It's only in hindsight I see the arrival of the rabbit for what it was, a herald of disaster to come.

Unlike the articulate, impeccably dressed bunny that led Alice to her fall into Wonderland, my rodent on the run was an ordinary rabbit. He didn't even have the distinction of being white. His coat, the standard, untailored, rabbit kind, was patched gray. He wasn't fluffy; he was scraggly and scarred. If bunnies could be street thugs, he was one.

"Is that your rabbit? What's wrong with it? Why don't you keep it in a cage?"

Standing at my open front gate was the small, demon son of my across-the-street neighbor. Five days a week he's sent out into the world, disguised as a normal child, to torment the teachers and students of the nearest Montessori school.

The evil spawn leaves home about the same time I do in the morning. Every time I see him, I wonder what new weaponry is concealed in his backpack and hope, sincerely, that his parents are now using a reliable contraceptive.

"That's the ugliest rabbit I've ever seen," Cupid said. "What do you call it?"

His parents named Cupid for the equally armed and dangerous cherub, the little nudist who flits about inflicting love. There's a strong, pink-cheeked resemblance between the two. It's an apt name, but Damien or Beelzebub would suit him just as well.

I had to come up with a plausible rabbit name. Letting Cupid know the rabbit was a stray would give him the incentive he needed to torture it to death.

Bugs? Br'er? What kind of a name is Br'er? Peter? Roger? Thumper? Hazel? *Watership Down* was full of bunny names. What were they? That invisible six-foot-tall rabbit in that old Jimmy Stewart film, what was—

"Harry," I said. Not quite it but close enough, though it was possible it needed elaboration. "Harry Rex."

"That's a really stupid name."

"It's not the only one."

Keeping his gaze fixed on the rabbit, Cupid picked up a stone from under my hedge, weighing it in his hand.

"If you throw that at Harry Rex," I said, "I'll do the world a favor and castrate you."

Cupid obviously had no idea what castration entailed, but he sensed its unpleasantness. Making a fist around the rock, he filed it away in his pocket and faced me, crossing his pudgy arms in front of his chest.

"My mother says you're a lesbian."

I had no ready comeback, but was saved from further conversation by the mother herself.

"Cupid?" Her screech carried across the street. "Come on, angel. It's time to go."

The angel stamped his feet. "No, I want to play with the bunny."

I was pleased to note a look of horror taking over his mother's face.

"Cupid. Get over here at once. Or there'll be no PlayStation. For a week."

Cupid screwed up his face to scream, then thought better of it. His features resettled into their usual cherubic curves, and he dutifully trotted across the narrow road separating his house from mine.

His mother ran a smoothing hand through his perversely angelic curls.

"You know how I feel about you petting strange animals," she said in her normal voice, a melodious shriek I could still hear clearly. "That animal could have rabies."

I had no idea what a rabid rabbit looked like, but that didn't prevent me from speaking up.

"He doesn't have rabies."

Her answering glare could not be interpreted as friendly. She took Cupid by his shoulders, turning him about to face her. "Now this is very, very important, darling. You must promise Mommy. We don't go near animals we don't know."

He must have agreed, as his golden head bobbed up and down in a good impression of obedience.

His mother fell for it. True, she could not, as I could, see the crossed fingers behind his back, but her failure to notice the fiendish nature of the smile lighting up his chubby face proved that a mother's love is as blind as any other kind.

I can't blame her for her lack of judgment. I've dated far worse than Cupid.

"If I were you," I said to Harry Rex once Cupid was safely restrained in the backseat of the family assault vehicle, "I'd be long gone before the Antichrist gets home from school."

Harry Rex cocked a disfigured ear, seeming to give the suggestion due thought. He hopped to the hedge and slunk into it—apparently taking my advice. He left behind the piece of paper, a flyer, he'd been nibbling on. The part of it he hadn't eaten announced that the end of the world was taking place the Sunday after next at exactly 8 P.M., Eastern Standard Time, 5 P. M. local time.

✝

The sense of impending doom, brought on by the discovery that the world had a rapidly approaching use-by date, abated when I reached the normalcy of my office. On my computer was an urgent all-staff memo calling for the owner of the dog that left a trail of poops on the floor near the library to come forward, presumably with pooper-scooper in hand. On my sofa someone was snoring under a newspaper. Outside my door our agency president, Larry Crawford, strode by, having a loud, one-sided debate with an entity only he could see— just another day at the office.

By the time the priest stopped at my door and asked the way to the bathroom, I felt like myself again. Only after I'd pointed him in the right direction did it hit me I'd seen an un-usual sight.

Larry was here and it was barely five past nine. I've only known him to show up before noon in cases of emergency, or when he knows cocktails are going to be served. No celebra-tion was slated for this morning. Which meant an advertising emergency was in progress.

I peeked out of my office to see what was going on, plan-ning to pull my head in before anyone could involve me. I'm the most senior woman in the planning department. That means I get all the shitty jobs the guys don't want. There'd been rumors flying around the agency for weeks. Members of the clergy showing up at work had to mean trouble. Unless I was careful, I'd be landed with it.

"Just the cranium I wanted to see," Larry said.

I jumped, for good reason. Larry's normal speaking voice is the sort usually reserved for getting the attention of someone standing on the other side of Wilshire Boulevard during peak-hour traffic. I'm accustomed to it, but he can still scare the crap out of me if he sneaks up.

My office faces the agency bar, a relic of a more prosperous, decadent time in the agency's history, but a relic kept fully stocked and in constant use all the same. Larry was filling a frosted glass with one of the three beers on tap. He offered to pour one for me as well.

"It's nine o'clock in the morning," I said.

He checked his watch. "So it is. Beer?"

"It's kind of early."

"For what?"

"Beer."

"Oh, I see." He turned to survey the top shelf, selected a bottle of scotch, splashed some into a glass, topped it up with a little water, and, with the two glasses in hand, cautiously approached my office door, where he stopped to scan the room.

"Where's the General?"

"He must be here somewhere." I pointed at a neat pile of papers on my desk awaiting my signature. "They weren't there last night. But I haven't actually seen him this morning."

Visibly relieved, Larry came forward to place the scotch in front of me, on top of a briefing document on my desk. He walked over to the couch and lifted the corner of the newspaper, nodding to himself when he saw who was sleeping under it. Replacing the paper gently, Larry found a spare chair and folded himself into it, regarding his beer in an amicable way.

"Out somewhere practicing his goose step, is he?"

"Patton's the best assistant I've ever had," I said. "He's just a little uptight, that's all."

"I still can't understand why you hired him."

"Nepotism. He's your nephew."

"Purely by accident. They weren't planning on having him, I can tell you that."

On the sofa, Noah, roused by Larry's not-so-dulcet tones, raised himself up on his elbows to look around. He lay back down and pulled yesterday's news back over his head as soon as he spotted Larry.

In a chair too small for someone of his height, chugging beer first thing in the morning, Larry still looked like the president of a large corporation. He's always expensively and correctly attired. You can see that he started out in a state of elegance at some point, even if he was unable to maintain it.

Silver hair makes people seem more respectable than they are, and Larry has plenty. Most notably in important eyebrows and a handlebar mustache that, legend has it, wilts into a Fu Manchu when exposed to undue heat or exercise.

"Enough pleasantries," Larry said, half his beer having been guided down his throat. "I've got a job for you. You're not going to believe who just walked in the door. I don't know if I believe it myself."

"Why, who walked in the door?"

"The Catholic Church." Larry crossed himself using his beer glass. "They need our help. They want the works. Complete image overhaul."

"The pedophile thing isn't working for them?"

Larry thumped my desk with the hand unencumbered by beer. A little scotch and water escaped my glass, finding a new home in my in-tray.

"I love sarcastic women first thing in the morning—or maybe I've just gotten used to them. What a pity you don't have bigger breasts. You'd be the perfect woman. Once you learned to hold your beer."

"Are we going to take on the Church?"

"Yes, that's where you come in. The Church is afraid people may see advertising as inappropriate, or worse, opportunistic. That's why they've asked for our help. They want to float the idea, to gauge the reaction."

"A research project?"

"That's right. You're going to find out how the plebs feel."

"You mean consumers."

"Okay, find out how they feel too."

"About being sold Catholicism?"

"No, definitely not. If people hate the idea then the Church looks bad. We can't have that. They look bad enough already. We keep things general. We don't ask: Can we sell Catholicism? We ask: Can we sell religion? Can we sell God?"

"What if people ask why we're asking?"

"We tell them it's a privately funded study, purely academic at this stage."

"We do it secretly?"

"No, right out in the open. Pass it off as an intellectual exercise. It's good PR for the agency. Should get a lot of press."

"Okay, but why me? I'm not the most—"

"No, but you're the third choice. If you don't do it we're fucked. We won't hit our number for the year."

"I thought we'd already made the number. We had a great start of the year. Two new—"

"We hit it too early in the year. The corporate bean counters just raised the figure again. What do you say? The guys won't touch it. Too volatile. They think if it blows up in their faces their careers will be over. They're not keen to jeopardize things just when they're on the verge of being able to afford trophy wives."

"What if it blows up in my face?"

"I wouldn't worry. You still have time to marry rich. You're a relatively young woman."

"You know, Larry, as the head of a public company it might help you to get a little more in touch with women born after the Civil War."

"What are you talking about? I'm a feminist from way back—ever since I found it could get me laid. I supported that job-share thing for the working mothers."

"Yes, you did. I remember. And that was good, but—"

"Good for the agency too. I'd rather have a smart woman three days a week than a dumb man for five, especially if she's good-looking. So how about it?"

"I've got a lot going on right now. I don't know if I can take on something this size. What about my other accounts?"

"Let them slide."

"Let them slide?"

"This is advertising. We don't care about the clients we already have, we only care about the ones we might be able to get. Haven't I taught you anything?"

"Do I have a choice in this?"

"You could always go back to wherever it is you came from."

The scotch and soda on the table suddenly seemed appealing. The industry was depressed—hence the never-ending scrabble for the few new advertisers out there—and I was at that difficult age in advertising: too old to be a wunderkind, too young to have my name above the agency door.

"When do I start?"

"Good girl. That's the attitude. Of course, it's in our best interest if you deliver a positive result."

"What are you saying?"

"Prove people will buy God and we land the most lucrative new account out there."

"What if people won't buy God?"

Larry twisted one end of his mustache, a silent-film villain. "Rephrase the question."

"How much money does the Church have to spend?"

Larry leaned over the desk and dropped his voice to his version of a whisper. People more than twenty feet away would now have some trouble hearing him clearly.

"More than God," he said.

"How much is that exactly?"

"In this country? About eight billion a year, and that's revenue alone. Then there's the real estate and—"

"Then why do they need to advertise? What? They need more money?"

"Our job is not to question why, our job is to make our twenty percent. If we could get them to spend what they spend settling lawsuits, we could turn the agency around. And there's always the potential this could go global. If it does . . . well, let's just say, the Vatican has its own bank."

"What's in this for me if I pull it off."

"The usual. A good bonus, a meaningless promotion, people kissing your butt for a week or two, you know the deal."

"I'm already due a good bonus."

"Well, you pull this off, you won't be the token female planning director anymore."

"What will I be?"

"The only female planning director."

"What's the difference?"

"Nothing really."

"What's my budget?"

"Whatever you need. And all the help you need, hire if you have to—get him to help you, he's not doing anything." Larry picked up a stress ball someone had left on the edge of my desk and pitched it at the outstretched form on my couch. The pitch was on target.

"What?" Noah peeped out from under the newspaper.

"Good, you're awake. You're going to save the Catholic Church. It's all up to you. Don't fuck it up." Larry stood. "That's today done then." He picked up the empty beer glass and took it back to the bar to rectify its emptiness.

Noah sat up. On his crumpled T-shirt was printed PEACE IS FOR PUSSIES.

"Help," he said.

I pushed the glass of scotch a few inches in his direction, leaving staggered watermarks on the document it rested on.

"Drink that," I said.

"Why do you let him get away with all that sexist crap?"

"Larry isn't sexist. He judges people on their work irrespective of what comes out of his mouth. Anyway, I prefer my sexism in my face. It's the guys who say all the right things, then skewer you in the men's bathroom, who you have to watch. All this political correctness hasn't made sexism go away, just underground. Now you don't see it until you step on it. Like a land mine."

Noah made a feeble effort to smooth down his hair, which, no matter what is done to it, always looks like a fierce sort of excrescence growing out of his head. "This is one hell of a project," he said.

"I know. But we'll humor them until someone in a position to do something about it realizes what a bad idea it is and pulls the entire thing."

"And if they don't?"

"Let's hope they do."

My computer made the sound it makes when new mail comes through. I opened the note marked urgent. Again it called for the owner of the defecating dog to turn himself in and clean up the shit. In the last thirty minutes, three people had stepped in it.

I knew exactly how they felt.

From: Sydney Welles <s.welles@fbmm.com>
To: God headgardener@gardenofeden.com
Date: Tuesday, May 17, 2005 9:02 AM PDT
Subject: Apocalypse Now?

Dear God,

Is the world going to end?

I don't usually pay much attention to any of the literature put out by the burgeoning Doomsday industry, but the end-of-the-world brochure I picked up looked as if it was published by the sort of people you like to associate with these days. It said everything would be over by Sunday after next. Is that the plan?

This is merely an opinion--and I'm aware you like to move in mysterious ways--but even given the problems in the world today, don't you think the Apocalypse is an extreme management solution?

Isn't it a little like stomping on the model airplane you made because it didn't turn out exactly like the picture on the box?

Sincerely,

Sydney Welles

I met Jake a few days after I met God and liked him better. He was celebrating his thirty-fifth birthday in a bar decorated to look like a large public toilet. What passes for cool these days is so inexplicable it's impossible to tell whether the interior design was intentional. Whatever the case, a row of urinals would've looked right at home against one of the tiled walls.

The place was two-thirds full of the usual mob: film, music, and media people out for the purpose of being seen out. Men wore the Friday night denim-and-leather-jacket uniform. Women exposed as much skin as you can expose without getting arrested.

Jake was with a large noisy group standing in the center of the floor, but I can't say that I noticed him when I walked in.

Anna I spotted right away. She's hard to miss: a redhead so tall all skirts are short on her. She scares most men. All men if she's wearing heels.

In the five minutes Anna had been waiting, she'd secured the best seats in the bar by one of her time-tested methods; hiding the sign reserving the VIP table—always empty on the off chance of an unexpected celebrity appearance—in her bag.

"So," she said after I'd taken a fashionably uncomfortable seat, "how did it go with the model?"

"Model-slash-poet. He was quite insistent on the 'slash-poet' part of the job title."

"Whatever. You went out?"

"We did. It was tragic."

"I thought you said he was gorgeous."

"Oh, he was. Still is. Looks like Jim Morrison at his peak. No . . . closer to Val Kilmer playing Jim Morrison at his peak."

"What was wrong with that?"

"He had a vocabulary of twenty-five words. Must write very short poems. Haiku, maybe?"

"There's nothing wrong with the strong, silent type," Anna said.

"No, not unless you want someone who'll talk to you on a date."

"We need to put you in a more reasonable mood before you meet anyone tonight."

"I have no intention of meeting anyone tonight. Do they have anything to eat here?"

Anna made a disgusted face. "The usual."

For a place like this, the usual means fusion food. One-of-a-kind fusion. Cuisines combined not for culinary compatibility but rather for no good reason. Alaskan-Korean-Scottish or some other synthesis allowing Haggis of Moose, served on a bed of Kimchi, with Mashed Potatoes and Bulgogi Sauce to appear, in all seriousness, on a menu.

"Gee, I'm glad we chose this bar over the other one," I said.

"You know I can't do that place. It's full of right-brained people. Too many drugs, not enough deodorant."

"I guess it's drive-through on the way home," I said.

"So, are you going to see the model again this weekend?"

"Are you kidding? I'm never going to date again."

"You have to. How else will you get even?"

"Well, no more model-slash-poets then. Or actor-, artist-, writer-slash-anything."

"Which leaves you with about ten guys to choose from in

this city. That's keeping your options open—hey, wait, I know that guy that just walked in."

"Who is he?"

"Tony-somebody," she said.

"Who is Tony-somebody?"

"I can't remember his other name. Vince knows him. He's a banker. That's all, no slash, only one occupation that pays. No sense of humor but filthy rich. I could introduce you."

"That guy? The one in the lawyer suit?" Tony was greeting someone he knew by winking, making his hand into a gun, and pretending to shoot him. "No. Thanks."

"It won't hurt to meet him."

A second glance revealed Tony pumping all his acquaintances full of imaginary bullets from his right hand while his left formed a permanent shield over his genitals.

"I think it will hurt." I closed my eyes to try to erase the image of Tony, pin-striped gunslinger. "A lot."

Anna means well, but she thinks love is distributed by a lottery system. The more tickets you buy, the more chances you have of winning. Substitute dates for tickets and you get the idea. Dragging me out to increase my chances of meeting potential jackpots has been her self-appointed task ever since I broke up with Matt, actor-slash-asshole.

That was over a year ago. Her desperation on my behalf has grown exponentially. She's now diabolically helpful in securing dates for me. Anna doesn't know about Charles— nobody does—but she won't be assured about my romantic future because I have a pen pal who happens to be a boy.

I go out with Anna for the company and the alcohol. I don't subscribe to her romantic-roulette theory. Anna tells me this is why I'm single and she's engaged to a multimillionaire. I remind her Vince was a client she met at work, not some random guy she picked up in a bar. We meet up almost every Friday to continue the argument over loud music and over-priced drinks.

Since her engagement, Anna spends most of her days shopping, but she continues her career vicariously through me. I tell her what I did at work during the week, and she points out what was wrong with what I did at work during the week.

That night in the bar I tried to scribble on a napkin to explain a concept to her, but my pen, a promotional ballpoint with the agency's name embossed on it, refused to work.

Frustrated, I threw the gimmicky piece of plastic over my shoulder.

Thirty seconds later a man approached our table. He was attractive in both the ways men can be attractive. Sexy enough to send warning pains through the scar tissue of broken hearts past, yet somehow still giving off a trustworthy, potential-first-husband vibe. For a breath, I entertained the possibility that Anna's love raffle had delivered a prize. Then I noticed he wielded my pen.

"Does this belong to one of you ladies?"

I pretended I couldn't hear him over the bar noise, but Anna nodded and pointed at me.

"This pen hit me in the head," he said.

"Really?" I slid several inches down in my seat.

He placed a hand on the arm of my chair and leaned over until our faces were almost level.

"Did you throw it at me?"

I could tell by his eyes that he wasn't angry. "No. Yes. I mean . . . I wasn't aiming at you."

"Who were you trying to hit?"

"Nobody in particular. I just wanted to get rid of it. I was mad at it."

"Why?"

"It wasn't working."

"So you threw it over your shoulder in a crowded bar?"

I began to see where he was taking the conversation.

"Do you know how dangerous that was? You could've taken someone's eye out."

I counted his eyes. "But I didn't."

"That's hardly the point."

Across the table Anna was not being helpful. Instead she carried out complicated maneuvers with her eyebrows and made jerky motions with her head toward my new friend.

Annoyingly, the guy had a legitimate complaint. Even I could see he was right.

I hated myself for being so reasonable.

"I'm sorry," I said. "I'm sorry you got in the way of the pen and got hit in the head. I hope you'll be more careful in the future."

"That's an apology?"

"How about if I promise never to throw a pen at you in this bar again?"

He smiled. A smile I could get used to. "What about other bars?"

"Or in any other bars."

"And restaurants?"

That was taking it too far. "You can't have restaurants as well."

"I guess it's enough I'm safe here for the moment." He eyed the one empty chair at our table.

Anna stopped wiggling her eyebrows and found her voice. "Would you like to sit down?"

I kicked her under the table.

"I'm Anna." She crossed her legs out of kicking range,

causing her skirt to get shorter and two men at the next table to spill their beers.

"Jake." He sat, placed the pen on the table, and turned to me expectantly.

I would've supplied him with my name then and there except I couldn't remember what it was.

"Jake, this is Sydney," Anna said.

I wondered if he'd heard Anna over the noise; Anna must have wondered something else entirely.

"You can call her Syd—if two syllables are too much for you."

"I can cope," Jake said. "Syd-ney. See. Hi."

"Hi," I said. And it took effort to come up with that.

Anna could see I needed help, but as usual she overestimated the amount required. "Syd-ney is single," she said, "and has no plans for next Saturday night."

I kicked her under the table again. Harder.

Jake clutched his shin. "What'd I do?"

Anna sniggered; I covered my face with my hands.

"I'm beginning to think you don't like me." Jake winced, rubbing his leg.

"I'm sorry. I was aiming for Anna."

"Your aim is off tonight."

I wanted to tell him he was fortunate I wasn't wearing my steel-capped boots, but decided he might like me better if I showed compassion instead.

"Does it hurt? Maybe we can order some ice for it? Should I call 911?"

"Maybe Syd can kiss it better." Anna again.

I glared at Anna until I realized Jake was looking at me as if I were dessert. I felt distinctly uncomfortable. It wasn't an entirely unpleasant feeling.

"I need a drink."

The others agreed with me. Jake made a movement with his hand and a waitress materialized at his right elbow. That annoyed me somewhat. I have to tap-dance on a table to get a waitress to notice me in a place like this.

"Champagne," Anna said, when Jake asked what we were drinking. She orders champagne when a man is buying drinks and cheap white wine if a woman is paying. It's her contribution to gender equality. As long as men are getting paid more than women are for doing the same jobs, they have to pay more for drinks when Anna is around. If you spend enough time drinking with her, it makes perfect sense.

Until the bottle arrived, Anna and Jake talked. About me and the damage I could do if someone gave me a pen made of metal. They promised each other never to give me one as a gift, finding themselves extremely amusing in the process.

I sat, mute and stupid, wondering why I'd lost the ability to speak.

Champagne came, was poured, and I faced a different problem. The bar served it in an old-fashioned glass, a wide shallow bowl on top of a tall glass stem, like the ones in old Hollywood movies. I have trouble keeping the champagne in those glasses on the way to my lips. Spill your drink and people think you're a drunk. Nobody stops to consider that you're far more likely to be a drunk if you can get the alcohol into your mouth.

On first impressions, Jake was going to think I was a violent drunk. But as it turned out, I needn't have been concerned about what he thought of me.

"Jay-ake. There you are. What are you doing?"

Jake raised his gaze to a point above my head. I turned around. A woman was standing behind me. She was attractive—if you find outstandingly beautiful women with long, blonde hair attractive. In particular that soft, butter blonde that's impossible to achieve in a hair salon without a Beverly Hills zip code.

I ventured a tentative smile in her direction. She looked me up and down as if I were a stain that had appeared on her wedding dress an hour before the ceremony.

I was tempted to offer her food. She was the size of your typical Hollywood starvelet. Not having eaten this month was probably what was making her irritable. However, I could see that such an offer might make me look like a bitch. I tried thinking charitable thoughts instead. Perhaps she'd had a few too many Botox injections and could only smile on the inside.

"Jay-ake, come on, everyone's here for your birthday. Why are you with these people?"

Why indeed? "You have to go, Jay-ake," I said.

"I should go." He made no move to get up.

"Jay-ake?"

"I'll be right there, Kim. Could you give me a minute?"

Clearly, Kim was more inclined to leave Jake in the clutches of the Swedish Bikini Team than in our company, but she turned and stumped her way back toward the bar. In awe, Anna and I watched her go, the poster girl for a carbohydrate-free world.

"Your pen." Jake held it out to me.

"No, it's your birthday. Keep the pen. We've got millions of them at work."

"Really? Gee, thanks." He slipped it into his pocket all the same.

"It's the least I can do. I didn't get you anything for your birthday and the pen doesn't work anyway."

He laughed, and soon after was gone.

"He left the bubbly. A true gentleman." Anna lifted the bottle out of its ice bucket to show me it was half full. "So what about him? He was nice. And he liked you."

I shrugged.

"Don't tell me you don't like him. He spoke in complete sentences."

"I'm trying to figure out how you failed to notice his girlfriend."

"I'm not so sure they're together. And if they are, it may not be terminal."

"It's terminal," I said. "You saw her."

"Okay, then why was he talking to us?"

"I don't know—to collect enough personal information about me so he can sue for hitting him with the pen."

"I see. You're in one of your glass-is-half-empty moods."

"Whether the glass is half empty or half full, it's still only half a drink."

Anna's eyes became narrow. "You did like him."

"It doesn't matter," I said, even though, for the first time in a long time, it did.

From: Sydney Welles <sydneywelles@yahoo.com>
To: God c/o moses@askmoses.com
Date: Friday, May 20, 2005 11:57 PM PDT
Subject: The Disgraceful State of Urban Dating Today

God,

Must you dangle intelligent, good-looking men in front of me, then have them whisked away at the last minute by Baywatch extras. Out of curiosity, when you made the girlfriend, how much silicone did you use?

Dating is hard enough without you having fun with it.

While we're on the subject, tell me, why has urban dating for women over 28 come to resemble a Road Runner cartoon? I see so many normally sane women devising elaborate plans to trap men. Yet in spite of genius-level plotting and state-of-the art accessories the man, no matter how dumb, gets away.

What is going on? Who is writing those books telling women how they ought to behave on dates? Is it Satan?

Sincerely,

Sydney

P.S. If you think I haven't noticed the priest you've installed in the office, think again.

Advertising is a particularly secular industry. Some would go so far as to describe it as godless. I've always considered that a perk of the job. So the idea of a marketing priest—a priest who secured an MBA before he decided never to have sex again—wasn't one I warmed to right away.

Father Bernadi is the business end of the Church. All business. But he's still a priest. Put me in front of a priest or nun, every inoffensive word I know flees my brain and I can't open my mouth without imperiling my immortal soul.

When I found myself waiting for the elevator with Father Bernadi, I was worried about what to say to him.

He remarked that it had been yet another nice day. I said it was a pity we were indoors for almost all of it. He said the irony of life is that, for all our complaints about it, most of it slips by without our noticing. I wasn't sure what to say next, as the only thing that came to mind was, Yeah, life sucks like that.

Luckily the elevator arrived. Everybody knows it's against the law to talk in moving elevators. I was safe. I'd managed to exchange the word or two required by politeness without a hitch. All I had to do now was stand next to the priest. Easy.

Until the elevator made a sick mechanical sound like a robot vomiting and crunched to a dark, silent halt.

"Holy shit," I said. I hit what I judged in the dark to be the open door button several times to no avail. "What do we do now?"

"Pray," the priest said.

I could just make out his silhouette. "Really?"

"It was a joke. We need earthly help. A little light to work by would be—"

Dim lights flickered on around the ceiling of the elevator, casting a ghastly glow, turning our skin an unwholesome green.

"That was neat," I said.

Father Bernadi examined the panels on either side of the door. "There must be a switch in here that gets the ventilation system working again."

As soon as he said that, I began to feel desperately short of breath. Then gears clicked in place; a low humming began. I felt a stream of fresher air on my face. I could see the benefits of having a holy man around in an emergency.

Father Bernadi read that in my face.

"It was a coincidence," he said.

"Two coincidences. First you said, 'Let there be light' and there was light, then—"

"The emergency system kicked in." He opened the little door to the phone and picked it up.

"What are you going to do with that?"

"Make a phone call—hello? Yes, hello, we have a problem."

While he conversed with elevator central, I helped. I pushed all the buttons several times.

I don't have much experience with the priesthood, but I'm sure that if every priest looked like Father Bernadi, the Catholic Church wouldn't need an advertising agency. Even tinted green by the unflattering overhead light, it was apparent God was this man's personal cinematographer.

Once he'd hung up, I followed his example and sat on the elevator floor opposite him, a little ill at ease being alone with a priest in a confined space. I was also beginning to feel cold.

My cardigan was hanging on the back of my office chair. I shivered.

The priest reached inside his jacket and produced a large hip flask made of dark leather and steel. Pouring colorless liquid into the miniature steel tumbler fitting over the lid, he handed it to me, indicating I should knock it back all at once.

It seemed like a good idea at the time.

Running down my esophagus like liquid lava, it danced a heated conga a couple of times around my stomach, leaving a trail of warmth in its wake.

"Christ," I said when I was capable of speech again. "What was that? It's fucking great."

✝

Everybody goes to hell. At least, all Catholics do. I gleaned that much from the priest in the elevator, who introduced me to the warming effects of grappa while we discussed the selling points of Catholicism—not too many that I could see. To prevent the enclosed space becoming a confessional, I kept the conversation confined to work.

"That is not precisely true," Father Bernadi said. "They go to purgatory, not to hell."

"Do they still get tortured?"

"Purged of their sins, yes."

"Then how is purgatory different from hell?"

Father Bernadi offered me the hip flask. "Hell is for eternity. Purgatory is only temporary."

"How temporary is 'temporary'?"

"It depends on the extent of your sins."

"Give me a ballpark figure for the average sinner."

"Some believe it could be centuries, or longer."

"You and I have very different ideas of 'temporary.' Hundreds of years of torture? What does Amnesty have to say about this?"

"They don't have an office in the afterlife."

"What about confession? All the Hail Marys and Our Fathers? What's the point of doing all that if you go to purgatory anyway?"

"You have to confess and repent your sins. That's essential—remember, the unrepentant go to hell—but sins have to be paid for."

"Is there parole in purgatory? Time off for good behavior—that sort of thing?"

"It is believed your suffering can be shortened if friends and family offer masses and prayers for you."

"Doesn't that mean a person who committed lots of sins, but has lots of friends, could get out before someone with fewer sins and fewer friends?"

"That's possible," he said, "but a person must have done some good to deserve so many friends."

"What if they were just rich and bribed a bunch of people to pray?"

"In those cases we refer to the 'bunch of people' as a 'congregation' and the 'bribe' as a 'legacy.' "

"I think, if I were Catholic, I'd want to stay alive as long as possible."

"That, I believe, is the general idea for everybody. However, purgatory does add incentive." Father Bernadi smiled. It hardly broke the surface at all, doing little to the flawless topography of his features. His amusement was iceberglike; a small part of it was clearly visible in his eyes, the rest hidden in what I suspected was a mountainous mirth inside.

"What about people who are very bad—just under the hell

requirement—with no friends or money? Do they stay in purgatory indefinitely?"

"Purgatory ends for everyone on Judgment Day," he said.

"Even more unfair. Some people will get off lightly by virtue of dropping dead just before Judgment Day . . . that's the end of the world, isn't it?"

The priest nodded.

"I hear the world is going to end this Sunday," I said.

"Ah, yes, according to that doomsday sect all over the news. Do you believe them?"

"Not really. I don't know. I guess it could happen . . . nothing surprises me anymore. It's all arbitrary anyway."

Father Bernadi was silent.

"You're looking at me funny," I said.

"I was wondering what it must be like to live like that, believing that everything that happens is arbitrary. It must be confusing."

"Life is confusing," I said. "So what about very good people? Do they get to skip purgatory?"

"Trust me. No one is that good."

A knock on the doors, the sound of metal on metal, was followed by a voice too faint to understand.

I knocked back from the inside. "Hello? We can't hear you."

The emergency phone in the elevator rang.

After a long explanation—involving facts about elevators I didn't even know I never wanted to learn—a painfully cheerful technician imparted the information that there was nothing wrong with the elevator except it wouldn't go.

"Never seen anything like it," the elevator technician said. "It's in perfect working order, but it won't work. Interesting, isn't it?"

"Yes, very interesting," I said.

"I won't be able to repair anything until I find something to repair. There's no one in there holding down the emergency stop button, is there?"

"No, there's not."

"Thought I'd check. I guess I'd better work on getting the doors open for you."

"That'd be nice." I hung up and relayed the information to Father Bernadi.

Catholicism 101 was a congenial experience under his tutelage. Unlike most men, Father Bernadi became more attractive when he spoke—without any accent that could geographically place him—in a sexy, sinister voice that made me think of fast women, hard liquor, and novel ways to dispose of dead bodies.

I learned that purgatory has changed a great deal since the first pope put on the first pointy hat. Even hell isn't like hell anymore.

"The idea of a demonic hell is still popular," Father Bernadi said, "but now we tend to believe in an abstract rather than a physical hell."

"What's abstract hell?"

"It's a state of being without life and without joy, as God is the source of these things. Hell is the absence of God."

"The absence of God. That's all? No torture, flesh-eating worms, or fires that burn but never consume?"

"No," he said. "But there is pain to endure."

"What kind of pain?"

"Mental and psychological torture. Much worse than fire and brimstone."

"I don't know. Mental and psychological torture is not that much different from normal life for most people."

"I hope that isn't what life is like for you."

"I . . . Why is the fire-and-brimstone version still doing the rounds if you God guys believe it's another thing entirely?"

"It's hard to let go of an idea you grow up with. It's also an easier concept for some people to grasp."

"I see. To reach the greatest number of people, aim for the lowest common denominator. Tap into what people already believe. Like advertising."

"Something like that."

We were both silent for a moment.

"You know," I said, "purgatory makes other religions look like Club Med."

Father Bernadi shrugged Italian-ly. "That is why we are here talking to you."

This struck us both as rather funny.

"I think," I said, "we should play down the purgatory thing along with that pesky theory of evolution. We'll put something in the disclaimer."

Light taps sounded on the door before it was wrenched open against its will. The lower third of the technician appeared through the partially open door. The elevator had come to a halt between the two floors of the agency.

The technician got down on his hands and knees to poke his head into the elevator.

"Hello," his large, square head said. "We're going to have to hoist you out from here. One minute, I'll be right back. Just want to make sure these doors won't shut on you."

We got to our feet.

"Well, that's the last time I take the elevator instead of the stairs in a two-story building," I said. "We've been punished for our slothlike ways. Thanks for keeping me company."

Father Bernadi placed a hand on my shoulder. I found myself staring into the most empathetic eyes I'd ever encountered.

"You will not always be alone," he said.

My shoulder must be connected directly to my tear ducts because I felt my eyes fill up.

"What do you mean?" The tears he was squeezing out of my shoulder slid down my face. "I'm not—"

"Right, who's first?" The technician's head was back.

"After you," Father Bernadi said.

The elevator guy held out a hand to me, and a Catholic priest grabbed my butt. It was only briefly, to give me the shove I needed, but not being Catholic myself I never expected to be groped by a priest. Nor did I expect him to say, "You made a choice to be alone, you can unmake it," even though I imagine it's just the kind of thing that priests like to say, to mess with your life.

The elevator technician had mysteriously disappeared by the time we dusted ourselves off. The mystery was how he did it in a vast open-plan space without us noticing.

It was past seven-thirty. But we didn't have the place entirely to ourselves.

Julie Ryan and Brad Pitt were waiting for us. Brad Pitt is a squat, ugly dog. His silhouette resembles a very large brick on legs. If he's built up enough speed, he's just the right height and consistency to take you out at the knees.

Brad Pitt is an English bulldog, but in many ways he's more qualified than Julie is to be Director of New Business Strategy. I'd say that even if I knew what a Director of New Business Strategy does.

Rumor has it Julie was promoted well beyond her capabilities because she's in possession of compromising Polaroids. I don't care why she was promoted. I'm just happy she was.

You can find quite a few women at the top these days. The

problem with them is they're all smart, talented, hardworking women who deserve to be there. Julie is all incompetence, yet still holds a senior management position.

Things won't be truly equal until the world hands out as many high offices to stupid women as it does to stupid men.

My feminist icon sidled up to Father Bernadi and asked him where he got his loafers. Brad Pitt tried to determine their origin by licking them. Once it was established which Italian leather designer was responsible for the priest's shoes, Julie plucked imaginary fluff from the shoulder of his suit, also expensively Italian.

"You're working late tonight." She executed a series of eyelash acrobatics. In less celibate circles they're quite effective. Julie's appealing if you like perky.

"I had not realized the time. If you both will excuse me, I must make a phone call." Father Bernadi gave me a surreptitious wink. He was ditching us.

"He's so hot," Julie said.

"For an older guy," I said. But she was right. The priest's sexual magnetism could be felt through walls.

"What happened with you two in the elevator?"

"Nothing."

"Nothing? You were in there nearly two hours, and nothing? Jeez. You had your chance."

"Oh, God, please tell me you're not going to come on to a priest."

"Why not? I didn't see a wedding ring."

"That would be because he's a Catholic priest," I said.

"What do you mean? He's either married or he's not."

"Listen to me. He took a vow of chastity."

Julie blinked rapidly. "Is that bad? Did they catch him taking it? Can't he just give it back?"

I made eye contact with Brad Pitt. He didn't think it was worth an answer either.

"Think about it," I said. "This is a Catholic priest we're talking about. You don't stand a chance. He's either gay or a pedophile."

"He's into guys?"

"Or kids."

"Kids?"

"Look, whatever he is or isn't into, don't try to sleep with him. Remember what happened the last time?"

"That was different."

"Yes, it was different," I said. "He wasn't a Catholic priest. This time the pope is going to be really pissed."

She blinked again.

"I'm going to wear my short gray dress tomorrow," she said. "The one that looks like a school uniform." Giggling in a decent imitation of a schoolgirl, she headed off in the direction Father Bernadi had gone.

I told myself the priest was safe. He had God on his side. I hoped that would be enough.

Brad Pitt knocked his dense head against my knees and waggled his ears, sticking out his tongue a little to show he was listening.

I told him I'd just learned purgatory is the all-expenses-paid vacation in hell you receive for being a good Catholic. He wasn't impressed. I couldn't imagine any sane person willingly converting to Catholicism.

All in all, my life was not going very well. I was telling my problems to a dog. I had to convince the Catholic Church to start advertising. Then I had to convince people they wanted to buy Catholicism. My most significant romantic relationship was with a right-wing newspaper columnist I've never met.

I was also slightly in lust with a guy I met in a bar, who I'll probably never see again. Both these men were romantically involved with women who weren't me. And if that wasn't enough, I was also developing a mild crush on a Catholic priest.

I think I could've coped with it all, unscathed by any inadvisable romantic attachments, if only there wasn't something about being privy to the knowledge that the world will end on the weekend, which encourages behavior more reckless than usual.

From: Sydney Welles <sydneywelles@yahoo.com>
To: God c/o presidentoftheunitedstates@whitehouse.gov
Date: Tuesday, May 24, 2005 8:12 PM PDT
Subject: The Easter Bunny

Dear God,

I recently acquired a pet rabbit. It's unfriendly and mangy, but even so, its coming has raised my level of rabbit-consciousness. It struck me as odd that rabbits are included in the most Christian and, if recent cinema is to be believed, most bloody of holidays. See, from an outsider's point of view, Easter seems to be all about persecution, betrayal, crucifixion, and resurrection. The bunny is not a natural fit.

At first I thought it was yet another marketing device foisted onto the unsuspecting public to sell something—chocolate was the first product that came to mind. It wouldn't be the first time the advertising industry has been guilty of messing with Christian holidays, under the radar of course. Putting Santa Claus in a red suit with white trim is still one of the biggest branding coups of all time, pulled off so well by the Coca-Cola Company that everyone thinks that's what Santa always looked like.

I did a little research on the subject of Easter. I was curious to see which multinational corporation was the culprit—the bunny-inserter—but I found that the bunny wasn't added to Easter at all. No, instead it turns out the bunny was there all along, and Jesus was added.

Well before the one-God-fits-all concept was adopted, back when people thought the coming of spring each year was a miracle, there was a goddess called Eastre who was credited with the miracle. This goddess liked bunnies, and they, being very fertile, were celebrated as an embodiment of spring.

It's funny that the two biggest pagan celebrations of the year, Christmas and Easter, are also the two biggest Christian celebrations of the year.

It's also funny that a pagan custom from tens of thousands of years ago, older than the passion play, older than Passover, older than the Bible, older than you if we take the Bible literally, has survived and is handing out eggs today.

Regards,

Sydney Welles

P.S. Look out for Father Bernadi. Julie is not as stupid as she seems.

There are places in the world where cars are considered utilitarian. This isn't one of those places. So much time is spent on the road in LA that getting from A to B is incidental. A car's primary function is to tell the world who you are. Cars announce your socioeconomic group and provide personality and character for those who have none.

The Germans and Italians, Porsche and Ferrari, make the classic compensation cars, but there are more reasonably priced American and Japanese versions for the less well-off underendowed men.

SUVs are usually just the result of bad judgment, but they can also double as compensation cars. For instance, any guy who drives a Hummer is compensating like crazy.

BMWs aren't, strictly speaking, compensation cars, but it's a well-known fact that nine times out of ten, guys who drive them turn out to be assholes sooner or later.

Some women I know won't even date a guy unless his car cost a lot of money. That's stupid. If you want to be with someone with money, why choose a man who's spent all of his on a car?

I avoid dating the owners of compensation cars. Relationships are hard enough without starting with a partner who brings so little to the party. Otherwise, vehicles don't factor into my choice of a partner.

When Jake picked me up for our first date I was grateful I didn't judge people on their cars. If I did, I'd have to conclude Jake was a pimp by profession, although he claimed to be a television producer. And that'd be unfair, considering he'd got everything else right.

The cozy French bistro on Beverly Boulevard was the kind of place I'd nominate if anyone asked me what sort of restaurant was right for a first date. It had authentic food, reasonably priced wine, and bossy, Gallic waiters. Real waiters. Not actors playing waiters.

Jake had chosen the place without any prompting from me, a point in his favor. He'd also sent me flowers at the agency. Another score. Getting flowers from a guy is pointless unless there are envious eyewitnesses to the event.

A regiment of crimson tulips in a square, glass vase was delivered to my desk. On the accompanying card, beneath a phone number, was written:

> *This is an invitation to dinner. Considering the head injury you caused, it's only fair you call and say yes. Also, you kicked me in the shin. If you don't come, I'll press charges.*
>
> *—Jake Reed*

Tulips are my favorite flowers. Another point to add to Jake's aggregate, even if awarded for a lucky guess.

Noah, who was loitering in my office when they arrived, said maybe it wasn't a coincidence. Maybe men are more perceptive than I give them credit for.

I told him to be serious.

All the same, I was impressed. With Jake's florist and his creative use of the Zagat guide. The only blemish on the evening was that he casually handed me a single orange gerbera when he came to pick me up. That was too much. Men in LA don't try that hard. They don't try at all.

The restaurant choice was probably a fluke. The tulips I could understand. Some men think a big, floral first impression gets them to the sex part faster. However, on top of the tulips, the gerbera was sweet and unnecessary. I had to suspect Jake was overcompensating because:

a) He was a pimp as his car suggested
b) He was gay but needed a womb-bearing beard to take to family functions
c) He was two-timing the blonde from the other night
d) He had a wife and family tucked away somewhere
e) He was two-timing the blonde from the other night and he had a wife and family tucked away somewhere

It occurred to me at this point that perhaps I was being too cynical, suspecting he was hiding something from me before we'd even been on a date. I decided to give him the benefit of the doubt—for the moment.

After we were seated in the restaurant, I ordered a glass of water for my gerbera.

"I think you should know," the waiter said, with a thick French accent, "that I was born without a sense of humor. Do you want the water with gas?"

I consulted the gerbera. "Sans gas," I said, giving our waiter the benefit of my most charming smile.

He stared at me for several seconds, dazzled, I suppose, by my smile, before saying, "You are making me afraid," and leaving to fulfill our liquid needs.

"He's very droll," I said.

Jake didn't even glance up from his menu. "Stop flirting with the waiter."

"You have nothing to worry about. In this part of town,

there's a good chance he'll like you better than me. Shall we ask him?"

"Let's not."

Our waiter returned with a bottle of mineral water and an extra glass for the flower.

He also carried a terra-cotta pot filled with ice and a bottle of wine, which he said was a couple of degrees too warm. He allowed us a scant quarter glass each, promising we could have more once it hit the appropriate temperature—room temperature in France.

"Well," I said once the waiter had taken his straight face away again, "if I can't flirt with the waiter and you won't either, what are we going to do all night?"

"We could try the first-date routine. Ask questions, get to know each other?"

"Fine, but I should warn you, I'm not very good at first dates."

"Perhaps you should let me be the judge of that."

"Oh, no. It's a well-known fact. I haven't had a second date in over a year, nor wanted to. I think I'd be much better at this if I could just skip the first two dates and start with the third." I downed the pathetic portion of wine in my glass. "I'm ready. Ask me a question."

"What do you do at Fisher Bennet McMahon & May?"

"That's easy. I'm a planner. Ask me a harder one."

"What does a planner do?"

"Plan things. Is it my turn?"

"Sure."

"Do you think we'll get married one day?"

Jake choked on his wine.

"Not a first-date question, huh?"

"No," he said.

"We'll move on. Do you feel comfortable going out with a woman who earns more than you do?"

"What makes you think you earn more than I do?"

"That program you produce for, it's quite worthy. People never get paid a lot of money for doing worthy things, only for un—"

French Poker Face, the waiter, was back to call out the specials and tell us what we should eat. For the most part we agreed with him. If this pleased him, we couldn't tell.

"Why do you think you earn more than I do?"

"I earn more than just about anyone I've dated," I said. "And it's not just because they've been losers. I actually get paid a lot. It bothers more men than you'd think. Also, there's your car."

"My car is a classic."

"From when exactly?"

"1989."

"No. There were no classics made in the eighties. Taste skipped that decade entirely. I have the photos to prove it."

"You don't like my car?"

It's important to men that you like their cars. Even the men who don't drive compensation cars feel this way. All men see their vehicles, if only subconsciously, as extensions of their penis. If you don't like a man's car but like the man, you lie.

"I like your car."

"What do you like about it?"

"Well . . . it has a lot of buttons to push. I'm looking forward to pushing more on the way home."

"You don't know much about cars, do you?"

"Not true. I know it's important that a car has chrome wheels. And . . . and I know that you use the steering wheel to aim it . . . okay, I don't know much. I've tried to learn, but anytime someone talks about cars, I fall asleep. But I bet I know stuff that you don't know. For instance, did you know there's a piña colada season?"

"No. I didn't."

"It's true, piña coladas are only good from the first of July until the end of August. If you order one out of season, they don't taste right. You really ought to know stuff like that."

"Why don't they taste right out of season?"

"No idea, it's just the way the world is. Who was that girl the other night?"

"Kim?"

"Yes, that's the one."

Jake took my left hand in his right. My own fault. I'd been careless, leaving it resting on the table well within his reach. He seemed reluctant to answer the question. The answer was going to be bad.

"She's . . . we used to go out."

It was as bad as I'd thought. "How long did you go out?"

"About two years."

Correction. Worse than I thought. "Who ended it?"

"I did."

"When?"

"Just under a month ago."

Wrong answer. "Why did it end?"

"Many reasons."

"Give me the top two."

At first I thought he was going to refuse, but then, "We want different things out of life. I want a family, she doesn't. And . . ."

"And?"

"She was convinced I was having an affair."

"Were you?"

"I'm not sure that's a first-date question."

"It isn't, but if you don't answer it, I'll be keeping up my poor second-date rate."

"I didn't have an affair," he said. "Not technically."

"What does that mean?"

"It means I wasn't having sex with anyone else."

"But?"

"But in a way, there was someone else."

"In what way? And where is that—no, wait, that's probably enough detail for me at this point. I'm hungry. I want the date to last until the end of dinner. Your turn to ask a question."

"Are you always like this?"

I patted his hand, the one holding my left hand captive. "I'll calm down once I eat something."

On cue, our waiter appeared at our table with his arms full of our first course. The steaming bowls of mussels kept us occupied for a while.

"I have one more question. It may not be a first-date question either," I said.

Jake had made a small mountain of empty shells in rapid time. He ceased adding to it long enough to say, "All right."

"Do you still want a family?"

"Yes, I do."

The odds on a second date were getting longer all the time.

✝

Later that night we found ourselves in a small, unfashionable bar we'd chanced upon on the way home. It was a Brad-and-Chad bar, a place full of people named Brad and Chad wearing button-down shirts tucked into jeans worn high and tight.

A dark corner by the bar had both privacy and a full view

of the Brads, Chads, and their main activity: Standing on a chair in turn, they'd drink a glass of beer while the rest of the bar cheered with a level of enthusiasm that suggested the task must've been more difficult than it looked to be or, more likely, that these guys didn't get out much. When we tired of watching their prowess, we picked up the conversation where we'd left it at the end of dinner.

"What are we up to? My religious beliefs or the number of sexual partners I've had?" Jake put his arm around me.

"The time has come, the Walrus said, to speak of many things," I said. "Of shoes and ships and sealing wax—why, how many sexual partners have you had?"

"You're a Lewis Carroll fan?"

"Of Wonderland, yes. But the guy was a pervert."

"A pervert?"

"Well, you see, he was one of the first photographers ever."

"And . . . photographers are perverts?"

"No. Well, okay, yes, the ones I know are. But Lewis Carroll, he was a pervert because he had a thing for the real Alice. The one the book was written for. He was kind of obsessed with her. And he took pictures of little girls naked."

"Where were the parents of these naked girls?"

"They were around. He'd ask their permission, but not all at once. First he'd ask to take normal clothed portraits of the girls, then move on to pictures in costumes, and finally pictures without clothes."

"Their parents allowed this?"

"They must have. The photos exist. Photography had just been invented. It had yet to evolve into a way to meet and date supermodels. Getting a photo taken must've been a huge novelty. Maybe the parents thought it was art. Or maybe they just wanted to have photographs of their daughters."

"In the nude?"

"Yes, well, this all happened before Freud. Until Freud pointed it out, we didn't know how sexually perverted we were. These days pedophiles are all over the news, so if some guy asked if he could take a soft-porn picture of our eight-year-old, we'd have him locked up."

"Probably why pedophiles no longer ask for parental permission. Lewis Carroll wasn't actually a pedophile?"

"I don't think he was out in a raincoat molesting kids, if that's what you mean. But he probably was a pedophile—a repressed one. All Victorians were repressed. Isn't that what made them Victorian? He was also a mathematician."

"Now that is unforgivable," Jake said.

"Do you know 'Lewis Carroll' was a pseudonym?"

"That I do know."

"Do you know what his real name was?"

"I do."

"Do you know one of your hands is on my ass?"

"I'm aware of it." Jake squeezed a cheek for emphasis.

"Have you been at sea for a year?"

"No."

"Well, I have a problem with being groped in public."

"We could go somewhere private."

"There's no point. I'm not going to sleep with you tonight."

"You forget. You have to sleep with me. I paid for dinner."

"Very funny, but I can't. Anna told me not to."

"Why would she go and tell you a thing like that?"

"Oh, everybody knows. You should never have sex on the first date because men are like dogs."

"I know I'll regret asking this. Why are men like dogs?"

"They try to hump everything."

"Harsh. So when does Anna say we can have sex?"

"It depends. It's all about obedience training. Sex is like a doggy treat. If the dog gets the treat before he's earned it, you'll never be able to train him. It's best to wait. At least until the dog learns to beg."

"Is that what you think?"

"Not really. I think if someone is an asshole, he's going to be an asshole whether you sleep with him on the first date or the tenth. The trick is to avoid dating him in the first place."

"Sounds logical."

"Only it's not that easy. For instance, at this stage I have no idea whether you're an asshole or not."

"When will you know?"

"Probably not until it's too late."

"I'm not an asshole."

"That's what all the assholes say."

"I see. I can't win."

"No, that's not true. It works the same way the judicial system is supposed to. You're innocent until proven an asshole. Sex is the litmus test. It shows up the inner asshole in otherwise nice guys. It's the only way to know for sure."

"If it's the only way, I guess I'll have to go along with it."

"That's another thing. Men are always ready to have sex. What is that? What would you think of a woman if she wanted to sleep with you on the first date?"

"I don't think I'd be doing all that much thinking."

"Would you think less of her than if she'd waited until the customary third date?"

"Sex on the third date is customary? I have to get out more."

"You haven't answered the question."

"I don't know. It depends on the woman concerned."

"What if I were the woman? If we had sex right now, would you think I was a slut?"

"Only if you wanted me to."

"Be serious."

"Okay." Jake smiled. "I think it'd be better to wait."

"Why?"

Jake's free hand linked up with his occupied one, behind me, south of my waist.

"It's not a good idea to have sex with me on the first date," he said.

"Why not?"

"I'll respect you less."

"You can't be serious."

"Deadly."

I took a protest step backward but Jake held me in place. I didn't really make much of an effort to put distance between us. Being chummy with Jake was no great hardship, but he was so perilously close to kissing me, I had a little trouble keeping up my end of the conversation.

"You'd think less of someone because they slept with you on the first date?"

"Yes," he said.

"But you're sleeping with them too."

"True."

"So what if they judge you the same way?"

"It's all right for me. I'm a guy."

"Obviously."

"You asked the question. You can't now complain because you don't like the answer. If a woman sleeps with me on the first date, I'd be unlikely to want to continue the relationship."

"You can't be this backward without a reason. Were you frozen in the last ice age? Did they only just find you and defrost you?"

"I think you'll find my views aren't uncommon."

"I think you have appalling views."

"What is so wrong with them?"

"They're just . . . wrong."

"I'm being honest. No one appreciates something that comes too easily. It's basic human nature."

"What? This is really annoying me. You can't get away with perpetuating this primitive macho crap. I can't let you. I won't. I'm going to have to sleep with you tonight."

"You are?"

"Yes. I have no other choice."

"Your place or mine?"

"Whose is closer?"

"Mine."

"Your place then," I said.

To make my point, I went with Jake to his place and slept with him. Twice. I did it mostly to do my part in the fight to change the double standards in dating. To take a stand—well, in this case, a recumbent position—for single women everywhere. But there were a couple of other reasons for my actions. I wanted to sleep with Jake, and the world was ending the following day. I had nothing to lose.

Hey God,

I know you're meant to be everywhere at once but you can't be absolutely everywhere, right? For example, you weren't at Jake's last night, were you?

I'm finding the idea of you being omnipresent disturbing. You're the ultimate voyeur. A great, cosmic pervert. Why is the creator of the universe even interested in watching my sex life? Which, let's face it, was a non-event before last night. Surely you have something better to do? There are children starving in Africa, you know.

By the way, I think I've found a loophole in this no-premarital-sex business: If I don't have any intention of marrying the guy then it isn't premarital sex, is it?

Best,

Syd

The sun dangled above a pointy tree in Vince and Anna's back garden. Even with the glare in our eyes, I could see that behind her sunglasses Anna was in mild shock.

"You slept with him?" she said for the second time.

"He tricked me into it. Did this whole reverse-psychology thing. It was quite clever. Anyway, he told me I had to sleep with him because he bought dinner."

"You said that?" Vince said.

Jake grinned. "I believe I did."

"I'm impressed."

Anna chose to ignore Vince, shifting in her seat to turn on Jake across the table. "How much was dinner?"

"About a hundred and fifty bucks."

"I have a feeling that won't be enough," I said. "You should've picked a more expensive restaurant."

"Did that include the tip?" Anna wanted to know.

Jake inclined his head to indicate it did. "She was cheap."

"I prefer the term 'on special.' Don't forget, he did send me flowers beforehand, so you have to factor in the cost of those too. But you're right, I should've held out for more." I squinted, sideways, at Jake. "How much would you have paid?"

"My entire net worth."

"How much is that?" Anna's voice held a shade too much innocence for it to be genuine.

"Why is sex a financial transaction even when there are no hookers involved?" Vince said. "And why are men always the ones expected to foot the bill? What happened to gender equality?"

"Nothing happened to it," I said. "Something has to exist before anything can happen to it. I know patriarchal propaganda says otherwise, but gender equality hasn't been invented yet."

"Due in no small part to closet chauvinists like you, darling." Anna patted Vince on the forearm.

"Yes, look at the unfair double standards we all cling to. Case in point—" I waggled a finger at Jake. "I didn't tie him up and force him to have sex with me, but you aren't judging him."

"He scored," Vince said. Though they refrained from high-fiving across the table, I sensed Vince and Jake shared a covert bonding moment.

"Yes. Exactly. I'm cheap, I mean, good value for money, while Jake here gets inducted into the stud hall of fame. If men are going to frown upon women who sleep with them on the first date, then they shouldn't go around sleeping with women on the first date. It's so hypocritical."

Everyone was silent for a moment.

"So," Jake said, "you think I'm a stud."

"I think it's possible you missed the point I was making."

"You were saying that you're a slut and Jake here is a stud—well done, son," Vince said. "Was there something else?"

"Yes. No. I give up."

✝

Jake told the truth last night. His house was closer to the bar than mine, two streets closer. I'd known we both lived in Venice, but I had no idea we were almost neighbors. I found it worrying. With the exception of urban wildlife and demonic children, I don't really get along with my neighbors.

"What if we have a horrible breakup? It'll be awkward if we keep bumping into each other," I said. "Maybe it's best we part on good terms now."

"We've never bumped into each other before."

"How can you be sure about that? We didn't know what we looked like before."

"Are you always this pessimistic at the start of a relationship?"

"Only if there's a guy involved."

Early this morning I found that Jake's fridge, though well stocked for a guy living on his own, held nothing resembling breakfast. I seized the chance to cite hunger as an excuse for a getaway. Leaving quickly was the polite thing to do.

Also, if the Final Judgment was going to take place at the end of the day, and cleanliness really is next to godliness, I had some tidying up to do that couldn't be delayed much longer.

I invited Jake to breakfast at my place, expecting him to refuse and mumble something noncommittal about calling me—the correct etiquette after you've had sex with someone you barely know. Jake was either ill-mannered or hungry. He accepted the invitation.

Found-food omelets are the breakfast special at my house. They're omelets filled with whatever I find in the fridge. Today it gave up green onion, proscuitto, cheddar, and shiitake mushrooms. The cheddar, from Vermont, is especially good. The cows there must be very sane.

Some friends are so familiar with the found-food omelet concept they've taken to slyly stocking my fridge with their favorite fillings. That's cheating. The challenge and charm of a found-food omelet lies in letting fate decide what you eat for breakfast.

I was sliding his omelet onto a plate when Jake wandered in from the street, clean and dressed as promised.

"I'm starving," he said by way of greeting.

His appetite confirmed his words. It was so hearty it reminded me of a character in a movie: Tyrannosaurus Rex in *Jurassic Park*. I donated half my omelet to the giant lizard, topped off his coffee, and toasted bread marginally faster than it disappeared down his throat.

"Do you have to rush off?" I said.

"No."

"Oh."

"Do you have other plans?"

"No. No plans."

"Is something wrong?"

"It's just that . . ." I decided to be honest about the way I felt. "It's just that I don't think I have enough food."

For reasons clear only to the scientists who study the male libido, and then only vaguely so, this admission made Jake want to kiss me. The kiss was just getting interesting when the phone rang.

On the other end, Anna said, "You haven't forgotten about today, have you?"

"Of course I haven't."

"When will you be here?"

"At your place?"

"Uh-huh."

"When do you want me?"

"How's ten thirty?"

"Ten thirty this morning?"

"When else? Can you still pick up the wings on the way?"

"Sure, no problem."

I put down the phone, checked my watch, and turned to

Jake. "I'm not sure why, but I have to be at Anna's in under an hour and I have to pick up wings."

"Chicken wings?"

I considered chicken wings. Raw chicken wings? Fried chicken wings in a bucket? Spicy buffalo wings? "No, I don't think so."

Then my brain kicked in. I hit my forehead with the heel of my hand. "Fairy wings."

"Naturally. I don't know why I didn't think of them."

"I have to go. I have to get to the Enchanted Grove on Robertson before ten to catch the fairy lady. Are you coming or staying?"

"I'll come. I think I should see this."

I saw him glance suspiciously at the bottle of multivitamins on the table as I opened the kitchen window and threw a piece of toast through it—for the rabbit.

"Harry Rex hates carrots," I said to explain matters, but Jake looked more confused as I rushed out of the room to find my shoes.

✝

We found Anna sitting sideways on a steamer chair by the pool, hanging onto an unlit cigarette, looking as if the world was about to end. A state in which she was best left alone.

Vince had greeted us at the door, relieving us of two sets of glittering pink fairy wings and two wrapped boxes from the trunk of my car, each containing a plastic, Barbie-sized Volkswagen Beetle.

His house, on the outside, is a replica of Tara. The interior is altogether different—it's Rhett and Scarlett's house in Atlanta after the Civil War. A splendid staircase confronts you in the foyer; perfect for grand entrances, climactic tumbles, or any kind of drama requiring steps. After the staircase, the ornate chandeliers are the next most dominant décor feature. They're everywhere, and of the sort you'd imagine Michael Jackson would buy on a whim. Everyone agrees they're well preserved, very valuable, and truly ugly.

Inside, the house looked as it ever did. It was the garden that was transformed. It'd been a normal garden—normal for a neighborhood where everyone has a full-time gardener. Now it looked like a theme park without a theme. In which two catering vans were starting to unload what looked like enough food for two hundred people.

"You have a housekeeper and a private chef, and yet you've hired a caterer—" I squinted to read what was written on the side of one of the vans. "—and a very good caterer at that. Whatever happened to birthday cake and pin the tail on the donkey?"

"When in Rome," Vince said.

"Or Beverly Hills."

A large pink-and-white-striped, fairy-tale-castle-shaped marquee had been set up on the lawn. Every tree was decorated, most with balloons or paper lanterns. One large tree was hung with wrapped gifts. Another dangled a vast number of piñatas.

"Syd-neeeee." Audrey and Lexie tumbled out of the marquee in perfect little fairy costumes, needing only wings to complete them.

Audrey launched herself at me from about three feet out with as little regard for gravity as a character in a Chinese martial arts epic. Once I'd caught her and restored her to the ground, both the girls doled out hugs, twirled so I could get the full effect of the tutus, and allowed Vince and me to help them on with their wings. Vince then left us in a hurry to cut off a tray-laden man from the catering company heading in a dangerous direction—toward Anna.

"Who's this?" Audrey held her arms up and in due course was picked up by Jake. Audrey is an accomplished five-year-old flirt.

"He smells better than the old boyfriend," she said.

After that auspicious announcement, I made the necessary introductions.

"What did the old boyfriend smell like?" Jake said.

"Smoke. He smoked, not just pretend like Anna. He's an actor. Anna says a bad one."

"Matt was pretty." Lexie, Audrey's younger sister by fifteen minutes, tugged on one of Jake's trouser legs. He put Audrey down, crouching so both girls could admire him.

"Was he prettier than me?"

"Yes," Lexie said. "Are you going to marry Sydney?"

"Do you think I should?"

"Do you have a house and a car?"

Jake nodded.

"Are they nice?"

"Very nice."

"Do you have a dog?"

"No, but I can get one."

Audrey and Lexie held a telepathic twin conference, coming to a quick decision.

"You can marry her," Audrey said.

"You're marrying me off for a car, a house, and a possible dog?"

Audrey gave me a grave look. "You can't be picky when you're old."

"How old is Sydney?" Jake—the sly bastard—said.

"Very old," Lexie said. "About nineteen or twenty." I'm thinking of adopting her.

"How old do you think Jake is?"

Lexie shook her head, the bearer of bad news. "Forty-six or fifty-three, I think."

Adorably identical, the twins are in demand as flower girls. In their experience weddings mean new dresses, being petted and admired, and cake. They try to arrange one for me at every opportunity. The girls also approve of divorce. They don't get to participate but they've learned that every divorce means there's a good chance of two new weddings.

Anna joined us on the grass, her cigarette now soggy. Audrey wrapped herself around Anna's legs.

"Poor Anna, she's having a bad day."

Me too, if I had to live in a mansion and throw kids parties on a competitive basis against Stepford moms armed with bottomless bank accounts. Okay, the mansion—apart from the chandeliers—isn't so bad if you have Southern belle delusions, but the mothers are terrifying.

I can't tell them apart. They all look like variations on the same woman. As if they got a group discount for going to the same dermatologist, beautician, hair colorist, plastic surgeon, personal shopper, and personal trainer.

Most of the moms are failed actresses and successful second wives. For them parenting is about redecorating a couple of spare rooms in pastels, producing a trophy child without it affecting their figures, and spoiling that child until the chances of it ever being able to do anything useful with its life are virtually nil.

Anna, on inheriting Vince's daughters, is three years and a

pound or two of collagen behind the crowd when it comes to parenting. But for someone who never planned on being a mother, she's come a long way.

The first time she and I had taken the girls out without their nanny, a Saturday not long after Anna and Vince became engaged, Audrey and Lexie grew restless and grouchy around noon. After a while I guessed what was wrong with them.

"I think they're hungry. We should feed them."

Anna nodded in agreement, then asked in a small, terrified voice, "What do they eat?"

✝

The birthday party was over by the time we'd gotten around to discussing how much I should've charged Jake for sex. Audrey and Lexie, despite eating enough sugar to fuel them for a week, were upstairs taking a nap. The rest of us collapsed on chairs around a table set up on the grass. Vince broke out monk-made champagne and an elderly single malt whiskey to celebrate the end of the party. We made our way through remnant pink-frosted, silver-sprinkled cupcakes.

In the twilight, three ponies, colored soft pink, lemon, and baby blue, grazed peacefully under a tree, waiting for the trailer to come take them back to wherever it is pink, lemon, and blue ponies come from. They, a stray, gutted piñata oozing candy entrails onto the grass, a deserted cotton candy machine, and the sagging marquee were the party carnage.

The cars I'd given the twins, now with plastic limbs and nylon hair poking out of the windows, were the girls' favorite nonrequisitioned gift of the day, which, though not all cupcakes and perfection, had been a great success.

The mothers wolfed down then purged the food prepared

for them according to the latest diet taking Hollywood by storm, received manicures, gossiped—not always viciously—and went home clutching vouchers for 25 percent off the procedure of choice from a well-known Beverly Hills plastic surgeon who happens to be one of Vince's friends.

Under the piñata tree, twenty or so daytime nannies took cover, dishing the dirt on their employers, taking mental notes for future tell-all memoirs masquerading as popular fiction.

Every child left, tired, cranky, and a little sick from too much cake and ice cream, with the innards of a piñata, a large stuffed toy from FAO Schwarz, and whatever else they could get their sticky little hands on.

Everything had gone well. Anna was no longer hyperventilating, having pulled off the most successful party of the year to date in the six-and-under category. She also had the distinction of throwing the first kids' party of the year to provide valet parking. The twins were happy and even when Arabella, a very sophisticated six-year-old, pointed out my nail polish didn't match my toe polish and asked, in a kind way, if I was a street person, I had to agree with Jake when he said, "Well, it's not the end of the world."

He was remarking that it was past sunset and the world had not gone poof, exploded cataclysmically, or whimpered to its end.

I was surprised. Given the right kind of scholarship and enough time spent with the Book of Revelations, the plagues, pestilence, and conflict predicted to herald the end of time were there at the party for all to see—if you were open to substituting Teletubbies for the four horsemen of the Apocalypse, and myself for the whore of Babylon.

On some level I registered disappointment. After all, the end of all things would've been something to see. Also, a timely Apocalypse would have saved me from having to actually work on the Catholic Church account. And it would've meant I didn't have to face the consequences of a relationship I'd leapt into without much thought, with a guy who, so far, was so absolutely perfect that there had to be a skeleton the size of King Kong in his closet.

However, at the time I was pleased we'd all survived.

Charles Turner
Los Angeles Times
202 W. 1st St.
Los Angeles, CA 90012

May 30, 2005

Dear Charles,

The only redeeming feature of a conservative male is that he tends to be a creature of habit who rigidly sticks to routine, if only because he lacks the imagination to do otherwise. He is reliable the way a Honda is reliable; reliable the way a bank is reliable. Boring, yes, but reliable all the same.

In view of this, I'm at a loss as to why you haven't replied to my last two letters after fifteen months of weekly correspondence. I can't imagine that I've offended you in any fresh way, not now, not after I've spent more than a year insulting you. So I'm assuming that one of the following has taken place:

a) You've run out of sexist ploys with which to put me in my place

b) Your girlfriend—the absolute doll—discovered our correspondence and, in spite of her frontal lobotomy or because of it, can't believe it's an innocent pen-and-paper affair and is forbidding any further exchange of fluids, inky or otherwise

c) You believed me when I told you the world was going to end and ran off to bungee jump off a bridge or to do whatever happens to be at the top of your to-do-before-Armageddon list

69

d) You've joined a monastery and aren't allowed contact with the outside world
e) You are dead and your last couple of columns were published posthumously

There is some evidence to support this last theory. Your columns did read as though a dead person wrote them. Only in the case of c), and perhaps e), will I forgive your neglect.

Yours (on paper),
Sydney

From: Sydney Welles <s.welles@fbmm.com>
To: God c/o theforce@lucasfilm.com
Date: Monday, May 30, 2005 7:40 PM PDT
Subject: Advertising is not going to work

Dear God,

Of all the gods available today, how did I get you? I'd have preferred the elephant-headed Hindu god, Ganesha. That religion offers yoga, curry, reincarnation, and Bollywood. And Ganesha is a remover of obstacles, a good-luck god. What's not to like?

Blessed with facial features only a pachyderm could love, encumbered by extra arms, and relying on a mouse as his only means of transportation, it's clear Ganesha doesn't go around taking himself too seriously.

A lack of pompous self-importance is so refreshing in a supreme being. Ganesha I could sell.

You, on the other hand, are a bad-tempered old man who sends people to hell. You're impossible to please. You've been pissed off with us virtually from the moment you created us.

And that's just the Christian version of you. The Catholic version is worse. There are so many reasons why, for you, advertising is a bad idea, not the least being that a good deal of a product's success lies in its name.

You are called "God."

Even as a proper noun, "God" is not a good brand name for a god. A good brand name for a god is Nike--Greek goddess of just doing it--or Mars or Mercury or anything short, memorable, and powerful. "God" is a no-name name, ambiguous at best. It's generic. Say it and people immediately think of the one they're affiliated with.

To successfully be the generic name in a product category, as Xerox is to copying or Kleenex is to tissue, it helps to be the first product of your kind to appear on the market.

You're far from the first. By the time Catholic God appeared there were already plenty of gods in existence. And, strictly speaking, Catholic God is a brand extension of Christian God, who is a brand extension of Jewish God, and Jewish God is a repackaged, relaunched version of a bunch of earlier pagan deities.

As a rule, brand extensions are unsuccessful and tend to eat into the market of the original brand, thus weakening it.

Sincerely,

Sydney

A Hindu, a Muslim, a Buddhist, a Jew, an Atheist, and a born-again Christian were sitting around a large table in a room in an advertising agency.

It was no joke. It was my job. I, a nonpracticing agnostic at best, had the job of moderating the group.

Religion was the topic they were being paid to talk about. Not surprisingly, it was the main topic of contention:

BORN-AGAIN CHRISTIAN: Atheists are ruining this country.

ATHEIST: Yes, I've heard that one before.

BORN-AGAIN CHRISTIAN: You're trying to take out God.

ATHEIST: I can't kill something that doesn't exist.

BORN-AGAIN CHRISTIAN: I was talking about the pledge of allegiance. What you're trying to do to it is evil.

ATHEIST: What am I trying to do?

BORN-AGAIN CHRISTIAN: To take out "under God."

ATHEIST: It's not something I'm personally seeing to. Anyway, it should come out. It was inserted in the first place. It wasn't in the original pledge.

JEW: I remember when that happened. I was in the third grade. My teacher told us they put it in to remind us that there's a power greater than a nation. She said they did it so that what happened in Nazi Germany could never happen here. I always thought it was a good thing.

BORN-AGAIN CHRISTIAN: We are one nation under God. No two ways about it.

ATHEIST: Whose God?

BORN-AGAIN CHRISTIAN: There's only—Jesus Christ—it doesn't matter.

ATHEIST: The "any god is better than no god" argument. Let me just point out that people who don't believe in God don't fly planes into buildings on purpose.

MUSLIM: Why is everyone looking at me?

MUSLIM: Now you're all trying not to look at me. I'm not responsible for the acts of a handful of extremists just because they claim to have the same faith I do.

BORN-AGAIN CHRISTIAN: Hitler was an atheist.

JEW: Hitler was raised as a Catholic. He was an altar boy.

MUSLIM: I've heard that too. Do you know he was never excommunicated? Don't you find that strange after everything he did?

BORN-AGAIN CHRISTIAN: Bullshit.

ATHEIST: It's true. Excommunication is reserved for pop stars.

BORN-AGAIN CHRISTIAN: Catholics are worse than atheists.

ATHEIST: I'm touched.

BUDDHIST [*pointing at me*]: Please remember, we're here to answer her questions, not to argue amongst ourselves. Perhaps we could all try showing more tolerance for other people's points of view.

ME: Well, if we could move on to the next—

BORN-AGAIN CHRISTIAN: Yeah, well, you know where you can stick your tolerance and world peace and movie stars. Keep your unnatural practices to yourself. If God had intended us to do that yoga crap, he'd have put instructions in the Bible.

HINDU: Er, yoga is more my department.

BORN-AGAIN CHRISTIAN: Where are you from? China?

BUDDHIST: Orange County. My racial heritage is Korean, if that's what you're asking. My parents are from South Korea. They moved here before I was born.

BORN-AGAIN CHRISTIAN: Korean, huh? You people should stop eating dogs.

BUDDHIST: I'm a vegetarian.

BORN-AGAIN CHRISTIAN: Well, tell your dog-eating friends back home to stop.

HINDU: Why should she?

BORN-AGAIN CHRISTIAN: You're not supposed to eat dogs.

HINDU: According to my beliefs, you aren't supposed to eat beef, but I'm not telling you not to eat steak or hamburger.

BORN-AGAIN CHRISTIAN: That's different. Dogs are pets to us. You can't eat them.

HINDU: Cows are sacred to us, but we accept that your beliefs are different to ours.

BORN-AGAIN CHRISTIAN: A cow is not the same as a dog.

ATHEIST: It's only different to you.

BORN-AGAIN CHRISTIAN: Dog is man's best friend.

ATHEIST: In some cases, the only friend a man can get.

BORN-AGAIN CHRISTIAN: Why is he here?

ME: There's no need to shout. He's here for the same reason you are. We're interested in getting as wide a range of perspectives as possible. All opinions are welcome. Why don't we all take a short break to calm—

BORN-AGAIN CHRISTIAN: This is about God. Why have someone here who doesn't believe in God? The rest of them I can understand. They believe in something, at least. But him?

ATHEIST [*pointing at Hindu*]: Wait a minute. Do you believe in his God? Sorry, I mean, his gods?

BORN-AGAIN CHRISTIAN: Of course not.

ATHEIST [*pointing at Jew*]: What about hers?

BORN-AGAIN CHRISTIAN: The only way to salvation is through Jesus Christ.

ATHEIST [*pointing at Muslim*]: What about his god?

BORN-AGAIN CHRISTIAN: You've got to be kidding. He's at war with Christ.

MUSLIM: I can't be at war with him. He's dead. They [*pointing at Jew*] and the Romans killed him. We had nothing to do with that one.

JEW: Hey, that's unfair.

MUSLIM: Sorry, I was just making a point. This guy doesn't seem to understand that, to me, he is the disbeliever.

BORN-AGAIN CHRISTIAN: Christianity is the only religion based on history and fact. Everything else is mumbo-jumbo.

ATHEIST: Well, I happen to agree with all of you. You don't believe in each other's gods, and neither do I. Probably for the same reasons.

BORN-AGAIN CHRISTIAN: Yeah, well, you can say whatever you want. Who do you think is going to get the last laugh?

ATHEIST: You born-agains are all the same. You do whatever you want to—things others wouldn't dream of doing—then as soon as you get that first taste of mortality, you run scared and get your slate wiped clean. Then you miss the fact that Christianity preaches humility and become the most self-righteous people on earth. I happen to think you have to live with whatever you've done, good or bad, for the rest of your life.

BORN-AGAIN CHRISTIAN: Enjoy hell.

ATHEIST: Yeah, yeah, I know. How does that old saying go? Choose heaven for the scenery and hell for the company? Well, for the record, I don't want to go to your heaven. I can think of nothing worse than having to spend eternity with narrow-minded idiots like you.

BORN-AGAIN CHRISTIAN: You're a servant of Satan. You just don't realize it.

ATHEIST: If I don't believe in God, it logically follows that I don't believe in Satan. He's your guy, not mine.

BORN-AGAIN CHRISTIAN: He's not my guy.

ATHEIST: Look, I don't care if you believe in a thousand gods. So why does it matter to you if I believe in none?

BORN-AGAIN CHRISTIAN: Because you're wrong. You're all wrong—

BUDDHIST: Oh, for Christ's sake, shut up.

From: Sydney Welles <s.welles@fbmm.com>
To: God c/o toptengods@godchecker.com
Date: Tuesday, May 31, 2005 5:50 PM PDT
Subject: Catholicism has no sex appeal

Dear God,

Nothing about Catholicism--with the exception of Father Bernadi--is sexy. This is very unfortunate because it's true what they say, sex sells.

Christianity has only one sexual position and you have to be married to use it. If you're Catholic, you also have to produce one new Catholic each time you use it. In any case, God forbid you enjoy it.

The most honored of Catholic figures, Mary, managed to get pregnant without having sex. Childbirth is incredibly painful for women who've had plenty of sex. What must it be like for a virgin? Words do not exist to describe the unfairness of the situation.

Not only does the Catholic Church forbid birth control, it, ideally, would like women to get pregnant without having sex. Two thousand years ago, women may have gone along with this. However, it won't go down well with women today. Let's not forget that women make up 51 percent of the population and make 80 percent of all purchasing decisions.

Syd

It's a great wonder that those working in the field of anthropology don't set up research camps in Los Angeles. The advances in human development originating here, spreading to the rest of the world through film, television, and celebrity magazines, are astounding. For instance, a completely new breed of woman has appeared in this city within the space of only one generation.

In the absence of qualified anthropologists, Noah is studying this divergent species and has classified them as Inverse Camel Girls.

Inverse Camel Girls are created when Hollywood starvelets hit puberty by way of breast implants. Puberty occurs when a starvelet realizes she's never going to be the next Julia Roberts and lowers her sights to nonspeaking parts in B movies, parts like Big-Breasted Girlfriend of Lesser Villain, or accepts the real-life role of Old Ugly Rich Guy's Girlfriend, which has very similar requirements.

Like camels, Inverse Camel Girls can survive without food for long periods because of the stores in their breasts. They're so evolved they have a secondary food store in their lips, which hold more each passing year. This combination of toothpick-thin bodies, obese lips, and breasts the size of their heads makes these girls singularly attractive. Men desperately want to mate with them. Sexual desirability is up there with adaptability in the natural selection process; the girls have to be the next step in the evolutionary process.

Whenever we begin a new qualitative research campaign, Noah rounds up flocks of Inverse Camel Girls, moderating the groups personally and wearing one of two T-shirts, I LOVE BIG FAKE TITS or FREE BREAST EXAM, until I notice what he's doing and tell him to stop. The purpose of consumer research is to find out what people are thinking, and thinking is not, generally speaking, an Inverse Camel Girl's forte.

Noah gets revenge on me by organizing interesting groups for me to moderate. The last-minute inclusion of an atheist in a group of mixed religionists was a Noah classic.

When he can no longer play with Inverse Camel Girls, Noah often turns to the only group of women more anthropologically remarkable. Noah calls them Permanently Startled Women. From an evolutionary standpoint, they're the forerunners of Inverse Camel Girls.

The difference between the two, apart from age, is that Permanently Startled Women don't carry food stores in humps out front: Breast implants were after their time. Permanently Startled Women don't need any food at all. As far as they're concerned, Atkins is for amateurs.

Permanently Startled Women are permanently startled because they went on "vacation," coming back "refreshed" when it was still the done thing for plastic surgeons to lift all the skin off a face, stretch it taut, and snip off the excess around the edges. Lift, stretch, trim, repeat every few years. A couple of decades go by and life is forever surprising you.

In meeting room number 5, a group of extremely slim women, wearing outfits in the same price bracket as a new Toyota Corolla, clustered around the light refreshment table. When I walked through the door, eight shocked expressions turned to greet me.

"I'll be right with you," I said before exiting the room the way I'd entered.

"Who screened this group?" I said to Patton who, in line

with his duties, had been following me around all day. He communed with his electronic diary. "It was Noah Glaser, ma'am."

Noah was, as I'd suspected, snugly ensconced in the observation room, mightily pleased.

I pointed at the women on the other side of the glass wall, a mirror if you were looking at it from their side. "Where did you find them?"

"Would you believe all in the one spot? Rodeo Drive, outside the very plush consulting rooms of doctors Williamson, Stafford, and White, plastic surgeons all. You can't complain. Every one of them passed the screening test. The right age group, the right income bracket, all churchgoing folk, or so they claim."

"They believe in God? Are you sure? Church attendance usually drops off once you reach that socioeconomic group."

"Maybe they have Him confused with Karl Lagerfeld?"

"You're getting back at me for sending you out there, aren't you? Well, I'm impressed with one thing. You got them to admit they're over sixty."

"We should get back in there." Noah stood. On his T-shirt was printed, JESUS HATES YOUR FACE LIFT.

"I don't know if that's appropriate."

"I have a spare in my bag. In case one of the babes from the media department drags me home for sex and I don't have time to go home before work in the morning."

"That ever happened?"

"There's a first time for everything." He held up the T-shirt he'd pulled out of his bag, which, as well as boasting severe creases, said RELIGION: KEEPING THE POOR FROM KILLING THE RICH FOR 2000 YEARS.

"Okay, I'll put on my jacket," he said, pulling on something black and hooded and zipping it. As he preceded me out of the room I saw that the words BABIES ARE ASSHOLES were sewn across his back in inch-high letters.

Back in meeting room 5, I surveyed our ladies' group, lined up in front of us like so many deer in the headlights.

"Do you want to moderate or shall—"

Noah got down on his knees and clasped his hands together. "Let me do it," he said. "Please, let me. I'll be good from now on. I promise."

With Noah steering it, the group progressed smoothly through the two hours allotted for it. Our Permanently Startled Women were, to a woman, quite prepared to purchase God, religion, and anything else we had for sale, but I couldn't help but feel that for these women, heaven would be a bit of a comedown.

"A rating," the woman name-tagged "Heloise" said. She was a dazzling woman who was the group leader in the if-you've-got-great-big-diamonds-wear-them-all-at-once category. "I think every church should come with a rating or something. Someone ought to go out there and review all the religions. Put it all in a Michelin guide."

"Yes," Jackie said. "Otherwise how can we be sure we're getting the best?" Jackie, according to the information I had in front of me, was sixty-two, thrice divorced, and the possessor of an annual household income of over $650K, all of it alimony.

"No, no, no, hon, what we need is not a rating," Victoria said—at seventy with a $1.8 million annual income, the oldest and richest of the group. She turned to me. "You see, honey, what we need is a guarantee of some kind. A rock-solid lifetime warranty."

This met with general agreement from the group. God needed to come with a guarantee.

"Okay," said Noah, "one more question. How would you describe your relationship with God? For instance, would you say God is a friend, a companion? Or would you say God is an authority figure, a judge, someone you have to please?"

The answer was "none of the above." To the best of my understanding, to this group God was first a kind of senior flight attendant who checked your tickets and made sure that coach-class people didn't get into the first-class heaven. Second he was the universe's greatest host, and heaven the house party to end all house parties.

"Unless there are any questions you'd like to ask us . . . we are just going to do one last exercise. This is heaven," I said, indicating a large piece of white cardboard propped up on an easel behind me on my right. "And this is hell." I pointed to a second piece of cardboard, also on an easel, next to the first.

Noah placed a large pile of glossy magazines on the table, heavy on travel and fashion, along with several pairs of scissors and sticks of glue.

"I'd like you each to go through these magazines," I said, "and pull three or four pictures that make you think of heaven and three or four that make you think of hell. We'll stick all the heaven pictures to the heaven board and all the hell pictures to the hell board."

The women, on their feet instantly, buzzed between the magazines and the boards like expensively attired, anorexic mosquitoes. Soon the magazines were drained, the two large pieces of cardboard swelling with pictures.

Heaven looked like a tropical island. A tropical island lousy with Tuscan villas and five-star holiday resorts, under blue skies dotted with fat, fair-weather clouds, oversized Cartier diamonds, and thin, tanned, blonde people in skintight white

Versace. Also readily available in heaven were cocktails, cabana boys, and several versions of George Clooney.

Hell was a dusty, third world landscape with tract housing, budget hotels, a couple of game show hosts, two or three politicians, several children who looked as if they could use a sponsor, and people wearing chain store clothing.

From: Sydney Welles <s.welles@fbmm.com>
To: God c/o thequeen@buckinghampalace.co.uk
Date: Thursday, June 2, 2005 4:32 PM PDT
Subject: Long Odds

Dear God,

I've been told several times now that getting into heaven depends on being a member of the one true church.

According to Father Bernadi, there are 19 world religions, which are divided into about 270 large religious groups, and these are further divided into subgroups. There are 34,000 separate Christian groups alone.

I'm curious, what are the chances of picking the right one? Higher or lower than winning the lottery?

Syd

Anna and I were in a bar in Venice—a classic midlife crisis bar catering to men of a certain age and socioeconomic group. Poor men can't afford to indulge a midlife crisis with money; there's no point catering to them. Women, given the gender difference in maturity levels, reassess their lives while there's still time to do something a little more constructive about it than mope around in a bar. Wealthy men in midlife crisis rarely do anything constructive. Instead they purchase convertible sports cars, which they speed around in, top down, hoping the g-forces will make them look younger.

It was just after opening time when we arrived, but three typical crisis cases, a ponytail, a comb-over, and a toupee, were already propping up the wood-veneered bar. By the way their reflections in the mirror behind the bar perked up when we walked in, we knew at least three rounds of drinks were headed our way.

Anna and I ordered Bellinis, requesting they be made with fresh, out-of-season white peaches crushed by hand into the most expensive Prosecco available. The bartender, with a nod of conspiracy, complied on the house.

An MLC bar survives by ensuring its wealthy male patrons spend their wealth over the bar. But these men, even in the throes of middle age imbroglios, can only drink so much on their own, and though they're incapable of fidelity in other areas of life, they remain faithful to the inexpensive drink they've been drinking since youth—commonly known as beer.

The bar's financial success requires a steady flow of cocktail-drinking female customers. Women, as long as they're young enough, don't pay for a thing. Your first drink is on the house and after that someone will buy you drinks. What patrons of an MLC bar lack in youth and hair, they make up for in a willingness to part with money.

Anna and I are exactly the right age for a midlife crisis bar. Old enough to know better, but young enough to look as if we don't know anything at all.

"So let me guess. Is this about Jake?" Anna said as soon as we'd settled in at a table.

"How did you know?"

"Let's see. You call me and tell me you have a problem you need to discuss. At the moment you're interviewing religious nuts for a living. For the past two years you've worked for a company that treats you like a highly paid intern, with male colleagues who take your ideas and pass them off as their own. You have no life outside of work except when I drag you out. You use alcohol as an emotional crutch—not that I'm hypocritical enough to judge—and you've been on six failed dates since you broke up with Matt the Rat. Despite this, recently, through no real desire or effort of your own, you meet a nice, intelligent, good-looking guy who is crazy about you. It's obvious he has to be the problem."

"Christ, you know me too well. I have to get some new friends."

"This is LA. The only friends you'll find here are on TV. You're stuck with me."

Our Bellinis arrived, Anna took a short break to taste hers, pronounced it not nearly as good as the one served at Harry's Bar in the other Venice, and was immediately back on my case. "So what is the problem, exactly?"

"I don't know, not exactly."

"I'm finding it difficult to see any problem. What? He wears women's underwear to bed?"

"That kind of stuff doesn't come out for months."

"Any disgusting personal habits or Freudian complexes?"

"No more than the next guy."

"Small dick, huh?"

"No."

"Well, then I don't know either. He looks like good raw material to me. I like him. Vince likes him. The girls like him—that doesn't count, they like everybody."

"He's likeable, I'll give you that."

"He was really good with the kids at the party."

"Why do we always assume that a guy who gets along with kids is a great catch? Why don't we assume he's a pedophile?"

Anna gave me the look she gives me when she thinks I've left my brain in a jar by my bed. "The kids liked him. You're going to hold this against him?"

"I'm not holding it against him. I'm just not holding it up as a sign that he's the world's greatest guy. When a man gets along with a bunch of small children, it's usually because they're all mingling at the same maturity level."

One of those cartoon lightbulbs appeared above Anna's head, or rather it should have, to add the finishing touch to the expression on her face. She said, "I get it. I get what the problem is. It's obvious."

"Do you think you could explain it to me?"

"Your problem is there is no problem. Don't you see? It's because there's no problem that you think there's a problem when there's not."

"I think you may have to speak slower so I can understand you."

"Look, with every guy in LA, every guy you've dated anyway,

there's always some insurmountable issue that prevents any relationship they're in from getting off the ground. Right?"

"I guess."

"I'm right. At the very least, it's the Hollywood Seven Week Itch. You know, that 'How can I commit to you when every week there's someone younger and better looking, struggling to make it as an actress and therefore desperate enough to date me, coming along?' Don't you see? You're so used to dealing with guys with issues that when you come across one without any, you think it's a problem. That's the problem."

I tipped the rest of my Bellini down my throat. "How do you know an issue won't kick in as soon as the next Hollywood starvelet crosses his path?"

"It won't," she said.

"How do you know?"

"I just know."

"Right."

"Okay, I know because of his ex."

"Because of Kim? I'm not following your logic."

"Well, she proves he's not in thrall to the Seven Week Itch. He didn't move on to a much younger, better-looking, bigger-breasted version of her, now did he? He moved on to you."

"I see what you're saying. Thank you. I feel so much better now."

She waggled a hand at me. "You know what I mean."

"I do. And that's weird right there. Between Kim and me, he chooses me. He's either insane or a typical guy, wanting whatever he doesn't have. Neither bodes well. And how can she and I both be his type?"

"I think she may be everybody's type," Anna said. "Even so, you're not exactly chopped liver."

"I think Jake's too sure about us—me and him."

"This is a problem?"

"I know, I know," I said. "But it is. It's too good to be true. It makes me suspect something else is going on. I'm killing myself trying to figure out what it could be."

Anna looked at me archly, like an actor in a BBC adaptation of a Jane Austen novel. "You might find out if you returned one of his calls."

We were no longer alone. The bartender was standing by our table with brand-new Bellinis. Going by the smarmy smile aimed at us by the man with the ponytail sitting at the bar, he was guilty of paying for them.

"Incoming," Anna said. She picked up her new glass and raised it to its sponsor, who immediately slid off his barstool to ooze on over. "Look, this is all very simple. It's that Groucho Marx thing—that 'I don't want to belong to a club that'll accept me as a member.' Jake is sure about you, so you're unsure about him. It's your own self-worth issue. You just have to get over it. Which is why we're here. Therapy."

Mr. Ponytail stood by our table, trying to look casual, as if he were just passing our table and happened to notice the people who occupied it were in possession of drinks he'd paid for. Even by the low standards of a midlife crisis bar, it was a little pathetic.

I'd called Anna earlier in the day to switch Friday night drinks to a Thursday-night crisis summit. We chose the bar for the free therapy: Spend five minutes with a man going through a midlife crisis and you'll feel great about yourself simply because you're not him. The free drinks are just a bonus.

MLC bars, like all natural resources, should be used sparingly. In the last three years we've visited only a few times.

Most recently, but over a year ago now, I called a meeting for the Soap Star Left Me For Someone Named Bambi—Or Was It Bimbo? catastrophe.

"Let me guess," Anna said. "Your wife doesn't understand you."

Mr. Ponytail was genuinely surprised. "How did you know?"

"A lucky guess," I said. "How long have you been married?"

"Three months," he said.

"And this is your . . . second marriage? Third? Fourth? Say when."

"Second."

"Just a beginner then," Anna said.

"We got married in Vegas, when my divorce came through." He sighed. "I was sure this time it would be different. Women are all the same. They change as soon as you marry them."

Anna and I traded looks but said nothing. I desperately wanted to point out to Mr. Ponytail that he was making a generalization about all women based on the only two stupid enough to marry him, but I restrained myself. Experience has taught me that irony is often lost on men in midlife crisis bars.

"The whole time you're going out with them, they let you think you're in charge. You think you're calling the shots. Then you get married and bang, you find out she's been in charge all along. She only let you think you were in charge while you were dating."

"It can't be all that bad," I said.

"It was great before we were married."

"Nothing's really changed," Anna said. "She was the boss then. She's the boss now."

"She just tells me what to do now. She doesn't even pretend anymore."

"Does she make good decisions?"

"Well, yeah, she's smart. Smarter than me."

"Then what's the problem?"

"I'm the man. I'm meant to call the shots."

"Let me get this straight. You don't really want to call the shots, you just want her to pretend that you're calling the shots, like she did before you were married," Anna said, gently. I'm beginning to suspect her upcoming nuptials are softening her.

"Is that too much to ask?"

Anna was being indulgent with him. That meant I was the bad cop in the situation.

"Oh, cheer up already. So you're number two on the totem pole, so what? It could be a whole lot worse," I said.

"How do you figure that?"

"Christ, think about it for a minute. You could actually be in charge."

Mr. Ponytail was clearly overwhelmed by this new perspective. He gulped and blinked several times in terror of the sheerest kind.

"You're right, that would be worse," he said. It came out in a whisper. He glanced at his watch. "I have to get home, it's getting late." It was a quarter to seven. "Bye."

"Bye," Anna and I said in unison.

Mr. Ponytail was already halfway to the door.

We grinned at each other. Our first crisis case of the evening was a success. Every time we've visited, we've scared at least one guy back to his family. We like to think we perform a community service in return for the money we save on therapists and cocktails.

An MLC bar also provides complete anonymity for our sessions. Unless all your friends are wealthy, middle-aged men with maturity problems, you're unlikely to bump into anyone you know. Until that evening we never had.

After the briefest of intervals, a fresh round of drinks arrived courtesy of Mr. Toupee, who got up to follow them to our table. A courageous move on his part after he'd seen us dispatch his fellow barfly.

However, his courage had limits. He never made it to our table, stopped in his tracks by another who reached our table first. Judging from the guilty look that appeared on Mr. Toupee's face—he blushed to the glue of his hair—and the speed he used to propel his portly body out the door, I assumed the man was Catholic, scared away by the specter of a priest in a place where he was hoping to sin.

I was a little startled myself. I managed to offer Father Bernadi a seat at our table and to blurt out something stupid like, "What's a nice priest like you doing in a place like this?"

Anna didn't say anything at all. Although I'd previously described him to her in some detail, it was the first time she'd seen Father Bernadi in person. She was busy trying not to drool.

"Hello, Anna. How do you do?" he said to her after I'd introduced them. She only managed a squeaky sort of noise in reply that could have been "hi" or "fine" or "eeee."

Beauty, like everything else, is relative. In a room with the men on *People* magazine's Sexiest Man Alive list, Father Bernadi would only be slightly above average—perhaps not in the number-one position, but certainly well ahead of the Scientologists. In an MLC bar, it was hard to accept he was the same species as the other men present. No wonder Anna was taking it hard.

Spending more and more time with him I was beginning to get used to his looks, but I still couldn't help but feel ridiculously pleased when he said, "I've been looking for you."

"For me? How did you find me?" I hoped I wasn't simpering.

"I asked your Patton. He told me you were here, then supplied me with a map, a car, and a driver to get me here."

"Sounds like Patton."

The place had filled since Anna and I had come in. It was a far more crowded bar Father Bernadi faced when he took in his surroundings: the Sean-Connery-as-James-Bond era furnishings; the abundance of middle-aged, hair-challenged men, all dressed as if they imagined they were twenty years younger; and an odd assortment of younger women scattered intermittently here and there, now all staring intently at our table. The quite large number of full drinks we had sitting on our table didn't escape his notice either.

"What kind of place is this?" Father Bernadi wanted to know.

I explained the concept of an MLC bar to him and the role it played from time to time in our lives, taking care to dwell on the charitable work Anna and I perform here. Anna was, for all intents and purposes, mute.

Father Bernadi gave me the benefit of his warm, steady gaze. "That explains a good deal. I have never seen so many obviously lost souls gathered together in one place like this."

I laughed, but it did cross my mind that he might have been including me in their number.

From: Sydney Welles <sydneywelles@yahoo.com>
To: God c/o professordumbledore@hogwartsschoolofwitchcraftandwizardry
.co.uk
Date: Friday, June 3, 2005 1:23 AM PDT
Subject: Male Chauvinist Gods

Dear God,

Pinning the blame for the fall of mankind on the first woman they could find was only the beginning of religious gender discrimination.

Ever since, every job opening above middle management level--disciple, ark builder, Red Sea parter, wise man, savior of mankind, etc.--has gone to a man. It's plain sexism and, in one case, also nepotism.

Religion even goes to the trouble of covering the signs of male pattern baldness. Two major religions have little hats designed to cover bald spots.

There is only one explanation for it. You must be a man.

Never mind.

Sydney

If the midlife crisis bar was a gathering place for lost souls, then the club lounge where I awaited my flight to St. Louis was hell.

I'd endured the LAX security measures requiring every reasonably attractive woman under the age of fifty to remove her jacket—even if the jacket was made of the lightest and sheerest of fabrics and would be classified by the garment industry as a blouse—while ugly men, wearing jackets that could hold enough arsenal to take out a dozen planes, strode through without being asked to disrobe.

Now, in a corner of the club lounge, I tried to close my eyes. Occasionally I'd take the time to glare at the people in suits invading the lounge. They had no right to look so pressed and fresh at five o'clock in the morning or to make cell phone calls when I was sleep deprived. Who did they have to talk to at this hour anyway? Even on the east coast it was only eight o'clock.

I'd spent the last three or four hours lying prone on my bed without managing to fall asleep. The only bright side was that I was now too exhausted to think. It was thinking that had kept me from sleeping, and it was Father Bernadi who had started me thinking, though Anna and Larry had also inconsiderately gotten in on the act.

Father Bernadi had sought me out last night to tell me something vital the Church thought I had to know before I left on my trip, and which I can't for the life of me remember now. While with us, the priest seemed intensely interested in the patrons of the MLC bar. I guess if you save souls for a living, then being in the midst of so many needing redemption would make you itch to exercise your professional skills.

I'm not a hundred percent sure but I think that he may have exercised some of his priestly skills on me, too, getting me to confess things I didn't want to confess while Anna was being accosted by an aging former child star who'd managed to corner her on her way back from the bathroom in spite of being at least two feet shorter than she was.

"These people are lost because the things they have based their lives on are things that essentially don't matter," Father Bernadi said. He's not much of a one for gossip or small talk.

"What are you saying? Porsches don't matter?"

"Yes, judging from the cars parked outside, they own a hundred times more than most people in the world will ever have, and yet here they are, miserable."

"Yes, here they are. In a bar avoiding their problems," I said.

"We all do that to a certain extent."

Did he have to look at me when he said that?

Father Bernadi made a gesture to include everyone in the bar. "It seems these people spent their youth wishing for all the things they have now, and now that they have everything they could possibly want, they are wishing for youth."

"The irony of life and all that," I said.

"Yes, we have more than previous generations could have imagined, but no time to enjoy it. Now that we are able to have all the things we want, those things are all we can have."

He'd obviously given the issue some previous thought. "You know what else is ironic?"

He didn't know.

"From what I can tell, religion has a great deal to do with being grateful for what you have. God is big on gratitude. Right?"

"Right."

"And advertising exists solely to show people all the things they don't have. It tells us that we need more. Even if you already have something, there's always a newer, bigger, smaller, better version you need. Right?"

"Right."

"Well, don't you think that a religion wanting to advertise is, well, kind of incongruous? It's like . . ."

About then, I realized that I was about to confess to a potential client of the agency, a priest no less, that I thought appointing us as their advertising agency would be akin to God appointing Satan heaven's general manager. At the same time I also realized that saying such a thing was not good for my career.

"Um, let's talk about something else," I said.

"What would you like to talk about?"

"Do you know what I most like about Catholicism?"

He said he didn't.

"I like that Catholics don't seem to have an issue with drinking, even though they have an issue with just about everything else. It must be because they can't be hypocritical about it, not when they serve wine in church."

"It must be," Father Bernadi said. "After all, religions are never hypocritical."

When he said that, I realized I'd lied to a priest. The thing I most liked about Catholicism was not the drinking. The thing I most liked about Catholicism was Father Bernadi.

✝

Patton had also informed Larry of our whereabouts. Unlike Father Bernadi, Larry didn't have anything important to tell me; he just likes to know where everyone is drinking so he can join in. He strode into the bar not long after Father Bernadi left. More accurately, he waddled in. At a certain blood-alcohol level, about point one-eight, Larry walks like a cautious duck, his feet splayed out. It's slow going on flat ground, but he can waddle pretty fast downhill.

He waddled over to us.

"Girls! Girrls! Girrrls!" he said, not unlike a hawker in front of a strip club.

Standing before our table, he was contemplating Anna and me as if we were drifting pleasantly in and out of his focal range. Larry is a notoriously happy drunk. His face begins smiling halfway through his second drink of an evening and doesn't stop unless LA County runs out of beer.

"Why don't you sit down, Larry," Anna said.

"Don't mind if I do. Don't mind if I do. I'm too old to be coy." Larry slowly lowered himself onto a chair. He relaxed into his seat but kept a sharp eye on his feet, as if he suspected they'd lead him in a Ukrainian Cossack dance if left to their own devices. Once he was sure his extremities were behaving, he stared at Anna until Anna came into focus for him.

"It's the lovely Ms. Perry. Where the fuck have you been? I haven't seen you for . . . it's been so long, I don't remember how long it's been. Too long. Have you been on vacation?"

"No."

"Then why haven't you been in at the office?"

"I don't work for you anymore. I haven't for over a year now," Anna said.

The ends of Larry's mustache lowered in surprise. "No, not that long? What happened? Why wasn't I invited to your going-away party?"

"You were the life of the party."

"I was?" Larry's mustache cheered up. "Good party, was it? Don't seem to recall it."

He caught the attention of a waiter, and, admonishing him not to be shy, Larry gave him temporary custody of a credit card so major it could purchase the place.

Larry surveyed the room. "What are you girls doing in this dump? You might be past your prime, but you can do better than these guys."

"Thanks," Anna said.

The bartender brought our drinks, which by any standards but Larry's were normal sized. After frowning at them, he then frowned at me. "What's wrong with you? Why aren't you drinking? Why are you so quiet?"

"Not much to say, I guess," I said.

"I know what's wrong with you. It's the damn Church. If I had to come up with a way to sell them, I'd be crying in my champagne cocktail too," he said.

"I'm not crying. It's not the Church."

"It should be. We don't land the account, we'll be fucked for the year. The vultures at Megacom will eat us for breakfast. I'll have to fire everybody. You know what the corporate boys are like."

I didn't know. I'd never met a soul from the Megacom Group, the holding company that owned our agency network and about a third of the other advertising agencies on the planet. But I did know from experience that the minutest of changes in figures, made by a faceless number cruncher at the Megacom level, could upset my life entirely.

"Okay, now I'm worried."

"Good," Larry said. "Worry a lot. You'll have it sorted when I get back, won't you?"

"Where are you going?"

"Switzerland. It's that time of year again."

Larry meant it was time for his annual detox at an exclusive Swiss clinic catering to well-heeled addicts the world over. The staff-to-patient ratio is incredible—twenty to one or close to it—and the facilities on par with the three or four hotels regarded as the best in the world.

Larry is only moderately wealthy as a result of his career in advertising. He can afford the clinic because he's obscenely rich in his spare time, a scion of an old tobacco family with numbered bank accounts to pay respects to in Geneva on his way to the rehab clinic in Zurich.

"Couldn't you wait to go until after this Church thing is over?"

"Nope, can't wait. Doctor says with any kind of delay there's a slight chance of death. How's it all going anyway?"

"Well, I have no idea how we're going to approach this," I said. "But at least the questionable morality of selling religion doesn't seem to be an issue."

"That was never going to be an issue. We ought to have seen that from the start. People will never see the real issues, not when they can focus on the things that don't matter. Have you learned nothing from presidential election campaigns? Getting around morality is the easy part. If you don't say it's an issue, no one will know it's an issue. Getting them to buy our brand of God is the trick. What have you tried?"

"All the usual ways of positioning it. Nothing's working."

"What's the problem?"

"Advertising is the problem. We've trained consumers to look for a product benefit, and we've trained them to be skeptical about that benefit unless we can provide them with a reason to believe it. You just can't sell snake oil anymore. Religion, as a product, is snake oil. The product benefits are all things that can't be proven or demonstrated. How do you package heaven when no one has ever seen it?"

Larry nodded in agreement. "You're going to have to pull something out of your ass."

"Maybe you just can't sell religion."

"Not true. Thank God. There are TV evangelists flying between their mansions on Lear jets because people are buying what they are selling, which, essentially, is nothing. You can sell religion. It's just no one does it with any kind of integrity."

"I don't have a working hypothesis to take into quantitative research yet. And I have no idea when I'll have one."

"Hell," said Larry, "Don't look at me like that. I don't know either. This wise old-guy exterior is just a facade. I look like Methuselah but only because I drink too much. I'm just a normal guy. I get up every morning. I shave. I have a beer. I go to work. That's all, just a normal fucking guy. I don't have any answers."

Neither did I.

✝

"Just call the poor guy," Anna said, as Larry's car—sans Larry; he was visiting another bar while his driver took us home—pulled up in front of my place. She was, of course, referring to Jake. She seemed to have appointed herself head of his fan club.

I looked around at the tan leather and burled wood interior of the golden Rolls Royce we were in. "I wonder how much this set Larry back?"

"Call him."

"Can't. It's too late to call him now and I'm getting on a

plane at six o'clock in the morning, which is too early to call him."

"Where are you going?"

"It's that research thing I told you about, the three-city sample tour, St. Louis, Houston, and Vegas."

"I thought you said you didn't have to go on that trip."

"I did say that. Strictly speaking, I don't really have to go, but I thought I'd keep my hand in . . . keep an eye on things . . . this is a really big project . . . if anything went—"

"You're running away. From Jake."

"You know, the world does not revolve around Jake. I'm not running away from anyone. It's work. Unlike those in the back of the car who are marrying money, I have to work for a living."

"You're running away."

"I am not."

"Are too."

"Am not—it's too late at night, I mean, early in the morning for this. I have a cab picking me up in four and a half hours. I have to go."

"Call him from the road. They have phones where you're going, right? Your cell phone still works?"

"I will if I can. If I'm not too busy."

"Yeah, right," Anna said. "Let me just say this for the record. You're making a big mistake. I'll be saying 'I told you so' just as soon as I possibly can."

"That certainly gives me something to look forward to."

"Me too," she said.

Dear God,

I told your priest that advertising and religion are incongruous partners, but I've been thinking about it since, and when you really look at them, advertising and religion have a lot in common. Both:

1. Have their fair share of false prophets

2. Are in the business of getting the public to part with their money

3. Distort the truth as it suits them

4. Have no basis in science

5. Claim miracles do occur

6. Want you to believe their version of the truth is better than the other guy's version of the truth

7. Use fear, uncertainty, and doubt as marketing tools

8. Are fond of making exaggerated claims

9. Promise acceptance and validation by your peers if you buy what they're selling

10. Offer intangible promises that can't be proven one way or the other

If you drink this sacramental wine you'll go to paradise, or if you drink this beer women barely in bikinis will wrestle each other in front of you, and this for some reason represents paradise for most men. What's the difference, really?

Best,

Syd

P.S. How is Elvis? Everybody wants to know.

One of the peculiar things about the U.S. is that fun is distributed on a geographical basis. It's contained entirely in a number of designated sites.

Childhood fun is enclosed in a series of artificial worlds, or theme parks, where junk food and rides—which cause you to vomit junk food—equal a good time.

Adult fun is allocated space in the real world. At times it has entire cities at its disposal. In the real world, fun is all about giving your money to a casino or a stripper. An adult good time always involves alcohol, which also causes vomiting. Sometimes it also requires a silly item of clothing so that those around you will be able to tell that you're having fun.

People behave so badly in fun places you'd think they didn't have any fun at home. This is probably true. For example, there's no fun in Houston. That's understandable. They keep NASA and oil companies there. If they had fun, something's bound to blow up.

The reason adult fun is restricted to certain areas is because fun in the adult sense is equated with sin in the mortal sense. God doesn't like it when you have fun. So to avoid the wrath of God, people don't want to live in fun places. They don't want them anywhere near their homes. But even God understands that a person has to work, so all business conventions are held in fun places.

While there are other notable repositories, Las Vegas is the main U.S. storage facility of fun for grown-ups, especially aging frat boys, conventioneers, and anyone who thinks getting a hotel room at a cut rate and then losing thousands of dollars in that hotel's casino is a good deal.

In spite of being in a casino, in Vegas, I wasn't having fun. The joy that comes from depositing a mortgage payment into a slot machine eluded me.

"What about a show?" Noah pointed at an indoor billboard featuring several women wearing only strategically positioned rhinestones and feathers. "They seem to be very talented dancers."

"They're topless dancers," I said.

"They're not," Noah said, "they're wearing—things."

He was right. They had rhinestones where their nipples should have been.

We watched security guards round up a nearby man who didn't meet the dress code and escort him out of the room. While the official dress code was more or less anything goes, the man in question was barefoot, claiming to have lost his shoes and socks somewhere near the blackjack table. According to one of the security guards, several people had complained about his foot odor.

"Amazing," Noah said. "You can piss in a plastic cup in here but you can't go barefoot."

"The irony," I said.

"It would've been more appropriate if he'd lost his shirt instead. What about a magic show?" Another poster featured a man with a supernatural tan, wearing a sparkling white suit. He was holding an orb of light in one hand, staring out from the wall in that intense, maniacal way only magicians can.

Both Patton and I pulled faces.

"We're not going to get into anything good at the last minute," Noah said. "We must accept this and choose from the available crap."

"It's all class," I said, "but I think I'll skip it. You guys go ahead."

"You're being such an old woman," Noah said. "You didn't come out in St. Louis either."

"I had to have dinner with my parents. They drove in from Chicago. I couldn't very well blow them off."

"Sure you could."

"I'll see you back at the hotel," I said.

A waitress bearing a tray walked past in what would've been a toga if it'd been a lot longer, taking all of Noah's attention from me.

"Okay, then," he said. "See ya."

"I'll come with you, ma'am." Patton was trying to take up as little space as possible, uncomfortable in this den of iniquity.

"No, you stay," I said. "You and Noah have a good time. Befriend one of these poor dancers who can't afford tops."

"I'd rather come with you, ma'am."

"You're old enough to drink and gamble, aren't you?"

"Yes, ma'am. As of January, ma'am."

"Then go drink and charge it to the project. Tell you what, if it makes you feel better, I'll give you a research assignment. Find out how many of these people will be in church on Sunday."

"All of them, I bet," Noah said. "Hypocrites."

"We're here," I said.

"We're here," he said, " but we don't go around thinking we're better than us because we spend an hour a week sitting in a building with a bunch of other hypocrites, wishing we were someplace else."

The shirt Noah had picked out for the evening read, RE-MEMBER THAT JESUS LOVES YOU. BECAUSE THE REST OF US

THINK YOU'RE AN ASSHOLE. He was clearly in an aggressive mood.

"Okay, I get the point," I said.

"What are you going to do?"

"I'm going to my room," I said.

"Do you want us to walk you?"

"It's in the building. I'll be fine. Take care of the little one."

Patton drew himself up to his full six-foot-three-and-a-half at being thus addressed.

"It won't kill you to have a good time," I said.

He looked pained, as if it would.

✝

I walked around for a while looking for the elevators to my room. They proved elusive, shrouded by the noise, lights, and garish décor of the casino. Instead, just past the high rollers' room, I discovered a bar. It was dark, quiet, and all but empty. I needed to escape the desperate atmosphere of the casino—the collective delirium of hundreds of people, each believing wealth would be theirs in the immediate future despite the overwhelming odds against that ever happening even in the infinite future.

Ignoring the crunchy quality of the tired carpet under my feet, I made my way over to the bar, perching on a sticky stool. The barman, looking as if he'd shaved for the very first time that evening, hovered behind the bar polishing a glass. He asked what I'd like to drink as soon as I sat.

I've noted, on more than one occasion, that my alcohol consumption has gained in momentum since I broke up with Matt the Rat. Actually, the escalation may have dated from the time I started going out with him. But now, in a town where everybody seemed to be drinking—that is, when they weren't busy throwing away their life's savings or spending quality time with sex-industry employees of their preferred gender—I didn't feel like drinking at all.

"I don't know, a Coke?"

The bartender showed his disappointment in me. "We can do better than that."

The bar had three other customers, one sitting at the bar like me. In a corner, at a table, two middle-aged, mustached men, dressed like cowboys, were arguing. When their dispute became louder for a moment, the snippet I overheard made me think they were disagreeing about the respective quality of two racehorses, although in retrospect they could also have been discussing two fast women.

The bartender put a martini glass in front of me and filled it from a little jug, which he also put in front of me. The liquid in the glass looked like the world's dirtiest martini, but tasted just like fresh apple juice.

Once he served me, the bartender did not appear to be the chatty sort. He went back to polishing the same glass he was polishing before—the glass he'd continue to polish for the rest of the evening. I was therefore forced to attempt conversation with the other person seated at the bar. He was the sort of guy for whom a light-blue button-down shirt, worn over a white T-shirt and teamed with jeans and sneakers, would always be the height of fashion.

"So," I said, "are you here for a convention or something?"

Brightening, he said, "No, actually. It's a funny story. An old college buddy of mine—he's a vacuum cleaner salesman— called me out of the blue and told me he'd won a trip for two to Vegas. It was for selling more vacuum cleaners than anyone else in the whole region for all of February. That's a tough month to win. On account of it has less days in it to make the numbers."

I nodded to show I was impressed at the February showing.

"Anyway, he didn't want to bring his wife—she didn't want him to come at all—so he asked me. I'm waiting for him now. I haven't seen him since college. Can you believe that? We're going to have so much fun."

"This is where they keep it."

He nodded in a way that made it clear he wasn't sure exactly what he was agreeing to. His left hand was curled around his glass. I checked his ring finger. It was occupied.

"What about your wife? Is she here too?"

"My wife? No, she's home. She didn't want me to come either."

"And yet here you are."

He looked guilty for a moment or two. "I'm going to do cultural things, too. Going to go see the Eiffel Tower tomorrow."

"Isn't that in France?"

"They have one here. Why go further?"

"Why indeed."

"You going to head out?"

"Me? No. No fun for me. I'm here for work—ostensibly. My best friend thinks I'm here because I'm running away from my life. She thinks I'm running away from someone, actually. This is my third city in four days, so I guess I'm doing a pretty good impression of being on the run. It's one of those if-it's-Tuesday-I-must-be-in-Texas trips. You know how it is."

"Er . . ." he said.

"Problem is, she's right. I am running away from him. Not just by taking this trip either. Since he and I, you know, got together, I've been on my way—this trip is just a kind of a physical exclamation point to the journey. You know what I mean?"

He didn't answer, but that didn't really matter. I was on a bit of a roll.

"The thing is—well—Jake seems just about perfect. But you and I both know there's no such thing. I mean, look at you. Your wife married you in good faith, and here you are about to play poker with your kid's college funds—or get friendly with a lap dancer—either way, I'm sure it's not what she had in mind when she got dressed up in that white lace airship, floated down the aisle, and said 'I do.'"

"I—"

"People have unrealistic expectations when it comes to love. I, on the other hand, don't. That's why I prefer dating people who wear their flaws on their sleeves. It's better to know upfront. However, if I continue dating this seemingly perfect guy, unrealistic expectations will set in. I'd just be setting myself up for a fall. What's the point? This way it ends quickly. No one gets hurt. No one gets left at home while others go to Vegas."

"Er . . . um . . ." He glanced around the bar for a way out of the conversation.

"It's just like you said. Why go further? Although in the case of the Eiffel Tower, it may be worth seeing the real thing over a replica in Vegas—but that's just my opinion."

He was cheerful again when he spotted someone outside the door of the bar, looking in. "Here's my friend, Richard."

Richard approached us. He was dressed in the same fashion as his friend, but unlike his friend had gone to the effort of combing his hair. Slicked down with a sticky-looking substance, it featured the most severe side part I'd seen outside of grade school.

The two men greeted each other not as old college buddies who hadn't seen each other in years but in an apprehensive way, as if any minute someone would tap them on the shoulder and tell them they had to go home.

"Are you ready to go?" Richard said.

His friend obediently stood up, and together they scampered out of the room as if a thousand disapproving wives were after them.

The bartender had discovered a whole pineapple somewhere under the counter and was holding it up to show me. "Pineapple juice?"

"Hit me."

A man in a tuxedo blew into the room. He took the seat on my left, placing a violin case on the bar.

"The usual, Nick," he said.

I was immediately impressed; I've always wanted to be able to walk into a bar, plop myself down, spout "the usual," and have the bartender know what that was.

The newcomer was a clean-shaven, slightly slimmer version of Santa Claus. He was all merry eyes and pink cheeks and had a smile powered by the same batteries they put in that toy bunny that plays the drums.

The usual turned out to be a tall pink drink adorned with a slice of pineapple, a plastic flamingo, and a pink-and-white-striped straw.

"Pink lemonade," the man said. "I don't drink."

I motioned my head toward the violin case. "Are you a gangster?"

The man clapped his hands together. "Oh, you think I'm wicked. I love it. I'm afraid I'm nothing so exciting. Just a violinist."

"Have you been out violin-ing?"

"I'm part of an eleven-piece orchestra for a lounge act—a tribute show."

"Who is the act a tribute to?"

"It varies. Depends who died."

"I'm Sydney," I said.

"Hello." He slid off his stool and bowed. "I'm Bartholomew. Bart, if you like."

We shook hands.

"Do you want me to play you something?"

"You take requests?"

"Naturally—only don't ask me to play 'La Vie En Rose.' Everyone always asks me to play 'La Vie En Rose.' I'm sick to death of it. I never want to play it again as long as I live."

"Go on, play 'La Vie En Rose.'"

"Oh, all right."

The men in the corner sidled two tables closer to us while Bart played. We were all silent until he finished.

"Where does one learn to play like that?"

"Boston Philharmonic. Played with them for years and years, until I came out of the closet, left my wife and Boston, and came here. Now it's weddings, parties, bar mitzvahs, and playing the dinner show for people who don't know the difference between a violin and a viola." Bart put down his violin. "But enough about me. What about you, what ails you?"

"How'd you know that anything ails me?"

"You're in this place of your own free will, aren't you?"

"Good point."

"I've changed my mind, let's talk about me some more. How old do you think I am?" Bart said. "How old?"

I looked him over, guessed an age, and added five years to it as anyone who asks you to guess their age generally looks younger than they are. "Forty-nine."

"No." He laughed, thrilled with my guess. "I'm over sixty."

"Are you sure?"

Bart was so pleased he wanted to perform again. He picked up his violin and tucked it under his chin in a well-rehearsed movement. His bow danced to the theme from *Carmen*, which he followed with a series of show tunes, each gayer than the last. The bar began to fill with people drawn by the spontaneous concert. How they heard the sound of a lone violin above the din of the floor of a casino, I'll never know.

"You know, Bart," I said, when he took a break, "if you weren't already married, over sixty, gay, and a teetotaller, I'd marry you in a minute."

Pleasure tinted his round cheeks. "Oh, you're just saying that." He patted my knee. "You know why else you ought not marry me?"

"Why?"

"No life insurance. No point marrying an old man if there's no life insurance. I don't have any kind of insurance at all. Don't believe in it."

"Why not?"

"I love to gamble—that's why I'm here—but I gamble to win. Insurance is gambling to lose. You're putting money on yourself to lose. Life insurance is the worst. You bet money on yourself to die. You live, you lose. The only way to collect big is if you die young, and then you're not around to collect it. It's a hell of a scam. The only thing we know for sure is that we'll die. Why bet money on it happening sooner rather than later?"

Bart picked up his instrument again. He placed the bow between his knees, holding it so it stuck out in front of him at a 45-degree angle, turned the violin upside down, and began to play a tune that he claimed was an Irish jig by rubbing the fiddle against the bow.

I sat there stunned, not because of his unorthodox violin playing but because he'd just inadvertently told me how to sell the Catholic Church.

I found a pen and envelope in my purse and jotted down the outline of the idea, then, realizing that there was something in the envelope, I peeked inside and found fifty unspent per diem dollars. I tucked the money into Bart's violin case while he was busy fiddling between his legs.

From: Sydney Welles <s.welles@fbmm.com>
To: God c/o info@hollywoodjesus.com
Date: Friday, June 10, 2005 12:32 AM PDT
Subject: Heaven is full of dead people

Dear God,

The one prerequisite for entry into heaven that everybody agrees on is death. No one gets in without dying. You get to live in paradise and have the best of everything, but only once you're a corpse. Am I the only one who sees a problem with this?

See ya,

Syd

P.S. It just occurred to me that you if you exist you might reply to one of my e-mails. I thought I should let you know that I'd prefer it if you didn't. It's just that these days, the people who claim you talk to them personally . . . well . . . they're not exactly Solomon and David anymore, are they?

Fisher Bennet McMahon & May

4848 Abott Way Los Angeles CA 90066 USA 310-807-3000 t 310-807-5000 f

Charles Turner
Los Angeles Times
202 W. 1st St.
Los Angeles, CA 90012

June 10, 2005

Dear Charles,

Thank you for your profuse and abject apologies. Consider them accepted and yourself forgiven, even though they could've been a little more profuse and a whole lot more abject.

It does sound as if you've been busy.

It is a good feng shui practice to get rid of old unwanted things on a regular basis. I'm pleased that you're doing what you can to unclutter your life and allow your energy to flow freely. But I'm curious. What exactly made you dump your girlfriend?

What happened? Did you just turn forty? Did she just turn twenty-six and become too old for you? Or did you see a more recent model of her and decide to upgrade?

For your sake, I hope you find a new girlfriend that:

a) Likes your new Porsche
b) Likes your new Ferrari
c) Likes your new Harley-Davidson
d) Is too young to recognize any of the above as midlife crisis accessories

If the answer is d), you can use one of those accessories to take her to her high school prom. Personally I'd go with the Harley. You'll be the envy of all those teenage boys.

Yours (but only figuratively),
Sydney

In spite of arriving in the office just before one o'clock after a turbulent flight only to face what looked like ten hours of back-to-back meetings, I was so cheerful and efficient at work that several people complained to management.

Everything concerning the Catholic Church account is supposed to be top secret, even within the agency. Any information regarding it is shared on a need-to-know basis, only with those directly working on it. This means that everyone who works at Fisher Bennet and its subsidiary companies knows more about the project than I do. The whole agency was keen to find out how our research groups had gone.

I left the recounting up to Noah, since recounting is one of his favorite things to do at work—that, taking naps, and eating plain saltine crackers, starting at a corner and nibbling his way through like a hamster, one after the other for hours on end. I had work to do, or rather I had meetings to attend.

I was in meetings that couldn't start because half the agency was supposed to be in attendance and nearly everyone was late; meetings that were really just group therapy for those who called them; meetings that were ego exercise sessions for those so senior in management they no longer had any kind of function to perform; and meetings with no discernable purpose at all.

All the meetings had two things in common. They ran overtime and no food was served. I found both annoying as I'd been up since six, had spent my morning with some of

Nevada's oddest Catholics, and had nothing to eat except for a couple of saltines filched from Noah's supply.

When I'd escaped the final meeting of the day, a brainstorming session to which most of the attendees forgot to bring their brains, it was late and I was tired. It was almost ten o'clock on a Friday night and about a quarter of the agency was still working. That wasn't surprising. As well as the Church project, two other new business pitches were underway, and all of them were conducted over and above the normal workload for the clients we did have.

Heading back to my office to gather up my things and leave, I heard a voice call out my name from the office that had temporarily been assigned to Father Bernadi. It was Larry's voice but it sounded thicker, higher than usual, as if it came from a Muppet of Larry rather than Larry himself.

The priest's office is a small meeting room, made over. The remarkable woman who manages the agency's physical space had obviously assigned this office for the benefit of the whole agency, displaying the priest like some precious artifact under glass, clearly visible from hip height to ceiling.

His feet on the footstool, in one of a pair of original Eames lounge chairs, Larry, using both hands, held onto an unopened bottle of beer as if it were keeping him afloat in the sea of whatever it was he was swimming in. He was helplessly happy. Squinting at me, he said, "Why are you fuzzy around the edges like that?"

"I'm not—in this case, I think fuzziness is in the eye of the beholder," I said.

"Oh, okay, fair enough. Do you have a bottle opener?"

"Not on me. Where's Father Bernadi?"

"I don't know. Does he have a bottle opener? I need one."

Larry held up his beer and tipped it upside down. "It doesn't come out otherwise."

"Give it to me."

Face pickled in a smile, he clutched the bottle to his chest. "It's mine."

"I'm not trying to steal it from you. If you give it to me, I can go open it and bring it back."

Larry looked at his bottle, at me, and at his bottle again. "No."

I picked up the phone on Father Bernadi's desk. Through it I asked Patton to find and bring a bottle opener to me. To the credit of his training, he only asked, "Wine or beer, ma'am?" before hanging up to execute the task.

Gratitude glowed on Larry's face—very pinkly in his nose and cheeks.

"You'll go far," he said. Then he blinked rather slowly. Five minutes passed between his shutting his eyes and opening them again, during which time I visited the bathroom and Father Bernadi returned to his office.

"When did you get back?" He half-sat on the edge of his desk, speaking quietly so as not to disturb Larry.

"Around lunchtime. And you?"

"About half an hour ago. I came by to pick up a few papers I'd forgotten. I didn't realize my office would be so lively at this time of night. How was the trip?"

"We got some interesting stuff. I'll take you through it first thing next week."

"And you? How are you?"

"Fine." Convincing, I thought, but the priest didn't buy it.

"Do you want to tell me about it?"

I wasn't surprised to find that I did. Ever since the elevator incident, he had that effect on me.

Patton tapped at the door, three bottle openers and one Swiss army knife in hand. Larry opened his eyes.

"Good work," he said when Patton was close enough for Larry to make out the tools he brandished. "You look familiar."

"It's me, Uncle Larry. Patton."

"General? Is that you? Are you sure?"

"Yes, sir."

"You never used to be so much taller than me."

"He's not," I said. "You're sitting down."

"That explains a great deal." Larry stood, and, after swaying for several seconds in a violent wind not felt by the rest of us, reached out to put an arm around Patton's shoulder. "Let's go get a bottle of beer for each of these fine devices you've found. Don't tell your mother."

"No, sir."

"Have a good time in Zurich," I said.

"It's not fucking possible to have a good time in Zurich. That's the point."

"You take care, Larry," I said.

"You take care of my agency."

"I'll do my best."

"S'all you can do. See you when I'm sober. You too, priest."

Father Bernadi settled back behind the desk in his chair, a black leather swiveling affair, his elbows on the armrests and hands constructing a pyramid below his chin. From there he studied me. Honeyed light from a recessed setting directly above his head created dramatic highlights and lowlights all over his person, and a filler light, source unknown, made sure his facial features were not obscured by shadow. He was a still from *The Godfather, Part II*.

"What?" I said, though he hadn't said a thing.

"Do you want to tell me about it?"

"About what?"

"What it is that is upsetting you."

Whether it was his posture or the lighting, I don't know, but I felt confident he could solve any problem put before him with or without God's help.

"No. Not really. Okay." I perched one knee on the footstool Larry had vacated. "There's this guy."

"In my experience, there is always a guy."

"Well, actually, there are two guys."

His Corleone composure trembled faintly. "You believe this to be a problem?"

"The problem is one guy is interested in me and the other one isn't—or if he is, he's doing a great job of hiding it."

"The situation inverted is preferable?"

"No, I'd like them both to be interested."

I thought I caught the inkling of a smile in his eyes.

"You sound undecided," he said.

"Tell me about it." I wondered what to tell Father Bernadi. That I sort of got involved with Jake, and then got cold feet, as he seems to be perfect and the sex was, well, pretty good, which makes me think that there must be something that's not quite right because nobody is that perfect and good and I don't want to spend the next few months waiting for the other shoe to drop. And now that Charles is single for the first time since I've known him, I'd really like to meet him. Only problem is that he hasn't expressed a similar desire to meet me. It seems as lost a cause as ever and yet a part of me thinks he's the one, even though that's completely irrational and I don't really believe in the whole notion of "the one." Of course, I haven't returned any of Jake's calls, so I've probably blown that. And in spite of my doubts about him, I have a feeling it might have been a huge mistake to ignore him, and Anna is going to say "I told you so" until I'm eighty.

"Dating is complicated these days," I said. "I'm beginning to think I'm just not meant to be in a relationship at all."

"I am sure it is not as bad as that."

"I think it might be."

Father Bernadi spoke as if he was considering every word. "A person's pain is always as great as the difference between the way things are and the way they want them to be. Happy people are not happy because of wealth or beauty or power. What makes them happy is acceptance. The key to happiness seems to be not about getting what you want but about wanting what you can get."

"You're a walking Hallmark moment," I said. "But I think that was exactly what I needed to hear. Thank you."

I paused on my way out of his office. "Don't take this in a *Thorn Birds* kind of way, but it's a great tragedy for women everywhere that you're celibate."

"Thank you," he said.

As I walked back to my office I realized what I needed to do. What Father Bernadi was talking about had to do with that bird-in-the-hand-is-worth-two-in-the-bush business. Birds in the bush crap in the bush, and that seems better than having one crap in your hand, but it really isn't because they all crap anyway. The priest tried to put a more positive spin on it but he was still right. I had to go see a man about a bird before it disappeared into someone else's bush.

From: Sydney Welles <s.welles@fbmm.com>
To: God c/o Secretary-General@UN.com
Date: Friday, June 10, 2005 5:41 PM PDT
Subject: American God

Dear God,

Up until this week I was under the impression that God and American God were the same guy. Now, after two weeks of research groups infested with his followers, I'm convinced American God is a deity unto himself.

This is a very religious country; perhaps that's why its been allocated its own God. Although with American God it's not entirely clear just who created whom. Either way, there's more churchgoing, Bible thumping, Jesus freaking, and born again-ing going on here than anywhere else on earth.

To his credit, American God has made it clear that we are the chosen people; chosen to have bigger cars and more stuff than anyone else in the world. No wonder he's the most popular god in the country (though it has to be acknowledged he enjoys little acclaim outside of it).

However, if I were American God I'd be worried. One day lawyers will find a way to prove, on some technicality and to the satisfaction of the American justice system, that he exists and is legally responsible for everything in creation. That day, American God will see that he has chosen for his flock the people in the world most likely to sue him for everything that has ever gone wrong in their lives.

Sincerely,

Sydney

Small armies have defeated great ones, armed only with surprise. It can be a formidable weapon. But outside the battlefield, surprises, especially if anyone involved has a weak heart, are generally not a good idea.

Of all surprises, surprise visits are the worst. They're always ill timed and half the time the surpriser ends up more surprised than the surprisee. I was fully aware of this and yet it didn't prevent me from paying one.

At just after ten thirty on Friday night when Jake opened his front door to me, surprise wasn't just written all over his face, it was tattooed on his forehead. I'd materialized on his doorstep without warning, well past normal visiting hours. His surprise was understandable.

What was disconcerting was that once the shock on his face subsided, it was replaced by another emotion I couldn't identify. I was only sure of one thing. Jake wasn't pleased to see me. Every self-preservation instinct I had screamed at me to turn around and leave.

"Hi," I said.

It took him fifteen abnormally lengthy seconds to respond.

"Sydney." There wasn't a great deal of enthusiasm behind it.

"Oh, good. You remember my name."

Given the lack of warmth in his welcome, it was better that I waited for him to say something next. At least in hindsight, it would've been better if I'd waited.

"I was hoping you'd be home."

I paused to allow him time to invite me in. He didn't.

"I tried calling your cell phone," I said. "I only got your voice mail."

"I've had my phone turned off."

"Which would be why I got your voice mail. I didn't have your home number at work or I would've called before I came—I just thought since you're on my way home, well, you're practically a neighbor and everything . . ."

Jake continued the man-of-few-words routine. The next thirty seconds went by like a snail with no sense of direction.

"Okay. Now I'm feeling that this is one of those ideas," I said. "You know the ones. They seem good at the time you think of them but go bad as soon as you try to execute them."

"Why are you here?" Not the most convivial thing he could've said, but that he spoke at all was encouragement enough for me to plow ahead.

"I wanted to see you . . . I was under the impression you might want to see me too."

Jake closed his eyes as if in pain, massaging his temples with his thumb and fingers. I seemed to be giving him a migraine. I didn't take it as a good sign.

"It's your turn," I said.

He opened his eyes. "My turn?"

"Your turn to add to the conversation."

The strong, silent act was beginning to get on my nerves.

"The way it works is, I say something, then you say something, and we keep taking it in turns to say things. Otherwise, it's more of a monologue than a dialogue."

Judging from the expression on his face, his migraine was getting worse.

"Have I come at a bad time? I can leave—"

"Your timing couldn't be worse."

"Oh . . . Okay. No problem. We can do this some other time—but, of course, only if you want to. It's not compulsory. We don't have to do anything at all. It's not like we're actually doing anything now. I'm just kind of occupying your stoop. Next time we could even go somewhere—or not—whatever you prefer—I'm going now. Bye."

I turned to face the street and wondered, in an out-of-body kind of way, if it would be possible for me to feel stupider than I did at that moment. It was.

A voice, calling out to Jake from inside the house, made me halt at the top of the steps.

"Who was at the door—" Kim stopped when she saw me.

At first I thought she was going to retreat back into the house, but she only moved back a foot or so to rest a hand on Jake's shoulder, standing by her man just as the song advised. Jake didn't fling her hand from his shoulder like a hot coal. I had to assume he didn't mind it being there.

My mind, traitor that it is, registered that they were wearing matching robes, but instead of thinking this was contrived and tacky, it thought they could pass for the kind of couple you see in catalogs, surrounded by things to buy so your life looks as good as theirs. Fleetingly, the idea I'd stumbled onto a catalog shoot occurred to me, but my mind rightfully dismissed this as a desperate, silly notion. Then it thought: Wow, their kids are going to be really good-looking. Then it decided it might be a good idea that I give up thinking altogether.

I took a deep breath and, foolishly, stood my ground.

"Right," I said to Jake, "this is the part where you tell me this is not at all what it looks like."

"I can't do that. This is exactly what it looks like."

"Well." I examined the finish on my boots and tried to

remember the last time they were polished. "If that's the best story you can come up with, I'm afraid I have to suspect that there's something going on here."

Nobody laughed.

"So," I said, "it's been lovely catching up with you but, um, I need to polish my shoes, so I'll say good night. Have a nice life, both of you."

Jake caught up with me at the bottom of his front steps, blocking the path in front of me.

"I called you eleven times," he said. "You didn't return a single call. I thought you weren't interested."

"You seem to have gotten over it."

"You don't understand, if you'd just picked up the phone—"

He broke off as he glanced over my head. I turned to follow his gaze and was surprised by a surge of empathy for Kim. She was standing half in, half out of the doorway, watching us, chewing a thumb, looking more like a normal woman and less like the pictures plastic surgeons show you to help you pick out new facial and body parts than I imagined she could.

"The strange thing is I think I do understand. If you guys have worked it out, that's great. Really. I should've called but . . . that's now irrelevant . . . I have to go."

"Syd, wait."

"Why? Is something more going to happen? If you don't mind, I think I'll skip the second act."

I skirted the outer extremities of Jake and took off as quickly as I dared to in high-heeled boots. I wanted to make it to the confines of my car in case I started to cry, and the sidewalk in front of his place is a little uneven. A prat fall was the last thing I wanted to perform in front of the happy couple.

"Shit," Jake said.

It summed up the way I was feeling precisely. I hadn't felt so depressed since the time I was too lazy to go beyond the D section at the video store—it's right by the front door—and I'd rented *Deliverance* and *The Deer Hunter* and watched them one after the other on the same Saturday night.

I headed straight home, deciding on the way to leave my luggage in the trunk until morning and spend what was left of the evening in close consultation with the bottle of vodka in my freezer. Other occupants of my freezer, Ben & Jerry, would also be consulted.

Vodka would help me see that I had no use for men like Jake and convince me that what just happened was not the result of my own stupidity but a blessing in disguise, albeit an exceptionally good disguise.

Vodka was better than sitting around wondering if Jake and Kim had ever been apart at all. Wondering if I'd been as much of a surprise to her as she'd been to me. Or asking myself why I was surprised when the pessimist in me suspected, as soon as Jake asked me out, that this was how it was going to end.

Vodka is a greatly underrated beverage. However, my plans to spend quality time with a bottle of the stuff changed dramatically when I reached home.

It's always quiet on my street at this time of night. The muffled sounds of HBO, the flickering glow of plasma screens in windows above the high walls the only indication my neighbors are home and awake. The only action was Harry Rex, sitting in the middle of the road, smoothing down his ears with his paws.

"What are you doing? You're in the middle of the road, you dumb bunny. You'll get run over."

He blinked and twitched his whiskers, giving the impression that he was surprised, pleasantly surprised, to see me.

"I live here, stupid. Come on, come into the yard." I took a couple of steps toward the gate. "Come on. I'll give you a cookie."

Harry Rex didn't budge.

A vodka-and-ice-cream-induced stupor was beckoning, and I felt too drained of energy to continue arguing with a rabbit in the middle of the street in the middle of the night. It wasn't my night. First Jake had ex-sex, and now my pet rabbit was trying to commit suicide.

Out of habit, I glanced up at one of the second-story windows of the house across the street. It was Cupid's bedroom window. I've gotten used to seeing the little guy's silhouette framed in it when I arrive home. He's taken to spying on my comings and goings. He wasn't there tonight. It was too late; even demon children need their sleep. Not seeing the imp up there, plotting my demise, made me feel lonelier.

I returned my attention to Harry Rex. "Fine. Be road pancake. See if I care." Problem was, I did. "If you don't come now, I'll give you away to some rotten kid who'll hug you every day."

I opened my white, waist-high, front gate to encourage him. The gate chose that moment to fall off one of its hinges, hanging, useless, from the other. It really wasn't my night.

Harry Rex wiggled his ears as if to say "whatever." Obviously he preferred being road kill to hanging out with me. I wondered, idly, if I'd have any ego left by morning, consoling myself with the thought that my life couldn't get any worse. The thing about getting dumped for the gorgeous ex is that once it happens, you don't have to worry about getting dumped for the gorgeous ex anymore. It'd all be on the up and up from here. I wasn't being optimistic. I was being realistic. Everything that could go wrong tonight already had.

That was when I noticed that someone had been sitting on my porch in the dark, and was now on his feet. And he was holding something the size and shape of a baseball bat.

From: Sydney Welles <sydneywelles@yahoo.com>
To: God c/o billgates@microsoft.com
Date: Sunday, June 12, 2005 3:30 PM PDT
Subject: Rewrite

Dear God,

I read your book. Okay, I admit, I didn't read all of it. To tell the truth, I skipped over most of it. It's not exactly a page-turner, is it?

Yet it's still the best-selling book of all time, and has been since Gutenberg first printed it, back when it was the only published book in existence. It even outsells Harry Potter and *The Lord of the Rings.* That is probably because you don't go to hell if you haven't read those other books.

The threat of eternal damnation is compelling but just think how many more copies you'd sell if it were actually readable.

Sydney

P.S. For people who are supposed to love their enemies and neighbors, Christians sure do seem to hate a lot of people.

I made a mental note to leave my porch light on to prevent people from lying in wait for me under the cover of darkness. Or I could get the kind of lights that turn on whenever they sense motion. Either way I'd have to get some of those long-life bulbs, the kind that last for years and years. I was wondering who made them when it occurred to me I should be concentrating on the situation at hand.

I'm usually much quicker but my head reeled from ocular proof that my new, sort-of boyfriend was still involved with his ex, a woman who made Malibu Barbie look homely. Although my life has been more eventful lately, it had still been a big evening for me. I didn't have the emotional resources to deal with a possible porch psychopath.

Screaming was the course of action I'd decided to take against whomever it was awaiting me when the silhouette brandishing the bat said, "Sydney, is that you?"

The voice sounded familiar. "Who's that?"

The light from the street revealed him in segments from the bottom up as he stepped out of the shadows.

Segment 1: Ostrich leather boots. I'm not a fan, but they meant my porch intruder could afford boots made out of a big bird, difficult to catch and make boots of, and he had tastes too expensive to want to steal anything I owned.

Segment 2: Blue jeans, frayed in all the appropriate places—could be anyone with a three-hundred-dollar designer-jean habit.

Segment 3: A long sleeved T-shirt picturing pouty, pubescent Rolling Stones. I used to date someone who thought

Mick Jagger was a minor deity. Someone with a blazing smile set in a tanned face just like the person before me, only his tan hadn't been spray-on when I knew him.

It was Matt, my ex, aka Dr. John Somers to daytime soap fans, aka fireman Gray Somers to those same fans before he came back from the dead as Gray's evil twin, and aka Matt the Rat by those not in his fan club, Anna foremost among them.

Life is very unfair. Right after my current, sort-of boyfriend dumps me, I am visited by the guy who dumped me before him. Reliving my most recent dating disasters was not the way I wanted to spend the night. First Kim, then Matt: My life had become some kind of B horror film. The Night of the Returning Ex.

"Hello," I said. "Why are you here? And what is that thing?"

In the light of the streetlamp, Matt's baseball bat appeared quite misshapen.

"This," he said, "is for you. A gift. It's an African rain stick." Matt tipped the stick upside down and I heard rain, showering for several seconds, before it cut off abruptly.

"Why does it do that?"

"It's full of seeds or something. You want to try?"

I took it from him and tipped it upside down a few times to the sound of precipitation. In the mood I was in it was challenging to drum up a lot of enthusiasm, but a gift is a gift even if it's a stick. Sadly, receiving a stick as a gift was without doubt the highlight of my evening so far.

"What is it for?"

"It's used for making rain."

"No, why are you giving me a gift? What's the occasion? You were afraid my crops were suffering from drought?"

He held up his hand like a non-Indian actor playing an Indian in an old Western. "I come to make peace."

"That's why you're lurking here late at night? I think that qualifies more as disturbing the peace."

"I wasn't lurking."

"It looked like lurking to me."

"Well, I had no choice. You've changed your locks, and your neighbor's kid was eyeballing me from across the way."

"I had a new security system installed; they changed the locks for free—wait, how do you know I changed the locks?"

He held up a key. "I was going to return this tonight, as well."

"As well as what?"

"Could we talk about it inside?"

Matt had a point. We were standing too far away from the vodka. "Sure," I said. "Why not? It's not like I have a life or anything—shit."

"What?"

I showed him my keys. "I picked up the old keys instead of the new keys. I was late for a very early flight to St. Louis and I was hung over. My brain wasn't working. Shit."

"You keep a spare somewhere, right?"

"Not yet. The locks were changed just before the trip. No time to give spares to my nearest and dearest. Shit."

"We could try a window."

"No. New window locks. And if we do get one open, we'll set off the alarm and wake up the whole neighborhood."

"Locksmith?"

"Good idea," I said.

✝

We sat on the old porch swing that had come with the house. We were no longer in the dark—unlike Matt, I was able to locate the outdoor light switch. I hoped the emergency locksmith would arrive soon; I'd used up all my awkward-silence conversation skills on Jake and had none left for Matt.

"I guess this is one of those moments we should be glad we live in LA," I said.

"Why?"

"Well, if we were locked out anywhere else, we'd have to deal with the weather, which we don't have to do here since LA doesn't have any weather." When in doubt, talk about the weather. "It's quite pleasant out."

"It's really good to see you," Matt said.

Well, if he was going to get personal. "If it's so good to see me, why did you wait over a year?"

"I had to work a few things out. You're not still mad at me, are you?"

"Mad? No, I'm not mad at you. I've moved on with my life. I'm now mad at someone else."

"I want to make it up to you."

I picked up the rain stick and showed it to him. "Oh, but you already have."

"Seriously, Sydney. I think I can help you, God willing."

I dropped the rain stick; it drizzled a little on impact. "Help me? God willing? When did you get religion? This is weird. You know, I think He's stalking me."

"I've spent the last few months exploring my spiritual side," Matt said without any irony whatsoever. He had either become an extremely good actor or was serious. I couldn't work out which was more unlikely.

"Okay. You've been exploring your spiritual side and now you're here. Why?"

"It'll take a little while to explain."

"I actually have some time right now."

Matt flashed his small-screen-heartthrob smile. It was the reason he'd landed the part of Gray Somers in the first place. It also had something to do with why I'd dated him. Although back then the smile hadn't been four or five shades whiter than naturally possible.

"What is that thing growing on your face?" I was being facetious. I knew perfectly well the thing growing on his face was a goatee.

"They made me grow it. To make it easier for people to tell the difference between Dr. John Somers and Gray Somers."

"I thought Gray Somers was dead."

"He is, but the art of the flashback is alive and well."

"One twin is good and one is evil. This isn't enough for people to differentiate between them?"

"You know what they say. No one has ever lost money by underestimating the intelligence of the American public. Or lost public office that way. If I recall rightly, it was you who passed that on."

"It sounds like something I'd quote," I said. "You were going to tell me why you're here."

"My guide—she's kind of my life coach and therapist— helped me realize that for me to move on with my life, I had to speak to you."

"You couldn't have picked up the phone?"

"She says I'm in debt to you because of the way I treated you. And to repay that debt I have to help you."

"Is this some kind of twelve-step program? Thank God. I was beginning to think you'd joined a cult."

"It's not a cult. The people who call it that have no idea what they're talking about—look, the thing is, I've discussed this at length with my therapist and I don't think you'll ever be happy unless you face your issues."

"Let me get this straight. You're telling me I'm the one with issues. And yet I wasn't the one who ran off with Bambi."

"Berry."

"Close enough."

Matt looked pained. In my opinion the look suited him. "I don't expect you to get this straight away, but this is my way of making things right."

Well, I had nothing better to do. "I'm listening."

Matt started squirming in his seat. Unfortunately, it was also my seat and a swing. I felt a little queasy from the movement, but not as queasy as I felt when he said, "I had your chart done."

"My chart?"

"Your natal numerology chart."

"Oh, that chart."

"I know, I know. I thought it was crap too," he said. "Only—I don't know why it works, but it works. And right now I'm prepared to accept anything that might help."

"Okay."

"You don't have any twos in your chart."

"No twos? I take it that's a bad thing."

"The number two is the number of emotion. The number of the heart, if you like."

"What are you saying? I have no emotions?"

"You have emotions, but you have trouble accepting them or showing them. You reason your feelings out of existence."

"I see." For someone who reasoned my emotions away, I was feeling unreasonably tired and emotional. So far this weekend sucked.

Matt took a deep breath. "The numerologist said you push

people away because the person you're most incapable of loving is yourself."

"That's deep," I said. "So no twos, no self-love. I think that you must have a lot of twos in your chart."

"Actually, that's true—but we're not here to catalog my problems."

"That's right, you're here to shed light on mine."

"Why did you get involved with me?"

"Um, I thought we were meant to be talking about my insecurity, not yours."

"Considering the mess I was, can you honestly tell me you thought we would end up together?"

"You forget: For some bizarre biological reason, any man who combines charm and a self-destructive urge is irresistible to women. People break up. It's not like everyone goes into every relationship thinking it's the one."

"Yeah, but they also don't usually go into a relationship because it's not the one."

"Oh really," I said. "Are you still with Bambi?"

"That's not the—no, Christ, the woman couldn't even read a map."

"See."

"I'm aware of the many mistakes I've made. But right now I'm trying to make you aware that you may be sabotaging your chance of happiness."

"You have no idea how disconcerting it is to hear you, of all people, talk like you're in the running to be the next Dalai Lama."

"I know."

"Oh well, I guess all this self-helping spirituality is healthier than doing coke every night."

"Yeah, you were right about that."

I didn't think I could take any more numerology so I changed the subject. "What's next for the dastardly Dr. Somers?"

"He devises a computer chip that he implants into the minds of several women who all need brain surgery at the same time—due to a rare, contagious tropical brain virus someone brings back from vacation. He turns them all into his personal sex slaves until he gets his comeuppance. The writers haven't figured out how that happens yet."

"Sounds like they're keeping up their high story standards."

"Are you seeing anyone?"

I was tempted to pour out the whole Jake saga, but suppressed the inclination when I realized it might give Matt material for his numerologist's misguided theories about me. "Not really, no. You?"

✝

When the locksmith van arrived, I thought I'd be free of Matt's newfound wisdom, but it wasn't the case. My two locksmiths shared a brain between them, and it was befuddled by the newness of my lock, one they didn't possess a master key for and hadn't yet learned to pick. For the two hours they attempted to open the front door, Matt felt obligated to keep me company and give me an in-depth analysis of my numerological chart.

Matt was still hanging around when Locksmith Number 1 told Locksmith Number 2 to go get a crowbar. Number 2 fetched, and Number 1 used the crowbar to pry open the front window, which it wouldn't do, my new window locks being every bit as strong as the security guy who installed them said they were.

Number 1, who went by the name of Joe, raised the crowbar and looked at me. I was ready for drastic measures. I nodded. He broke the window and opened it that way, at which point my new alarm system started screaming into the night and Matt, rather abruptly, said his see-you-laters.

After waiting for Joe to fumble around with his flashlight and point it inside the window so I could see the glass I should avoid, I scrambled through the opening, sprinted to the control panel, and punched in the code that would silence the alarm. The alarm kept wailing. I pressed the code again. And again it didn't work.

Joe was behind me.

"It's not shutting off," I said.

Joe asked me what the code was.

I told him and stood aside. Locksmith Number 2, whom Joe called "Eddie," was through the window now too. He ambled over to see what Joe was doing.

"You sure that's the code?"

"Yes," I said.

"Well, it ain't working," Eddie said.

"We know that," Joe said.

"Can't you do something?"

"She wants us to do something," Joe said to Eddie.

Eddie held up the crowbar.

Joe started pressing more buttons.

I went to the front door and opened it to look outside. Lights were coming on in my neighbors' houses. This was going to make them hate me—those that did not hate me already. I headed back to the kitchen.

"Please make it stop," I said. "Any way you can."

"Right," Joe said.

Eddie hit the panel with the crowbar. The alarm stopped.

Joe and Eddie were quite a help after that. Using a piece of cardboard and duct tape from their van, they covered the hole where the glass in my window had been, and even offered to come back during normal business hours to fix my useless gate and, as Joe said, put a decent lock on it, all for a reasonable cost.

I looked for Harry Rex. The alarm must have sent him into hiding. He was nowhere to be seen. A couple of my neighbors had come to their doors and windows and glared at me while I was looking, but most of them had turned out their lights and, I assume, gone back to bed, which was where I was going. The vodka would have to wait until morning. I was too exhausted to drown sorrows.

I'd just locked up, feeling grateful this day was finally over, when someone rapped sharply on my door, which was odd for two reasons:

1. It was now nearly two o'clock in the morning.
2. I have a doorbell.

✝

Detective Karl Lauderdale wore plain clothes and a uniform face. Deep lines radiating from the outer corners of his eyes were his only distinguishing features. For my sake, I hoped they were laugh lines.

The LAPD doesn't respond to house alarms. It rarely responds to 911 calls. But there is something in LA that can get a senior officer from an overextended police force to make a house call in the middle of the night, and that something is a movie star. To be specific, the movie star who lives in the biggest fortress on my street, several fortresses down from me. Like the pigs in *Animal Farm,* movie stars, in a classless society, are more equal than anyone else.

From the moment I'd made his acquaintance, the detective had spent a great deal of his time gazing at the kitchen ceiling. Nothing up there excited interest. It was plain white plaster, alleviated only by a rather utilitarian light fixture in the center that I've been meaning to change since I moved in. Yet while I told him the story of my evening, he kept tipping his head back, only occasionally checking to see if I was still seated across the table.

True, I probably did tell him more than the cold hard facts he required, but it was a relief to get it all off my chest, especially the bit about Jake and Kim in matching robes, and since he didn't seem to be in a hurry to go anywhere, I also told him about Matt's numerologist and the whole sordid Bambi affair.

From time to time, the good detective glanced down at his pad on the table and seemed surprised to find it still blank. He'd give his pen an accusing look, crinkle his eyes and smile, in a sheepish way, at me. He was such a good listener that when I made us a pot of coffee, I regretted not having any doughnuts on hand—cops like doughnuts.

"So, you see," I said, "in the end Matt came here for selfish reasons. He didn't do it for me, he did it for his chakra."

"His chakra?"

"To clear bad energy in his relationship chakra. A clogged relationship chakra will prevent him from having fulfilling relationships in the future."

Detective Lauderdale gave me a scrunched-up look.

"I'm just repeating what he said. You know how actors get when they find themselves spiritually."

Detective Lauderdale inspected the ceiling again. I looked

up. We both stared for several seconds. Nothing happened up there.

"Can I call you Lauderdale?"

His eyes crinkled up again as he smiled. "I wish I could think of a reason why you can't."

"You can call me kid."

"Okay, kid, I guess everything is under control here. Do you have someplace else you can stay?"

"Why?"

"This is a pretty high crime area."

"Oh, I know. That's why I had the security system installed."

"That security system?" He pointed at the bashed in control panel. "Maybe you can get someone to stay with you until you get that window fixed."

I nodded. "I can sort something out tomorrow."

"Good." He handed me one of his cards. "Call if you need me."

"So in spite of everything I told you, you can't arrest Matt?"

"Numerology is not against the law."

"And not Jake either, I suppose?"

Lauderdale got up, and he and I looked up at the ceiling one last time for old times' sake.

"Is that it?" I asked.

"Yep." The lines around his eyes crinkled. "See you, kid."

"Later, Lauderdale."

What a night.

I decided that whatever happened, I'd blame Jake. Then again, if it weren't for Charles, I probably would've called Jake and he might not have gone back to Kim, so maybe Charles was more to blame for my current predicament. And if Matt hadn't broken up with me, I may never have gotten involved with Charles, so it was Matt's fault first. I saw that I could keep going backward until eventually I'd run out of men I've been involved with and have to blame myself.

It was God's fault. He was responsible for creating two genders and allowing them to mingle. Having assigned blame I felt better, and fell asleep almost immediately.

Dear God,

Some of your followers believe that the only way to live life is in absolute fear of going to hell, that the Ten Commandments need to be followed to the letter, and that a God who showed leniency on these matters would be a bad God, a God not worth believing in.

If you are that kind of God--the severe, unforgiving kind--why are there only ten commandments? If you're going to have a list of things we shouldn't do, the danger is in leaving things off the list. Omission implies that those things are okay to do.

For example, we're all agreed that rape is not a good thing. Yet something like one in three women are raped. Less than 60 percent of convicted rapists admit to reading porn, but 95 percent of them admit to reading the Bible. A commandment about not raping other people would go a long way.

May I suggest a comprehensive addendum?

Here are a few more just off the top of my head: thou shalt not start wars in My Name; thou shalt not abuse children; thou shalt not beat up thy wife or girlfriend; thou shalt not sell heroin to twelve-year-olds; thou shalt not be an asshole; and so on.

If you really want everyone to take everything literally, you have to get more literal.

Regards,

Syd

P.S. Almost forgot one: thou shalt not practice numerology, not even on people who work in advertising.

Chirping birds and an indecent amount of sunlight let me know that morning had broken too soon for my liking. Sunshine and birdsong prevented me from going back to sleep, but I stayed in bed, trying to avoid thinking about the previous night, trying to avoid thinking at all, until the doorbell rang enough times to get me up to stop whoever it was from ringing again.

It was Cupid. For a moment he stood looking at me in a way that would've made me think he was glad to see me—that is, if I didn't know him better. Then he pulled a grotesque face.

"Did you have burglars last night?"

"I had ex-boyfriends and locksmiths and policemen, but to the best of my knowledge, no burglars."

"There was a man on your porch."

"He was just a mistake I made once."

"Nobody stole anything?"

"No, sorry to disappoint you."

He pointed to my new cardboard window. "What happened to your window?"

"I locked myself out and we had to break into my house last night with a crowbar."

"Cool," Cupid said, smiling, looking like the angel he wasn't.

I patted him on the top of his head to annoy him.

He said, "Don't do that."

So I fluffed his curls. They were hard to resist. In the sunlight they sat like a golden halo around his head. It made him look ethereally beautiful in spite of the scowl on his face. "I'm just checking to see if there's a three-digit number tattooed on your scalp."

"Why do people always do that?"

"It's a reflex action."

"Do you have the crowbar?"

"No," I said. And that ended Cupid's interest in me for the day.

Cupid's visit triggered a sort of nostalgic rash to do with my own childhood, and to scratch it I was tempted to call my parents. But what would I tell them? I try not to tell them anything that will upset them until at least a year or so after the event—so they think I'm still dating Matt. I called a window-repair place instead. Then I headed for the bathroom to take a shower.

The doorbell rang again as I was running a comb through my towel-dried hair. I grabbed my rain stick on the way just in case it was Matt or anyone else offering spiritual guidance.

"There better not be Mormons out there," I said through the closed door. Is it just me, or do others also think it strange that some religious groups claim to revere God but then peddle Him door to door as if He were nothing but a second-rate insurance policy?

"It's Jake."

I opened the door. It was Jake, as promised, and he carried a large shopping bag in one hand. A bunch of daisies peeked out the top.

"I hate daisies."

He looked at the stick I was resting on my shoulder like a club, grabbed the daisies, and tossed them over the hedge into the street. "So do I. What happened to your window?"

"It's a long, complicated story."

"I have all day."

I stood aside to let him pass.

"Where's your girlfriend?" I followed him down the short hall into my living room. "I miss her."

"That was a mistake. It's over."

"Again? I have to start taking notes. I'm having trouble keeping up with your love life."

"Give me a chance to explain."

I sank into the sofa and pulled my feet and rain stick up after me. "No, sorry, I can't take an explanation right now."

Jake knelt in front of me. "I think we can work this out."

"Maybe we can. I don't know. All I know is I can't deal with it now."

"Okay." Jake's gaze shifted to what I was wearing: Marvin the Martian flannelette pajamas. I'd fallen asleep in my clothes the night before and so had decided to spend the day in my pajamas to redress the balance. "Nice pajamas," he said.

Unfortunately for Jake, it was precisely then that my body's supply of adrenaline—the only thing that had seen me through the night—ran out. I burst into tears.

"I'm sorry. I like your pajamas. I really do. Jesus. I'm sorry. Please don't cry." He found a box of tissues for me, then joined me on the couch and held me. In return I made the front of his sweater wet. I also built up a good-sized collection of soggy tissues.

"Do you want to talk about this?" To his credit, he'd figured out I wasn't as sensitive about my sleepwear as I appeared to be.

"No." I treated us both to a series of sniffs before rubbing my nose with a handful of tissues for what I hoped would be the final time. "What else is in that bag?" It was now sitting on my coffee table.

"Things to make you like me again."

"Then it should be a bigger bag."

"Is this about me?"

It was, but I wasn't going to let him know that. "You're really not as cute as you think you are. This is . . ." I didn't know where to start. "I need to get my window fixed." I started crying again. "The police said I shouldn't stay here alone with it broken like that."

"No, you probably shouldn't. Look, I can call someone to come fix it."

"I called someone. He's so busy he can't come until Tuesday." It takes forever to get any kind of non-emergency contractor or electrician or painter or plumber or anything to come to your house in LA. I think it has something to do with the traffic.

"So you stay with me until it's fixed."

I raised an eyebrow.

Jake held up his hands. "Just to make sure you're okay. A purely platonic arrangement if you like."

"Platonic? No, I don't think so. What's the time?"

"Nearly noon."

I poked him in the chest. "Okay. You need to make someone bring a very large pepperoni pizza. It has to have a thin crust. The crust is very, very important, a matter of life and death. Then you can give me whatever is in that bag. But be warned: Tomorrow, when I have more energy, I'm going to kick your two-timing butt."

"I understand."

I realized, even in the state I was in, that agreeing to stay with Jake before we'd talked about the Kim issue was not my best next move. But somehow, now that Jake was no longer perfect, I felt more capable of having a relationship with him.

It was now far less daunting because there was less chance of it working out.

I was, of course, much too vulnerable to dwell on how this gave credence to everything Matt had tried to tell me about the way I approached relationships.

Fisher Bennet McMahon & May
4848 Abott Way Los Angeles CA 90066 USA 310-807-3000 t 310-807-5000 f

Charles Turner
Los Angeles Times
202 W. 1st St.
Los Angeles, CA 90012

June 15, 2005

Dear Charles,

Last Friday night I stayed out practically all night. Unfortunately it was due to locking myself out of my house. I had to wait around until the locksmiths came, but Matt, my awful ex-boyfriend, kept me company.

As far as locksmiths go, mine were quite nice. Their names are Joe and Eddie and they came back a day later to fix my gate for a very reasonable price. It's fixed so well that now I can't open it and have to scramble over the top of it to come and go.

I don't think I've mentioned Matt. He was before your time. BC. Before Charles. Get it? Sorry. Anyway, Matt has acquired spirituality since I last saw him. I think he's joined one of those cults populated with movie stars, sons and daughters of the rich and famous, and others leading lavish lifestyles with no visible means of support, all searching for a way—other than cocaine— to alleviate the guilt of having much more money than talent. Matt is now very compassionate and caring. He's terrifying.

Suffice to say that he, even more than you, is a good indication of my appalling taste in men. How was your weekend?

Love,
Syd

The venue for the evening came down to a choice between two bars. One is popular because it's almost impossible to find. In an industrial district, housed in an unremarkable, unmarked warehouse, the only visible indication of its existence is a tiny valet parking sign stuck, seemingly, in the middle of nowhere. The second is popular because it's located far away from anything you'd want to be near. It has the added enticement of being extremely seedy-looking on the outside. No one is quite sure what the interior looks like because no one has seen the interior.

Because the first bar is attached to a restaurant that features mediocre food at fine-dining prices, we chose the second bar. It serves only alcohol. Anna and I felt it'd be easier to manage our disappointment in the food if there wasn't any.

Still blinded by the ironically tacky neon sign above the entrance, it took a while before my eyes adjusted to the darkness inside. Finally I made out a soft line of light glowing behind what I assumed was the bar. I knew I'd guessed right when I heard the reassuring sound of glass and ice clinking and alcohol being poured in the generous amounts you get in LA, where bartenders never use measuring tools and everyone drives home after drinking.

Slowly the shapes of people perched on barstools came into view. Their silhouettes outlined the spiky haircuts and retro glasses of LA intellectuals, who dress to show they're not influenced by fashion and who are each working on an angst-ridden screenplay which opens on a depressed protagonist waking up in the morning.

The rest of the room, even more dimly lit than the bar area, held table-, chair-, and people-shaped shadows. I noticed a person shape, seated alone at one of the table shapes, either waving vigorously or having a convulsive fit. I made my way over to it.

"Is that you?"

"Yeah," Anna said. "What do you think? Is this a lighting concept or did they forget to pay the power bill?"

I groped around under the table, found a stool-like object, and sat on it. "I could go either way."

"If I'd known, I wouldn't have bothered to put on makeup. I think there's a martini list on the table. Only you can't read it. It should be in braille."

"We can't read braille."

"A mere technicality. They have braille on drive-through ATM machines, why not here? It'd be just as useless. What do you want? I'll go to the bar. If there's table service I can't see it."

"Vodka martini, dirty."

The long black shape that was Anna got up and disappeared into the gloom.

"Maybe it's a celebrity privacy thing," I said when the silhouette of Anna reappeared with martini glass silhouettes in its hands.

"What is?"

"The lighting. A celebrity could come in here, drink all night, and never be spotted."

"You think there could be someone here now?"

We tried to see who was sitting at the other tables, and the other tables, it seemed, were trying to see who was sitting at ours.

"Or," Anna said, "they want us to think there are celebrities here when there aren't. Cheers. Here's to the latest in the sorry tale of your romantic life."

"Why don't we talk about your wedding instead?"

"The wedding is a full-time job for me. This is my leisure time. And anyway, I can hardly show you swatches. I don't think we're really going to be able to tell the difference between Pearl, Ivory, or Mist in here."

"Work is going really well."

"I don't care. I'm ecstatically engaged, soon to be happily married. Where am I to get my fill of relationship drama if not from you?"

"You're as bad as my sister," I said.

"I have a long way to go before I get quite as bad as that."

True. My sister, Morgan, married her high school sweetheart about two minutes after high school was over, then moved to a small midwestern college town—full of other people who've had sex with only one person in their entire lives—from where she is scandalized by my life. She, of course, calls me constantly for fear of missing anything.

"Well?" Anna waved at me in the dark, or at least I think she did.

"Well, what? What more do you want? What could possibly top finding the guy I was sort of seeing having sex with someone who wasn't me?"

"Only after you didn't return his calls for two weeks."

"Let me just take a moment to remind you that you're supposed to be on my side."

"I am," she said. "Usually, I'd be the first to say dump the two-timing rat-bastard on his fat head. But in this case there are extenuating circumstances. You guys only had one official date before you stopped speaking to him for two weeks."

"Are you going to keep bringing that up?"

"The point is you weren't exactly in a committed relationship. What he did was bad, but not unforgivable."

"It happened last Friday night. Less than a week has passed. I'm allowed to hold it against him a little longer. It's not like I've dumped him."

"No," Anna said. "You are living with him."

"Yes, even if it's only for reasons of personal safety, I am living with him. I'm living with him and yet I'm not really sure if we're still seeing each other."

"Are you sleeping with him?"

"If you're going to get technical about it, yes—but it doesn't count."

"Why not?"

"Well, if it weren't for the window, then Jake and I wouldn't be together now, not after the Kim incident. Therefore any sex that occurs is purely circumstantial and not to be held against us as evidence of a relationship."

"I thought the window was fixed days ago," Anna said.

"It was. But now we're waiting for the security system to be fixed. You know, to be safe."

"Right."

"The alarm is being replaced on Saturday. I'm going back to my place on Sunday. Then we'll see."

"See what? He may be your last chance for a heterosexual guy with a job and a full head of hair without two ex-wives, three kids, or a drug addiction."

"Your expectations for me are so high it's touching."

"Come on, you really like him, or you would've stayed with me."

"Ah, but I have notoriously bad taste. Take Matt, for example."

"Is what he said still bugging you?"

"Oh, only all the time."

"He obviously hit a sore spot."

"You're really not getting the whole friendship-and-loyalty thing tonight, are you?"

"I never thought I'd say this, but for the first time in his life, the Rat is right. Mind you, he had professional help. It's not like he figured it out all on his own with his tiny rodent brain."

"I can't believe you're taking his side."

"Nobody, least of all you, thought that relationship would work."

"Everybody makes mistakes."

"Yes, but not everybody is as determined to make them. Look at what you're doing now."

"What am I doing now?"

"Looking for a reason to dump Jake."

"Looking for a reason? Exchanging bodily fluids with Ex-Girlfriend Barbie not good enough a reason for you? The visual is indelibly etched in my mind, thank you. How do I know he won't do it again?"

"You don't. But I think it's worth sticking around to find out. Trust me, I'm almost married. I know everything there is to know about men."

"I'm so glad we're sharing like this," I said.

"Saying 'I told you so' is getting tired."

"I'm sure that won't stop you." I stuck my finger in my glass to see if it really was empty. "I guess it's my turn to grope my way to the bar. What will you have?"

"Same again, thanks."

"What was that? I can't see."

✝

"A Detective Lauderdale called your cell phone," Jake said after he'd met me at the door, propped me up against the doorjamb, and waved Vince and Anna, similarly propped up in the passenger seat, off. "He said he was checking up on you."

"Oh, boy. More police business. Maybe I ought to call him now?"

"That's not a good idea. It's very late."

"Were you waiting up for me?"

"I was."

"That's nice. Nice that you waited up, I mean. Not that it was nice for you—you'd probably like to be in bed asleep. It's nice for me. Not for you. I wasn't saying it was nice for—"

"I get it," Jake said.

"You're nice and I like you."

"I'm glad."

"Do you like me?"

"Yes."

"How much?" He needed some sort of scale with which to judge his feelings for me. "This much?" I spread my arms as wide as they would go.

"Sure, now come on." Jake turned me around in the right direction and prodded me in the butt to get me moving. It didn't work. With my arms outstretched I was too wide to fit through the door.

"You like me"—I assessed the distance still between my arms—"a whole lot. And, though you have no concept of personal space when it comes to ex-girlfriends, you are an intelligent human being. So it stands to reason. I can't be all bad."

He pushed my arms back down by my sides and guided me through the door. "You have one or two redeeming qualities."

"Yes, that's my point exactly—oops." My purse had somehow come loose from my grip and fallen to the floor. Jake picked it up and threaded it back on my arm, tucking it under my shoulder.

"Thanks," I said. "I like you."

"Yes. You like me. I like you. We've been over that."

"That's right. You like me. I'm okay. So what if I don't have any twos? Is that really such an issue? Is that why you went back to Kim, because I don't have any twos? Do you have any twos?"

"I can't say."

"Never mind. It's okay. I'm not a numberist." I patted his cheek. "You're prickly. Who is he to tell me I need therapy anyway?"

"I can honestly say I don't know."

"The only thing he's managed to get out of all those twelve-step programs is the ability to count to twelve. And that, it seems, makes him a numerologist. Only in LA."

"I have no idea who you're talking about."

"Rat. The Matt. I mean, Matt. Rat is his middle name."

"Who is he?"

"He's my . . . he's my Kim, only without the antigravity breasts."

"I see," Jake said. "Have you spoken to him recently?"

"Oh, yeah. That night. The Kim and broken window night—I squeezed a lot in that evening. But seriously, if anyone is incapable of love, it's an egotistical actor with the emotional range of an eggcup. How can he say that I'm the one incapable of love? I'm the one incapable of showing emotion? He can't show emotion even when they pay him to. This is all pots and kettles and degrees of blackness. And it's not true. It can't be true. I mean, what about you?"

"What about me?"

"Well, you're Exhibit A. You're hard evidence. You're living proof."

"Proof of what?"

Really, Jake was being quite dim tonight.

"Hello? Proof that I'm quite capable of being in love with someone, thank you very much."

The silence that ensued made me think Jake's ability to take in information dwindled drastically after midnight.

"You see," I said, speaking slowly so he could follow me, "your very existence proves he's wrong. And that I'm right."

"I'm not disagreeing with you."

"Exactly. I have emotions. I'm in love. True, I don't think I've ever been in it before, but he doesn't know that, does he? For all he knows I could've fallen in it all over the place. Right?"

"Right."

"The guy hasn't a clue. He's on daytime television and what? That makes him Oprah? Men. They think they know it all."

Looking at Jake, it occurred to me I'd said something I ought not to have said.

"Uh-oh," I said. "I shouldn't have said that. You're a men."

"I'll overlook it this once."

"Will you? That's nice. I like y . . . oh . . . I don't feel so good."

"We need to get you to bed."

"Okay."

At the bottom of the stairs I motioned Jake closer to let him in on a secret.

"I'm drunk."

"I know," he said. But I felt I owed him more of an explanation.

"You see. I've been drinking."

"That's the way it usually happens."

I had plenty more to say on the subject but before I could, Jake had picked me up and, judging by the way they were falling away from me in an alarming manner when I looked down, I was on my way up the stairs through no exertion of my own.

"Look Ma, no legs," I told Jake's left ear.

There was a lot of giggling on my part and quite a bit of patience on his when we reached his bedroom. I entered the room in a thoroughly good mood, but as I lay in bed waiting to fall asleep I felt unsettled. More unsettled than the bucket of martini I drank could be held accountable for. It was as if I'd eaten something I shouldn't have. Or said something I shouldn't have. The more I thought about it, the more I was sure it was the latter. I hadn't eaten anything. Besides, there was something suspicious about Jake's behavior once we were in the bedroom, a kind of watchful speculation in his eyes that wasn't there before. But my mind was balancing precariously between vodka-induced paranoia and sleep and I didn't want to nudge it in the wrong direction by recalling what it was I'd said. In the morning I'd be hung over and wouldn't remember anything at all. Comforted by this, I spent the night in fitful sleep, visited by several strange dreams, all involving me being caught flying around in public places without a stitch of clothing on.

Dear God,

Who turned all the water into vodka? My head feels as if several thousand freed Israelites are holding a dance party on it. I swear I'm never ever going to drink again.

Actually, I don't swear. I know you don't like swearing and it probably isn't wise to bandy words like "ever" about when talking to an immortal being, especially one who's been cranky for at least two thousand years. So let's just say that in the future, I'm going to try to rethink my beverage choices.

I have to go sit on the bathroom floor for a minute now.

Bye,

Syd

From: Sydney Welles <sydneywelles@yahoo.com>
To: God c/o melgibson@reformedmoviestarswithamessage.net
Date: Sunday, September 25, 2005 3:21 PM PDT
Subject: Update

Dear God,

How are you? It occurred to me today that you probably only hear from people when they need something--that is, apart from those sickeningly cheerful people who feel the need to constantly bombard you with their gratitude, which must be annoying in a different way.

I haven't been in contact for about three months, since that world-class hangover I had in June: for one reason. My life has been going exceptionally well. And, as is the case for most people, when life is going well, you aren't a priority.

I'm really only getting in touch now because I have work news to share. You are, ultimately, the head client on the Catholic Church account, and you have a right to know. Since we hit upon the strategy of selling the Church as an insurance policy against hell--which, let's face it, is actually what it is--everything has been going right. The rest of the qualitative groups responded very well to the idea. People have health insurance, car insurance, home insurance, mortgage insurance, travel insurance, disability insurance, and life insurance. Afterlife insurance isn't much of a leap. It was the only strategy we took into quantitative research.

After a sample of eight thousand people, it looks as if we're onto something. It's only a matter of time before you are available at a supermarket near me.

Being omniscient, you probably already know all this.

You probably also know, because you like to watch people have sex, that I still have the boyfriend I sort of had when we last spoke. He's just finished that piece on drug lords in custody. Everyone thinks it worthy of some kind of award. It certainly is very gritty and real. At the very least, Jake has a dozen new contacts for discounted drugs should he wish to become an addict.

Life seems to be going frighteningly well. No doubt something will happen soon to mess it up. Even in California, people can only go around following their bliss for so long before it all goes to shit.

Hope everything's okay in heaven,

Syd x

Charles Turner
Los Angeles Times
202 W. 1st St.
Los Angeles, CA 90012

September 26, 2005

Dear Charles,

I've given the question you put to me in your last letter a lot of consideration. I think it odd that you've asked me to lunch now, after all this time. Especially after you pointedly ignored the unsubtle hints I dropped in every second letter telling you where I'd be so you could easily bump into me if you wanted to.

However, my answer is yes. There was a time when our letters were embarrassingly long, when we poured our insides out on paper for each other's perusal and I wrote things to you I wouldn't dare say to anyone. It was the only time in my life I think I've ever been that open with another person—and, Christ, I put it in writing. I don't know what made me do it. If I remember correctly, that period of candor lasted about seven months before our correspondence regressed to become, more or less, what it had started out as. To this day I have no idea what happened.

It is because of the letters we wrote during that time that I'd like to have lunch with you. I think it best to go along with whatever you say. After all, I'd hate for the world to find out what really goes on in my head, and you have the evidence in writing.

See you there, noon, Saturday.
Syd

For most of Thursday morning I tried to shake off my conscience. There was nothing wrong with having lunch with Charles. It was just lunch, in a proper restaurant, in full view of the world. I wasn't going to have sex with him on the table between courses. I'm familiar with the restaurant. The tables are too small.

Besides, by asking me to lunch instead of dinner, Charles is indicating it isn't a romantic date. According to those dating books full of dating rules, if a man is interested in you that way, he asks you out to dinner. Preferably on a Saturday night, as Saturday night is the only night of the week that men have serious intentions toward women—those books are very specific.

If a man asks you to lunch as a first date, he's deliberately keeping things neutral. He's not sure whether he's interested in you but would like to have sex with you anyway, or he's interested in you but only for sex, or he just wants to be friends—friends who have sex. So in truth it isn't a date at all. The only flaw in this logic is that there's a good chance Charles hasn't read those dating books and may not know it isn't a date.

There's also the distinct possibility Charles is unattractive; newspaper columnists, especially the humorous ones—not that his columns are always intentionally funny—aren't known for their good looks. I also have to allow for the possibility he might find me unattractive. There's no accounting for taste these days.

By all standards it was an innocent excursion. It wasn't

much use telling myself this. Since being exposed to Catholicism, my sense of guilt is more highly developed.

However, it's not as if Jake and I are in a committed relationship. Since the Kim episode, we see each other—to the best of my knowledge—exclusively, but, so far, have avoided any kind of serious state-of-the-union discussion.

Lately, though, Jake has been talking about future events in his life as if I'll be concerned in them. The "we" and "us" business of romantic partnerships has snuck into his vocabulary and, I'm ashamed to admit, mine, and we've come to take it for granted that, unless one of us is away or otherwise engaged, we spend our free time together.

Just this morning he'd admitted to me what it was that had made him fall in love with me. Well, actually, that wasn't exactly how he phrased it. Love wasn't really mentioned at all. In fact, I think it was me who asked him what it was he liked most about me. I was curious.

He'd replied without hesitation, "Your nose."

"My nose? The thing you like most about me is my nose?"

He'd said, "I think you're underestimating your nose," which was nice, but even if I were underestimating my nose, it still doesn't strike me as much of a basis on which to build a relationship.

I blame proximity, that consummate enabler of romance, for the ease with which we've fallen quickly into what from the outside looks like an established relationship. In Los Angeles, distance is the most important contributing factor—after silicone, of course—to a successful relationship.

In a place made up of a series of sprawling suburbs cobbled together by a freeway system that sometimes works, it's entirely possible to have a long-distance relationship with someone who lives in the same city. The average person spends over two hours commuting to and from work. There are not enough hours in the day to also commute for sex. I know many men who won't ask a woman out if she lives more than twenty minutes away.

When I consider the very minimal distance between Jake's house and my house, and that he has not officially declared his feelings for—or intentions toward—me, I could come to the conclusion—especially if I've just been reading one of those dating books—that for him, the relationship is convenient rather than serious. According to the aforementioned books, I'm not in a real relationship for two reasons:

1. There is a list of things, rather like commandments, that you're not supposed to do if you want a guy to take you seriously, and everything that you're not supposed to do—sleeping with the guy on the first date comes pretty close to the top of the list—I've done.
2. Until he declares himself one way or the other, he is not committed to me—these books state that only the man can decide if a relationship is serious or not—so therefore I'd be stupid to consider myself committed.

By this reckoning, I've no reason to feel guilty for agreeing to a blameless lunch with a newspaperman, but, as I strongly suspect that these dating books are full of shit and emotions can't be reduced to a few arbitrary rules, I was wallowing in guilt.

My conscience annoyed me for the better part of the meeting I was in; a meeting held to determine the way we should run meetings. After going over it in my mind and weighing up the possibility of upsetting my relationship with Jake against a strong desire to finally meet Charles, I knew what needed to be done.

It was obvious. I had to break the plans I'd made to spend the entire weekend with Jake—at least for Saturday around lunchtime. Of course, I couldn't tell Jake I was ditching him to have lunch with some other guy, so what I needed was an alibi, someone to cover for me, someone I could say I was having lunch with in case Jake became suspicious. The only question that remained was who it should be.

It had to be someone no one would suspect of being capable of deception. Someone who didn't really have any kind of moral or ethical code that I'd have to worry about. Someone who doesn't stop to think things through before they agree to them.

I found Julie Ryan in a small meeting room near her office. Her constant, constantly panting companion, Brad Pitt, was nowhere in sight. She was with Patton, who looked as if he'd dearly like to be gone.

Julie tapped the pen she was holding on Patton's notebook. "You got all that?"

"Yes, ma'am."

Julie wriggled around in her seat, coming to rest in what looked to be an exceptionally uncomfortable position, at the same time spotting me in the doorway.

"Oh, hello," she said.

"What's wrong with you?"

"New kind of pube torture."

Patton looked to me, confused. "Pube?"

I translated for him. "Pubic hair. I think Julie's just had a bikini wax."

Blushes, like concentric circles on the surface of water, spread across Patton's face, each more crimson than the last.

"I should get going, ma'am. Don't think I should be present for . . . for . . . secret women's business."

"Fine, off you go then."

Patton began gathering his notebooks together.

"Spill," I said. "What did they do to you?"

Julie used to be in the habit of having her pubic hair waxed and trimmed into the first initial of whomever she was dating. That fashion ended when she found she was going through men too quickly to allow time for the regrowth required between different letters of the alphabet. Only seeing men with the same first initial—she tried "M" for six months—was too limiting.

Since then she's been experimenting with a series of pubic hairstyles and colors, all of which she's prepared to describe in detail to anyone who'll listen.

In my opinion, what she does only serves to perpetuate the grossly unfair private-parts situation between men and women. Women undergo the pain and humiliation of paying a complete stranger to rip the hair out of their genitals, to appear more attractive to men. They trim, shave, wax, dye, plait, and pierce according to the current definition of vaginal attractiveness as dictated by the old men who publish girly magazines—who, I daresay, have never allowed hot wax anywhere near their nether regions. In return, men occasionally wash in their genital region to appear more attractive to women.

While I stand by my opinion that the excessiveness of her pubic grooming is ideologically unsound, it's still fascinating to hear what Julie's had done.

"It's called a Tiffany's," she said.

"Is there jewelry involved?"

"No, just the packaging. All they left is a small square, dyed the same blue as a Tiffany's box."

Patton, on his way out of the room, walked into the door frame.

"That must have hurt," I said.

"No, ma'am, not at all. I'm fine."

"I meant her, not you."

Julie screwed up her cheerleader face. "The bleach was the worst—I'm not going to make it to the gym tonight."

Patton, who couldn't leave the room effectively, was blushing again. Red rose slowly from his neck and crept up his face like sunrise. The boy possessed the widest variety of blushes I'd ever seen.

"That reminds me," I said. "Patton?"

"Ma'am?" He turned back to face me from the doorway.

"Could you please call my trainer and cancel my appointment on Tuesday—I'm not going to be able to make it, not while getting this presentation together."

"Where do I find the number?"

"It's under *E*—for Evil Josh—in the old Rolodex. You know, while you're at it, you may as well cancel the next week's appointment too."

"No problem."

"Only don't do it until this time next week. Just make a note of it so you remember. In fact, make a standing note to cancel my Tuesday-morning appointment every Thursday or Friday afternoon. Okay?"

"For how long, ma'am?"

"Forever, I should think."

Patton looked puzzled. "If you aren't intending on keeping any of the appointments, why don't I cancel Mr. Evil altogether?"

"I can't cancel him altogether," I said. "I'd have no trainer at all. That would be really letting myself go."

Julie agreed. "You can't not have a trainer."

"It's true—like she says—it's much better to just cancel every week. You understand?"

"No, ma'am, not at all."

"Will that prevent you from completing the task?"

"No, ma'am, not at all."

Patton managed to leave the room successfully.

"There goes military training at its finest," I said.

Julie appeared to be lost in deep thought. It's an optical illusion she performs from time to time. When she spoke, it was clear her thoughts had not strayed from the pelvic region. "Do you think he's still a virgin?"

"Who? Patton? Don't even think about it. Keep your jewelry box away from him."

"I'm too sore to try."

"Stop doing this to yourself."

"Guys really like it."

"I'm sure they do, but there's no need to spoil them. Listen . . . I need to ask a favor."

"Okay."

"If it's all right with you, I'm going to tell Jake that I'm having lunch with you on Saturday. So if you should see him and he should ask—"

"Are we having lunch on Saturday?"

"Well, no, we're not."

"You just said we are."

"Yes, but—"

"Then why did you say we aren't having lunch on Saturday?"

This might be harder than I thought. "We're not having lunch. I'm just saying that we are."

"But if we're not, then that's a lie."

"Yes, yes, it's a lie."

"Why are we lying?"

"Because I don't to want tell Jake who I'm really having lunch with."

"Who is that?"

"A . . . friend," I said. "It's nothing. Just lunch. I'd just prefer that Jake doesn't know."

About then Julie's intellect grasped the situation entirely.

"Oooh, I get it. This is like a cover-up."

"That's right."

"I pretend that I had lunch with you so Jake doesn't find out you're having lunch with this friend. I can do that. Don't worry about a thing."

"I really appreciate this. It'll—what is it?"

Concern had wrinkled Julie's usually unnaturally smooth brow. The time for another round of paralyzing poison to be injected into her brain cavity must be close at hand.

"What should I say I had for lunch?"

"What?"

"If Jake asks me. What did I have for lunch?"

"I don't know," I said.

"Did I have a starter?"

"No. Maybe. I . . . does it matter?"

"What about wine? Did we have wine?"

"Um . . . okay, sure, a glass or two."

"Red wine or white wine?"

"Red?"

"I can't drink red during the day, it's too heavy."

"Okay," I said. "White then."

"What about dessert? I think it'd sound more realistic if I say we split a dessert. Profiteroles?"

I was seriously questioning my choice of accomplice. "Fine," I said. "Have the profiteroles."

"Nah, I'm not in the mood for profiteroles. Can I have crème brûlée instead? With something interesting in it, like lavender or citrus. That's very trendy right now." Alarm grew in her eyes as she blinked at me. "Where did we go?"

"Sorry?"

"For lunch. Where did we go? What if the things we had aren't on the menu at the place we say we went to? He'll go there and see right through the whole thing. We've got to be careful. Where did we go to lunch?"

"We're—I am going to that wine bar on Abbot Kinney."

"I know the one. I've never been there. I should go beforehand."

"I don't think that will be nec—"

"With you. I'll have to go with you. What if he asks what you ate? Or what we talked about? We'll have to go there for lunch by Saturday."

"But that's the day after tomorrow—"

"Good idea. We'll go today." Julie looked at me in a satisfied way. "This has worked out so well. I didn't know what I was going to do to fill the rest of the day and I really wanted to go somewhere nice for lunch. Are you ready to go now?"

"Where's Brad Pitt?" He was my last hope. Julie insists on taking him everywhere and the restaurant wouldn't allow him in.

"Doggy-daycare day today. For his social development."

"I . . . I'll just get my bag."

Not for the first time, I wondered if Julie was really as silly as we've all been led to believe.

From: Sydney Welles <sydneywelles@yahoo.com>
To: God c/o theholyghostguy@holytrinity.com
Date: Thursday, September 29, 2005 6:39 PM PDT
Subject: Miracles Are No Longer Miraculous

Dear God,

Miracles aren't what they used to be. These days they're all about statues and some form of liquid: statues weeping, statues bleeding, or statues drinking milk.

Face it, you've lost a good deal of your showmanship over the years: Manna never rains from heaven and water never morphs into wine. No one is parting seas. No one is walking on water. And no one is rising from the dead.

While fairly stupid on a number of counts, the average consumer is, thanks to modern cinema, very sophisticated when it comes to the quality of their special effects. They like them big, bold, and believable. They like things to blow up. They like to see tricks they've never seen before.

If you want to put butts in pews, you're going to have to do better than a leaky statue.

Sydney x

Theologians define miracles as God-willed transgressions of the laws of nature. In LA so much contravenes the laws of nature that, God-willing or not, these violations, for the most part, occur without incurring much comment. This is understandable. Miracles need to be rare to be classified as such. A surfeit of anything lessens its value, as our consumer society demonstrates on a daily basis. The supply-and-demand equation that applies to the most popular handbag of the season also applies to God's handiwork.

That is not to say that all marvels go by completely unnoticed in this town. I personally am witness to one on an annual basis, as are at least several hundred other people. I've seen the Crawford Transformation three times before. But for those beholding it for the first time—and there are always plenty of virgins in an agency of five hundred with high turnover and burnout rates—just seeing Larry Crawford not drunk must seem quite miraculous.

In my opinion, our agency is full of miracles. After all, it is also somewhat of a wonder that Noah never seems to need to leave the sofa in my office—a sofa which I've never considered mine, because I've never had the chance to sit on it. Reclining like a Roman emperor, eating saltines instead of grapes, Noah was distributing cracker crumbs with surprising range, still wearing yesterday's T-shirt, which still said: FUNDAMENTALISM MEANS NEVER HAVING TO ADMIT YOU'RE WRONG.

I was at my desk, imprisoned by piles of paperwork, trying to tailor a presentation to suit men of the cloth. "You want to take a crack at part of this?"

"As I'm paid far less than you, I feel my job is to lend moral support. That's best achieved from over here."

"Why are you always in my office?"

"Because my office doesn't have any walls. No privacy."

"Not much in my office either. Shouldn't you be working on . . . something?" What was he supposed to be working on? I'd lost track of all our other projects since becoming embroiled in Catholicism.

"God before Country Style Frozen Dinners," he said. "And you need me."

"Hardly. This is the easy part. The hard part begins when we're awarded the account and have to produce something."

"Details, details. All we need to do," Noah said, "is ask ourselves what kind of advertising campaign Jesus would do."

A deep voice boomed into the room. "You think you're being funny, but you're not. Jesus, ultimately, was the one who kicked off this campaign."

The man who stood at the door of my office was almost too elegant to bear. His suit bespoke, his collar painfully crisp, his tie exhibiting equal amounts of good taste and individuality, he was too well-groomed for real life, giving the impression a team of professionals had polished him until he gleamed, arranged him in my doorway, and now waited off camera for any touchups required.

"Larry," I said. "You're back."

"Yes, all wrung out and ready to go again." Larry noticed Noah on my sofa. "You look famished," Larry said. "Go to lunch."

"I'm not—"

"Did your mother drop you on your head as a child? Go, before you waste away."

Noah does look undernourished. He's one of those tall,

skinny people who can and do eat a horse, never gaining an ounce. He eats constantly during his waking hours, so it's inconceivable he could ever be famished, but he could take a hint. Grabbing his precious saltines, Noah threw me a look of commiseration and left.

Larry immediately took Noah's place on my sofa, first fastidiously dusting off the crumbs.

"How was that girl I sent you to interview this morning?" Larry said. "India Walsh—"

"India? Well, put it this way: When I asked her about her work experience, she told me she once took golf lessons every day for three months, and didn't that count as kind of like a job?"

"That good?"

"She doesn't seem to have any skills at all."

"Well, we have to give her a job."

"We do?"

"Sure. Her father is one of the biggest advertisers out there, and not yet gracing our client list."

"I see. Only I didn't keep her résumé. I did give her my business card at the end of the interview, but I doubt she'll know how to use it. How do we get in contact with her again?"

"It's okay, I know her godfather. I sent her to you to see if you could use her at all. It doesn't really matter what she does, but we should try and make it look good—or at least make it look like she was hired for her looks."

"I don't know—Julie thinks she needs an assistant. She's been using Patton a lot lately. And I think he's scared of her."

"He's scared of women in general. But that could work. We get Ms. Walsh on the payroll, and next time Daddy reshuffles his deck of advertising agencies—something he does fairly often—he'll have to throw us a bone."

"Very Machiavellian of you."

"Yes, isn't it," he said. "Have you solved our little church problem?"

"As a matter of fact, I have."

"Tell me everything."

"Well," I said, "turned out I was looking for something about religion that people would willingly buy, when I should've been thinking of it as a necessary evil all along. To cut a long story short, I'm now using insurance as a selling model. It works because of—"

"Brilliant," Larry said. I'd forgotten that Larry, sober, doesn't need anything explained to him. "Makes perfect sense. How's it doing in research?"

"It's researching its balls off."

"Good. Good. We're ready to go then—on this, at least. I wish I could say the same for the rest—they're all performing to expectations, saving up the problems on their accounts all year for me to deal with post-rehab—no wonder I'm an alcoholic. At least the Church will come good."

"Well, if it does, I hope it keeps the bean counters at bay."

"It will, for a while, until they want more beans to count."

"If we get the Church account, we'll have grown twenty percent for the year, and the year isn't over yet. They can't expect more. Everyone is working well above the call of duty as it is."

Larry shook his head. "You seem to be under the impression that there's humanity, or at least consideration for human beings, involved in the running of a public corporation. There isn't. Try to get over it. All that matters is the share price."

"It has to be enough. We've been going after new business since this time last year. If we get this one, that makes five wins in a row. Everyone is exhausted. There has to be a saturation point. They can't expect us to do this again."

"That's exactly what they will expect. What we've done in the past year will be the benchmark for the next."

"It's like trying to fill a bottomless pit."

"Exactly," Larry said. "Now you're getting it."

"What's the point if nothing we do will ever be enough?"

"Can't tell you that. I know what the point is for me. It gives me something to do between cocktail hours. What the point is for you is something you're going to have to figure out for yourself."

"Yes, Obi-Wan."

"You jest, but this is important, life-changing shit . . . speaking of shit, I think it's about to catch up with me."

I glanced up to see what Larry was referring to. His rather formidable personal assistant, trailed by several account-management people meekly walking in single file, was on her way to my office to collect him.

"Here come the please-fix-the-mess-I-made suits."

"Good luck," I said.

Noah returned to take up space on my couch soon after Larry was rounded up and marched off. Noah's hair was damp and he had a fresh T-shirt on. Actually I didn't know how fresh it was, but it was certainly a different color from the one he'd been wearing when he left the room. He'd taken a shower. Sometimes I wonder if he lives at the agency.

Not that I can talk. LA has an indecent 329 days of sunshine a year, yet I seem to spend most daylight hours in here, basking in fluorescence.

Noah shifted into a more relaxed, open position on the couch, enabling me to read his new shirt: GOD HATES HOMO-SEXUALS, BUT LESBIANS ARE THE SHIT!

"Did Larry like the work?"

"He didn't look at anything," I said. "But he did say the selling model was brilliant."

"We keep our jobs for another year then."

"It seems so."

Satisfied with his tenure, Noah yawned, stretched out, and settled in for a nap.

Briefly I wondered where on earth he obtained his unending supply of sacrilegious shirts, but I soon went back to wondering what I'd been wondering before he came back into the room.

What was the point for me?

From: Sydney Welles <s.welles@fbmm.com>
To: God c/o info@churchofscientology.com
Date: Friday, September 30, 2005 4:59 PM PDT
Subject: Heaven is designed to keep people out

Dear God,

More and more people now live in gated communities. I used to think it was because people like to live near other people who are scared of the same people they are.

Now I'm wondering if they're actually attempting to create heaven here on earth. After all, heaven is the ultimate gated community. Is this because heaven has only a limited number of places for the right kind of people?

Or are you the Greta Garbo of supreme beings? Do you just want to be alone?

Best,

Sydney

Pulling up at the valet parking stand that serves several restaurants at the Main Street end of Abbot Kinney, it dawned on me I couldn't possibly have lunch with Charles. It wasn't cold feet, though mine seemed frostbitten, or my sudden loss of appetite. It was Jake at home, innocent, unsuspecting, and probably trying to fix something, while I was out on what may or may not be a date with a newspaper columnist.

If I'd examined my feelings a little more closely at the time, I'd have also seen that I was terrified. Meeting Charles after he'd existed, perfect and fictional, in my imagination all this time was bound to be a disappointment. I feared he'd fall far short of my expectations, but not as much as I feared he might live up to them. Luckily I didn't examine my feelings any more closely than was required for me to change my mind about lunch. Panic then took over as I tried to think of a way to extricate myself from the situation.

The right thing to do was to stop in and inform Charles of my change of heart:

A) "Hi, nice to finally meet you after all this time, but I can't stay and break bread with you. I just wanted to see whether you were cuter than my boyfriend, and, well, now I see that you're not."

B) "This is all your fault. If you'd only dumped your girlfriend and asked me out sooner, I'd be able to eat now."

C) "I only have two weeks left to live and only want to eat lobster, which they don't serve here. Sorry."

Or, I could sneak around like the coward I was and leave a message with the hostess without being seen. That shouldn't be too hard. Charles didn't know what I looked like; it wouldn't matter if he did see me. It was the best solution.

Stepping on the accelerator, startling the valet parking attendant, whose feet just escaped being flattened, was the chickenshit thing to do, but also the choice I opted for.

I soon came to a halt, mostly because of a stop sign and partly because I hadn't any idea where I was headed. The bullying horn of the black SUV behind me forced me to make a decision. Turning right was easier than turning left. I turned right. That turn came off without a hitch. I turned right a few more times and after a while found myself turning onto Jake's street.

Shortly afterward I was ringing his doorbell. He didn't answer. Odd, since he'd told me he'd be home all afternoon. He'd even told me what he'd be doing, cleaning his outdoor furniture and assembling his new patio umbrella so we could eat outside when we felt like it—we were experiencing a bit of an Indian summer in Los Angeles.

Now it struck me as odd that he'd tell me that. He doesn't usually go into details of domestic chores—it's one of the things I like about him. I began to wonder: Had I been so busy deceiving him about today that I completely missed the possibility he might be doing the same to me? Telling myself I was being paranoid, I sat on his front steps and waited. And waited.

I was still waiting nearly an hour later, by this time thoroughly convinced something was going on, when Jake's car pulled into his driveway and stopped just before hitting his garage door. He was whistling cheerfully but not terribly tunefully as he got out of the car. The whistling chafed me a little but I couldn't pinpoint the reason why.

Walking around the back of his car, he glanced across the road, registered my car parked there, and looked around for me. I was still camped out on the steps; his search was short and successful.

"Hey," he said, bounding up to the stairs in a way I found as irritating as his whistling.

I stood up and dusted my butt. "Where have you been?"

Jake, in a disturbingly cheerful mood, picked me up and spun me around, in the process even helping a little with the butt dusting.

Once the dizziness subsided, I tried again. "Where have you been?"

"Getting something to eat."

He unlocked the door, holding it open for me. "What happened to lunch?"

"I, er, finished early."

"You're all dressed up."

"This? No, it's an old dress—I never wear it—I just thought I should this once—rather than—I never wear it—it's old."

"It doesn't look old."

"It looks new, but it's old. Because I never wear it."

"You're still too well dressed to help." Jake had begun to rummage around in the storage cupboard under the stairs. He soon found what he was looking for, a wooden, malletlike object.

"What are you going to do with that?"

"Wait and see. Why didn't you just let yourself in?"

"Why didn't I break into your house? I didn't have one of those things." I pointed at the mallet.

"But you have keys, right?"

I did? I'd forgotten that I did, but when I checked, there

they were on my key chain. "I'm not staying here anymore, so I can't use these keys. It's against the rules. Sorry. I should've returned them to you. It's your fault too; you ought to have asked for them back."

Jake headed toward the kitchen. "Keep them."

I followed him. "Why?"

"They're very useful for opening the door when it's locked."

I detached his keys from the others on my key chain, at the cost of a fingernail. I held them up. "I can't keep them. We're not ready for this."

"For what?"

"Keys are a commitment," I said. "We should wait."

"How do they suddenly become a commitment? You've had them all this time."

"That doesn't count. I didn't know I had them. Now I know, so now it counts as a commitment."

Jake was looking for something under the sink. He emerged from the cupboard to squint at me. "I think you may have a commitment problem."

"No. I don't have a commitment problem. I'm the girl. Historically speaking, my gender does not have a problem with commitment. I just think we may be getting ahead of ourselves."

Jake stood, brandishing the booty he'd discovered under the sink, a couple of T-shirts turned rags. "You're being really silly. Keep the keys."

"But these things snowball. Once you start there is no turning back. I don't nip it in the bud now, and next thing you know I'm in Reno, waiting for a divorce, with issues that could cost me years in therapy."

Jake put the rags down on the counter. "You're sane most

of the time, so I'm going to forget we had this conversation."
He took the keys and key chain from my hands, reattached
them, and put them back in my purse on the kitchen counter.
"See, now everything is as it was before. If it helps, you can
pretend you don't know you have them. Either way, cease and
desist with the commitment dementia."

"Now I'll have to give you keys too, won't I?"

"Syd?"

"Yes?"

"Shut up."

"Shut up? Oh, we are definitely headed for divorce."

"You're under no obligation to give me your keys."

"You don't understand. I have to give them to you now. I
can't not."

"Why?"

"If I don't, I look like the one not coming to the commitment party—I'll be the bad guy. I can't be the bad guy because
I'm the girl."

Jake stared at me closely for quite a while. "You have a real
gift for complicating the simplest things."

I did what I was taught to do when someone pays you a
compliment that most likely is not a compliment. I smiled and
said, "Thank you."

✝

Sunday morning we were up and out of bed early. Slipping on
sweats and flip-flops, we set off on our usual Sunday forage
for breakfast, walking down to the farmer's market on Main
Street, where there were French pastries sold by Ukrainian
people to be had in exchange for very little money.

Within seconds of arriving at the market I regretted setting out. There, between two rival flower stalls, I spotted a woman and a dog I knew. After my abrupt change of luncheon plans yesterday, quite possibly the last owner and pet I wanted to see.

Julie approached us, Brad Pitt reaching us a leash length ahead of her.

"Hi Julie," I said in a way I hoped was laden with warning. "You remember Jake, don't you?"

"Yeah, we met at the agency one time. Hi." She paused dramatically. "So, Syd, how'd you pull up after that extremely long lunch?" Her question was accompanied by an unsubtle wink.

Thankfully, Jake was crouching to take a closer look at the resplendent ugliness of Brad Pitt. I took the opportunity to give Julie a meaningful glance and a shake of my head, mouthing "No" to alert her not to say anything more. It was all lost on her.

"Syd and I had the nicest lunch yesterday—went for hours," she said.

Jake looked up with interest. "You did? Yesterday?"

"How's the interviewing for your new assistant going?" I said.

"Fine. So, Jake, have you been there?"

I tried again. "You're up early for a Sunday, aren't you?"

"What?" she said. "Anyway, get Syd to take you there. The food was good—lots of little courses. I liked the lamb, and the ribs. All of it really."

Jake stood back up. "This was yesterday?"

"Thursday," I said. "It was Thursday we went to lunch."

"No, it was Sat-tur-day, re-mem-ber, Syd-ney?" She was winking again.

I cringed.

Julie went on. "It was full, but we got a table outside without a booking. No wait at all. Turned out I'd slept with the head waiter in my early twenties. Lucky, huh?"

"Very lucky," Jake said.

I bent over and rubbed Brad Pitt's head.

"Help me, doggy," I said.

He cocked his head as if to say he was on the job. He started barking, pulling Julie in the direction of a passing golden retriever, who was barking in return.

"Oooop," said Julie, "looks like he's spotted a friend. He goes on play dates with that dog—wish the owner was more attractive—I could play with him as well. Gotta go say hello. See ya."

"Play dates for dogs?" I said. "I thought doggy daycare was excessive. What next?"

"That was odd."

I shrugged. "Not really, not for Julie. We had lunch on Thursday—I guess she just got the days mixed up."

"She seemed pretty adamant."

It was a good thing I was wearing dark glasses. "Yes, didn't she?"

"Come to think of it, when I dropped you home Friday night, you mentioned you were having lunch with Julie yesterday."

"I did?"

"You did."

"This presentation I'm working on is making me forget whether I'm coming or going—"

"Where were you yesterday?"

"Yesterday? Oh, yesterday. It was a work lunch with work people, a working lunch—oh look, fresh chocolate croissants, shall we get some?"

"Sure," Jake said, and that put an end to the subject.

Jake wasn't at all suspicious—quite the opposite, in fact.

His lack of suspicion made me suspicious. Not for the first time since the night I surprised him and Kim, it occurred to me that he was hiding something. Call it women's intuition, or call it paranoia; somehow I was sure there was something he wasn't telling me.

He was whistling tunelessly again. That's when I realized what had bugged me about his whistling the previous day. I knew why he was whistling today: sex. Men are inordinately pleased when they can put their early-morning erections to use. I didn't know what caused him to whistle yesterday, except that I had nothing to do with it. I began to wonder just who did.

Fisher Bennet McMahon & May

4848 Abott Way Los Angeles CA 90066 USA 310-807-3000 t 310-807-5000 f

Charles Turner
Los Angeles Times
202 W. 1st St.
Los Angeles, CA 90012

October 3, 2005

Dear Charles,

You may have noticed that I did not join you for lunch on Saturday. I offer my deepest and sincerest apologies, but can offer no explanation of my absence at this time—well, no explanation that you'd buy. I will explain this all to you one day in person if you're still speaking to me at that stage.

In the meantime, please accept one of the following pathetic excuses:

A) My house burned down
B) My car wouldn't start
C) My rabbit ate my homework (this one is definitely not true as my rabbit has run away from home and I haven't seen him for a couple of weeks)
D) I was upset about my rabbit running away

Even if none of these excuses suit, I hope you can forgive me,

Syd

Any psychiatrist could have told me it was my own guilt over Charles that made me suspicious of Jake. They say it's always the less-than-faithful partner in a relationship who is more mistrustful, while the innocent party trusts implicitly; since each is guided in their outlook by their own behavior. I became convinced he was hiding something from me because I was hiding something from him.

Had I a psychiatrist, he or she would've probably told me just that, but as I'm one of the handful of people in Los Angeles not currently in therapy, no one told me anything. My paranoia, which grew rapidly the weekend I was supposed to meet Charles, was allowed to blossom. You could say, the night I broke into Jake's house, my paranoia had reached full bloom.

Once inside, I slipped out of my shoes. I had no intention of turning on any lights. Espionage is traditionally carried out in the dark. I'd gone over the layout of his town house in my mind and was pretty sure I could find my way. Waiting only until my eyes adjusted, I walked straight into an armchair and stubbed my toe.

Shit.

Fortunately I had a small flashlight in my jacket pocket. My keys and purse were in one hand and my shoes in the other, so I used one of my other hands to go for the flashlight. Everything I was carrying hit the ground.

I decided it would be okay to turn on the living room light for just a minute. Long enough for me to gather my belongings and tiptoe to the kitchen. It was as good a place as any to start. In the flurry of planning a crime I'd forgotten to eat dinner. Investigating the fridge first, I made myself a sandwich—avocado, ham, cheese, and mayonnaise—and ate it.

My search of the kitchen turned up nothing else. I moved on, taking only the flashlight with me. I was pretty sure now that the best spies didn't bring their purses along on jobs.

The only room I hadn't spent time in was Jake's study. I had no reason to be in there. So that's where I headed.

His desk was clean except for a pile of bills, a few charity solicitations, and his computer. I opened the laptop and turned it on, looking over the desk while I waited for it to come to life.

The top drawer was full of bits and pieces—paper clips, staples, glue, tacks, scissors—it was a mess, but not an incriminating one. The second drawer held checkbooks, postage stamps, a letter opener shaped like a miniature sword with its own little scabbard, and, in a small, plastic, resealable bag, a locket. It was too heavy to be silver, too silver to be white gold. It had to be platinum. A beautiful, delicate, feminine platinum locket on a threadlike chain.

I lifted it out of the drawer. I didn't need three guesses to work out who it belonged to.

The locket found its way into my pocket. I wasn't stealing it, just temporarily seizing it as evidence. My plan was to . . . well, I didn't know what my plan was, but I was sure I'd think of something.

Jake's computer made a ploink noise; the screen asked me to enter the access password. Password? Who did he think wanted to get into his computer? I thought I was paranoid.

The third and largest drawer was locked. I was paralyzed by the discovery. This was it. Whatever I was looking for would be in that drawer. I was sure of it.

The phone on the desk rang, startling me so much I shrieked like a girl. This was okay because the ringing drowned out the shrieking and, well, I am a girl. After a few more rings, my heartbeat returned to normal and the machine answered the phone.

"Jay-ake, it's Kim. Please pick up if you're there." She waited for him to pick up. He didn't. Neither did I, though I was sorely tempted to. "Can you call me as soon as you get this? It's important. I need to speak to you. You know the number. I really need to talk."

I bet she did.

I played the message back, listening for anything that might indicate there was still something going on between them. Her words didn't tell me anything one way or the other. It was clear she needed to talk to Jay-ake. I wasn't so keen on the idea. My right index finger liked it even less. It depressed the "Erase" button and the message was gone.

It wasn't one of my finest moments. Then, neither was breaking and entering. If Kim needed a kidney or something, she'd call back.

I knelt in front of the drawer. If I were Jake, where would I keep the key to a drawer I didn't want me to look in? Well away from me. He had to have the key on him. Only a complete idiot would lock a drawer, then leave the key lying around.

Defeated by my logic, I pulled myself up into the chair. And found myself staring at a key stuck to the inside of the metal shade of the lamp on the desk. I picked it off. It was the right size, too small for a door, too big for a padlock. I tried the key in the drawer. It slid in smoothly and released the lock without any pressure.

A door slammed shut. It sounded like the front door. I

stopped breathing. Someone was in the house, someone with a key, someone who was home a full hour before he said he would be—Jake, obviously.

What do I do? Lock the drawer. Replace the key. Hide under the desk.

Plan A: Stay under desk all night and let myself out after he goes to work in the morning.

Brilliant—provided he wasn't planning on using the study in the meantime and I didn't need to go the bathroom during the night. It also didn't help that tomorrow was Saturday.

Jake was moving around downstairs.

Plan A (modified): Stay under desk until he falls asleep, then sneak out and blend fluidly into the night, not unlike a ninja.

Simpler. Better.

"Sydney?"

I hit my head on the underside of the desk. He knew I was here. How did he know I was here?

My purse. I'm a moron. I left it in full view on the kitchen counter. Then there were my shoes, the plate, bread knife, and half a sandwich. I'd also left the living room light on.

Oops.

"Sydney?" He sounded as if he was at the bottom of the stairs.

Plan B: I needed a plan B.

Wait. For all intents and purposes I was Jake's girlfriend.

I dashed into his bedroom, peeled off my clothing down to my underwear, and threw myself onto the bed. I shook out my hair, hoping it would look disheveled in a come-hither way rather than disheveled as a side effect of turning to a life of crime. I arranged myself on my side across the bed in a seductive pose. I hoped it was seductive. It was hard to tell. It certainly wasn't comfortable. Too late. I could hear footfalls at the top of the stairs, and no other seduction positions came to mind.

Jake stopped short in the doorway when he saw me. He was grinning, and it was one of those grins that you can't wipe off.

It was just possible I was going to get away with this.

He leaned up against the doorjamb.

"Hello," he said.

"Hi." I tried to be casual, as if lying around in my underpants in other people's bedrooms was something I did on a regular basis.

"I thought you had to work late."

"Not as late as I expected. I came to return that CD I borrowed."

He glanced at the pile of discarded clothing on the floor.

"Where is it?"

"What?"

"The CD. You don't seem to have any pockets in that outfit."

"It's, um, I think I forgot to bring it." That sounded suspicious, even to me, and I was on my side.

"Aren't you cold?"

Freezing, actually. "No."

"You look cold." He dropped his gaze, pointedly, to nipple level.

"Maybe I'm just pleased to see you."

"Are you trying to seduce me?"

"Why, is it not working?"

"If you're going to all this trouble, shouldn't your lingerie match?"

"Oh." There was that. I'd dressed for espionage, not seduction. People like Mata Hari must dress for both. Note to future spy self: Wear interesting underwear at all times.

My bra was the main offender, worn thin and, worse, gray. Gray is not a color that reminds men of sex. My underpants had potential. They were black. Black is officially sexy.

There was only one thing to do.

"Close your eyes."

He was instantly obedient.

As all fashion editors know, less is more. I sat up, removed the bra, tossed it on the floor, then resumed the position.

"Okay, you can open. Is this good?"

"Better," Jake said.

He didn't question my presence in his house. Nor did he ask how I knew he'd be home an hour early. He didn't question anything. His complete lack of curiosity led me to think:

A) He was hiding something from me—guilty people can't see past their own guilt.
B) He wasn't hiding anything from me—innocent people can't see anything either.
C) Men are easily distracted.

While I was convinced one or two of these theories applied, I felt pretty awful about getting away with what I'd done—or rather, tried to do. Whatever his reasons, Jake trusted me. I wasn't sure whether or not he'd betrayed my trust, but I was sure, by nosing around in his office, I'd betrayed his. I began to wonder how I'd gotten worked up enough to do it. Emotions are strange things.

There was only one thing I could do to make up for it. I had to wake up before he did and steal his car. I'd been planning to do it all week anyway—as a kind of belated hostess gift to thank him for letting me stay while my window was being fixed.

From: Sydney Welles <sydneywelles@yahoo.com>
To: God c/o info@kabbalah.com
Date: Saturday, October 8, 2005 8:12 AM PDT
Subject: Discrepancies

Dear God,

Jesus Christ was Jewish. And Buddha was a Hindu. I just thought I'd point that out.

Syd

In Marina del Rey, a gold Mercedes cut me off as I was turning into the driveway on Washington Boulevard. It parked haphazardly, blocking off most of the entrance to the auto shop. Two men got out of the car. The first was silver-haired and dressed in a handsome silver suit, the fabric of which shone dully and expensively in the sun. Though elegant, he had a sharp edge to his polish that suggested that he did not pay much, if anything at all, for his finery. The other man was much less august and about twenty years younger, thuggish in his appearance, slightly softened by shoulder-length hair glossy enough for a shampoo commercial.

I lowered the driver's side window to ask them to move their car, but then thought better of it. They looked like Russian mafia to me.

The older, silver man glanced at me, then at the narrow space his car had left in the driveway.

"You can fit," was all he said to me, before entering the building through a side door, closing it behind him.

His hit man stayed behind to see that I didn't scratch anything I shouldn't scratch, and to toss his European soccer-star hair and smoke a cigarette. To his credit, he smoked exactly the way a gangster should.

Being unfamiliar with the outer reaches of Jake's car, I maneuvered around the gold Mercedes awkwardly.

"I know this car," the hit man said. "This is a good car."

Reluctant to end up a headline on the six o'clock news, I inched by the other car cautiously and did not answer him.

"This is not your car."

"No," I said, "it's not."

"You steal this car?"

I had managed to get past the mafiamobile alive. Relief flooded through me. "Yes."

He nodded. "You want to sell?"

I shook my head.

"Okay." He flicked his cigarette butt out into the street and took up sentry outside the door the older man had disappeared into.

I parked on the other side of the building, well away from the gold Mercedes.

The old, rotund Russian who was the Pete of Pete's Auto Body Shop came out of the office to greet me loudly.

I rummaged around in my purse and produced a bottle of paint, about the same size as a bottle of nail polish but ten times more expensive.

"Mercedes Black from the dealer, like you said. Are you sure that will be enough? It doesn't look like much."

"It plenty enough. I make very nice touch-up for you, young lady. Like new."

Pete was giving me a tour of the spots on Jake's car where the paintwork was not all it should've been when the side door of the building opened and the man in the silver suit came out. He and his hit man exchanged a few words. The younger man pointed in my direction. Nodding, his boss got into the gold Mercedes and drove away, leaving him standing by the building. Before long, he was sauntering over to us. He stopped by the car and tapped the scratched front bumper bar with the tip of his shoe.

"Peter, this car need new bumper bar to be perfect." Walking around the back, he said, "Back bumper too."

Pete examined the bumper bars. "You have to order this things ahead. I have not part."

"No parts," I said, apologetically.

"I know where are parts," the hit man said. "You have cash?"

"Some," I said.

He dropped his cigarette, flattened it with his foot, opened the passenger door, and got into the car. "Come, we get bumper bar."

I looked at Pete. He did not seem at all disturbed by the turn of events or alarmed for my safety.

"Get bumper," he said. "I install for you."

New bumper bars would surely make up for breaking into Jake's house. They'd probably make up for burning it down.

"Okay. Where are we going?"

"My friend live very near to here. Eight blocks. He has many bumper bar. I make him do good deal."

Less than fifteen minutes later I was the owner of two new bumper bars. The hit man, who gave his name as Eryk, helped me put everything in the trunk, then stood back as I got into the car.

"I stay here," he said. "Visit friend. He has sister."

So far I'd seen no friend. It was Eryk who found the bumper bars in his friend's garage, after forcing the door up, and he who had sold them to me.

"You take this," he said, handing me a card. "You call if you need more."

"Thank you."

I took the card and put it in my wallet.

He tapped on the hood of Jake's car. "You steal more like this?"

"No, probably not," I said.

Eryk bore his disappointment stoically.

As I pulled out of the driveway, a woman in a short silk

kimono and sheepskin boots emerged from the small house to watch me leave.

"Who's that girl?" the woman said.

"She is business," Eryk said, waving me off.

Pete was waiting when I arrived back at his shop. I opened the trunk, proudly displaying the new bumper bars.

"How much you pay?"

"Fifty dollars for both."

He grinned, wide as his face. "Normal price two hundred. You steal them."

"No, but I think somebody might have."

"This your car too?"

"No."

"This nice car. Better than your car. This real car, your car, girl car. Your husband?"

"Boyfriend."

"How much he pay?"

I repeated the amount Jake had told me he paid, telling the story about the little old lady in Florida who had bought the car new and kept it garaged in Beverly Hills for the occasions she visited LA. She didn't like to drive rental cars; they were dirty.

Pete walked around to peer in at the odometer. He tapped on it.

"Too low, not original miles. They turn it back," he said.

"No, it's original."

"Original? No one drive this car. No one drive it. You pay so little. You steal this car."

"Yes," I said. Jake was going to be so pleased that I did.

✝

Detective Lauderdale examined the crack in my kitchen ceiling that runs from the base of the light fixture to the cornice.

"I'm not sure I understand," he said.

"Which part don't you understand?"

He sighed. "I don't understand any of it, kid. It's a mystery."

"Do you want me to explain it again?"

"Go ahead. Start from the burglary."

"It wasn't a burglary. Not precisely."

"Yes, you said that. Something was taken?"

"A locket."

"A locket. Good, we're getting somewhere. What was it worth?"

"I don't know."

"What was it insured for?"

"I don't know if it was insured or not. It didn't belong to me."

"Can you describe it?"

"Yes. It was a platinum locket, about so big. Quite exquisite workmanship—I think it may be vintage. I've never seen anything like it." I pulled it out of my pocket and placed it front of him. "It was like this."

Lauderdale picked it up off the table; the locket and chain looked positively ethereal in his large, square hands.

"How much like this?"

"I'd say pretty much exactly like that."

Lauderdale looked me in the eye. "Is this the stolen necklace?"

"Yes."

"Did you steal it?"

"I did, but it was an accident. I only took it out of a drawer and put it in my pocket."

"Accidentally?"

"No, I meant to take it. Only I didn't mean to leave the house with it. That was the accidental part. You see, I got caught and I had to take my pants off—"

Lauderdale put up a hand to stop me from going on. "This is where you lost me the first time. Back up. Where did you get this necklace?"

"From my boyfriend's house. I broke in."

"You broke into your boyfriend's house?"

"Yes and no. I have keys, but in spirit it was a break-in because I knew he wasn't home. I stole the necklace while I was there. It was an accident."

"An accident?"

"I only meant to move it around a little—actually, to tell the truth ī didn't know what I was going to do with it. Now I'm stuck. He must know it's not there. Of course, he doesn't know that I know it's gone. And he doesn't know that I know that he knows it's gone."

"You've lost me."

"You see, he won't be discussing it with me on account of it belongs to another woman that he doesn't want me to know about. I know—he just doesn't know that I know. That's why I took the locket in the first place."

Lauderdale cast his eyes upward, beseeching heaven. "I'm not even going to try to understand. Just tell me how I can help you."

"Well, I figure that you, being a detective, must have, in the course of your career, been in this kind of position before."

"Not that I recall." The skin around his eyes crinkled in amusement.

"Okay, so not exactly the same position, but there must

have been times when you have acquired evidence in a way . . . well, in a way that may not stand up in court."

"I guess I've been in that situation. What has that got to do with this?"

"The necklace is evidence."

"Evidence of what?"

"That Jake may still be involved with his ex."

"Now you've really lost me."

"See, I need to know how I can still use this evidence to confront Jake, without him finding out how I got it."

"Okay, I think I understand."

"So how do I do it?"

"Have you tried just asking him?"

"I was thinking more along the lines of making something up."

"Like what?"

"Well, we could say that you recovered it through quick and daring police work. I could be there when you tell him. Then I could ask him why he has it."

"Difficult, considering it hasn't been reported stolen."

"Oh. Well, this sort of thing must happen all the time, right?"

"No, not really."

"Maybe the thief, just before he became a chalk outline, wanted all the things he ever stole to go back to their rightful owners. He gave you the names and addresses of everybody he stole from, along with the items he stole."

The detective was inspecting the crack in the ceiling again.

"Come on, Lauderdale. Help me out here. I don't want to mess things up. Everything has been going so well since I stole Jake's car."

That got his attention down from above.

"I gave that back."

"Why can't you give the necklace back and ask him why he has it?"

"There really has to be another option."

"I could arrest the thief."

"What should I do?"

"You want to know what I think?"

"Yes."

"You're going to have to come clean. Tell him what you did and why. Then ask him if he's still involved with his ex."

"That would be even worse. He'll hate me."

"Just pick your moment. Courage, kid. He'll understand."

"Do you think so?"

"I'm sure if anyone can get away with it, you can."

"Thanks."

We both sipped our coffee. Lauderdale's gaze was drawn naturally upward again.

"You know, I think I knew I had to tell him but I had to hear it from someone like you; someone with a gun."

His gaze remained fixed on the ceiling, but he said, "You're welcome."

I scrutinized the patch of ceiling he was staring at. "Have you been to the Sistine Chapel?"

"No," he said. "Why?"

"No reason in particular. I just think you might like it there."

That got me a crinkly smile from one of the LAPD's finest.

I knew Lauderdale was right. I'd known what he was going to say before he said it, but I needed to be told to confess by a secular authority. If I'd sought the advice of a religious authority—Father Bernadi being the most likely candidate as he is the only religious authority I know—no doubt he'd have said exactly the same thing, but I didn't go to him for three reasons:

1. If I told Father Bernadi what I'd done, God would also find out. He has a commandment against swiping stuff and may not see the subtleties of stealing by accident, as He's old and grumpy and has been doing this for a long time without a break.

2. It would be too easy to disagree with Father Bernadi, on the grounds that I didn't believe in his God. Besides, Catholic priests prescribe confession to anyone and everyone as a matter of course, making it easier to dismiss it.

3. He is a client, used to seeing me as calm and professional—well, for the most part—and shouldn't be privy to the woeful nature of my private life any more than is absolutely necessary to win the Church account.

Furthermore, Father Bernadi's authority is only good in the afterlife. Detective Lauderdale, on the other hand, could arrest me now. I guess I chose him because I was too ashamed to tell anyone else and I figured that compared to the hardened criminals he encountered on a daily basis, I'd seem not so bad by comparison. Also, Lauderdale and I have kept in touch by e-mail since the night we met and found each other amusing. We mostly just forward things that we find funny, but it'd be true to say he's now my closest policeman friend.

I considered telling Lauderdale about the suspiciously well-priced bumper bars I'd purchased from a low-ranking member of the Russian mafia, then decided against it. One crime at a time. I first had to come clean with Jake. I was going to follow police advice and tell him everything, regardless of the consequences. Well, almost everything.

From: Sydney Welles <s.welles@fbmm.com>
To: God c/o vicepresidentoftheunitedstates@whitehouse.gov
Date: Thursday, October 13, 2005 6:33 PM PDT
Subject: Science 101

Dear God,

The universe is a big old place. Big enough for you and Darwin. The idea of a divine initiative to get the ball rolling, combined with evolution to keep it rolling, is not incompatible with Catholic dogma. A couple of popes have even said as much.

Even if you forbid evolution from being taught in schools, everything will still keep evolving. You'd do much better to embrace Darwin and claim credit for his work.

Or, failing that, some religions avoid having to deal with the theory of evolution altogether simply by implying that supreme beings have no concept of time. This allows you to incorporate all the sciences without having to concede a thing. Seven days to a god is like four and a half billion years to us. You know how it is. When you have stars and planets and large primates to make, and there is no one around to help, time just gets away from you.

Syd x

They say a woman can confess any sin to a man, and provided she picks her time correctly, he will forgive her. Unfortunately they never say exactly when that time is. Up until now I've always assumed the correct time was sometime during sex. This is not the case. Men do not multitask well during sex. Coitus confession is a waste of breath.

Confessing directly after sex doesn't work either. It is only in French films that men lay about carrying on meaningful postcoital conversations, smoking Gitanes. For noncelluloid, nonsmoking men in Southern California, this time is nap time.

When can you admit to murder, or casually mention you were raised by wolves and on occasion still like to howl at the moon, and have it not affect the way a man feels about you? This magical time of assured clemency continues to elude me. I'm hoping, however, that it's around dinnertime.

After all, they also say the way to a man's heart is through his stomach. Most men, no matter what they may claim, do not have sex three times a day, but the majority do eat three meals a day.

The locket weighed heavily on my conscience all weekend. By Monday evening I was bursting to confess, if not everything, then at least the part about me snooping in Jake's study. He would probably want to know why I'd snooped, so I'd tell him why, but no more. Jake was still pleased with the improvements I had made to his car with the help of Eryk—hit man and spare parts distributor. I wanted to strike while Jake's goodwill toward me was high, but I didn't want to strike too hard.

To stir up more goodwill, I offered to cook dinner: a shrimp and pasta dish I was pretty sure he'd like, since he seems to like most everything I like and I like anything with vodka in it. After installing him in a chair with beer, cheese, and crackers within his reach, I beheaded shrimp in my kitchen sink. I hoped it wouldn't give Jake any ideas. He couldn't get too mad at me. I was the one holding the knife.

To say he was astounded at my confession would be a technically correct description of his reaction, but the word doesn't do justice to the full breadth of his bewilderment and bemusement. Predictably, he wanted to know why I felt the need to break into his house. I told him I'd suspected he was still seeing Kim and wanted to find out one way or another. He quite reasonably asked why I didn't just ask him. I said I didn't know why I hadn't just asked him. So he asked why I thought he was still seeing Kim. By this point I was a touch defensive.

"Gee," I said, "maybe it's because Kim has been calling you, desperate to get in touch."

Jake was surprised. "How did you know that? I only spoke to her this morning. She called me at work."

Oops.

"How did you know?"

"I . . . okay, that night when I broke into your house, she called and left a message on your answering machine. I couldn't help but overhear it because I was in your study at the time, trying to get into your file drawer."

"Did you get into my file drawer?"

"No, that was when you came home and I had to stop what I was doing to seduce you."

"That, I remember," he said, smiling a little before frowning. "There weren't any messages on the machine that night."

"That's right. Her message sort of got erased."

"How?"

"Um, I erased it."

"You erased it," he said. "You erased it." He seemed to have lost his sense of humor as well as his ability to form interesting and original sentences.

"It was kind of an accident."

"Why didn't you just give me the message?"

"Okay, when I say it was an accident, I mean that I did it on purpose, only I wasn't fully in control of my actions at the time due to paranoia. I didn't pass on the message because I didn't want you to know what I'd been doing. I suppose I also didn't want to pass it on. But you have to understand that the necklace was truly an accident. I did mean to take it, but not to take it out of the house."

"What necklace?"

Oops.

"What necklace?"

"Okay, I found a locket and chain in the second drawer of your desk and I was sort of pissed that Kim was still leaving her jewelry lying around at your house, and I . . . I took it. I don't know why. I guess I wanted to piss you off. To make you think you'd lost it. I was going to put it back. At least I think I was, but then you came home. By the next morning, I forgot it was in my—"

"It doesn't belong to Kim."

"It doesn't?"

"I hadn't noticed it was gone."

Damn. Damn. Damn—wait a minute. "I'm sorry," I said. "Which of your girlfriends does it belong to?"

Jake gave me a look that, well, let's just say "loving" was not the descriptive term that came to mind. "It belongs to you," he said.

"I'm afraid you're mistaken. I've never seen it before. You must have me mixed up with some other girl."

"I bought it for you. I haven't gotten around to giving it to you yet."

"Oh." I deserved to be demoted to the bottom of the food chain. "Why?"

"You had a lot of trouble accepting keys. I wasn't sure what kind of scene truly precious metal would produce. Let's just say I needed to build up to it."

I wondered if I'd be allowed to live at the base of the food chain or if the other bottom-feeders would blackball me. "No, I mean, why did you buy it for me?"

"No reason. I thought you'd like it."

The basement level of the food chain was officially above my reach.

Jake, seeing my misery, let me sink in it for a few moments more before saying, "I got it at that seized-goods auction we covered for the show."

"The drug lord story?"

"I thought you'd like that the locket had a sordid history."

"I do. I like the locket. Very much."

"I guess you must. You did go to the trouble of stealing it."

"I have it in my bag, I'll go get—"

"No, no. Now you have it, keep it. Saves me giving it you and introducing God knows what for you to worry me about."

There wasn't a lot I could say besides "thank you."

"You're welcome."

Jake got up to get another beer out of my fridge. I decapitated the last shrimp. I rinsed the little slimy creatures—which, considering my new status in the ecosystem, ought to be eating me for dinner—with several changes of water before washing my hands with toothpaste to get rid of the smell.

"I'm sorry," I said.

"You should be."

"I thought you'd be angry with me."

"I am."

"I thought you'd be angrier. You're taking this very well."

"There was no real harm done. If I look at it another way, it's quite flattering. Your psychotic jealousy is strangely endearing."

"Thank you," I said.

"You're going to be saner in the future, right?"

"Yes," I said. "No more paranoia."

"Good."

"What did Kim want when she called?" I don't think Jake was taken in by the seemingly casual way I asked the question.

"She wanted to tell me she's relocating with a new job."

I could live with that. "Where's she going?"

"New York."

Even better news. "When does she go?"

"Tomorrow."

Detective Lauderdale and Father Bernadi are both right. This confession business is good for the body and good for the soul.

"I hope she's happy there," I said. I even meant it. I placed the herbs I'd been washing on the chopping block.

"So," I said. "You still want to go to this charity thing in Brentwood on Friday?"

"I'm not sure I'll be back in time. What time does it start?"

"Back from where?"

"I have to go away for a few days, background check on a story. I'm back Friday evening."

"What time? I can leave your name on the door, you could come later."

"My flight gets in at seven forty-five. If I came straight from the airport, with traffic, I doubt I'll be there much before nine."

"Well, come if you feel like it."

"I will."

"Where are you going?"

My question brought on a strange mix of wariness and amusement in Jake's eyes. "New York," he said.

"That's . . . nice."

I pretended to be intensely interested in the Italian parsley I was mincing. It was taking all the self-restraint I had to keep from commenting. Jake was fully aware of this and, it seemed, found it mildly comical.

Unfortunate, then, that I'd just confessed my dirty deeds to Jake and he'd been so reasonable. Now I was in no position to be angry with him over what was—if he was to be believed—a work trip and one of the world's most remarkable coincidences.

On the slight chance it actually was a remarkable coincidence, I didn't want to enact a jealous scene now and make Kim, replete with a Manhattan backdrop, even more attractive by comparison. Or make Jake so angry he'd go see Kim to spite me—if there was a chance he wasn't already planning on it.

"When do you go?" I asked when the Italian parsley could be minced no more.

"In the morning."

"Tomorrow?" Chalk up another extraordinary coincidence. "Well, have a nice trip."

"Thank you."

I didn't mention his New York trip again for the rest of the evening. No jealousy, no distrust emanated from me, at least not that I noticed. I was proud of myself. I was so magnanimous I offered to wake up at six to drive him to the airport. An offer he refused on the grounds that it'd be easier for him to have his car at the airport if he was to come straight from the airport to the charity do.

"You could catch a cab to the thing. That'd be cheaper than parking your car at the airport for four days."

"Work covers parking. Do you know how long it can take to get a cab at LAX?"

"It can take a while," I said. His logic was sound, irritating.

Jake came over, close to me, to look me in the eye. "It's a coincidence. That's all."

I'll say this much for him, he had a convincing act going.

"Yes, of course it is," I said. "Anyway, it's a really big city."

Was New York big enough that they could both be there at the same time without having sex? It was hard to know. I tried not to imagine the two of them strolling around Central Park together or, for all I knew, meeting at the airport and taking the same flight over, canoodling all the way to JFK. I was not going to lose a minute's sleep over this. I'd just wait until Jake got back from New York. Then I'd kill him. And dance the haka on his grave.

From: Sydney Welles <s.welles@fbmm.com>
To: God c/o headsheep@sheepusa.org
Date: Tuesday, October 18, 2005 2:28 PM PDT
Subject: A conflict of interest

Dear God,

Do you know you have a commandment that forbids advertising, albeit indirectly? You spake against ads in Commandment 10:

It tells us, "Thou shalt not covet the cool stuff your neighbor has." This has to be the least successful commandment of all. Our society is based on coveting what our neighbors have. House, ox, ass, George Foreman grill, plasma screen TV, RV, SUV, all of it.

And advertising is an industry set up to tell you what stuff your neighbor is likely to have, so you can get on with coveting it.

The point of living for most people is not just to covet but to get the stuff their neighbor has and, if possible, get bigger, better things to get their neighbors to covet back.

If anyone paid any attention to this commandment, the country's economy would collapse.

Still, I think it makes advertising a bit of a gray area, don't you?

Cheers,

Sydney

Fear is the greatest motivator there is. Anyone in advertising can tell you that. And religion has been using the two greatest fears—the fear of death and the fear of God—to great effect for at least two thousand years. For advertising, however, using these fears is a new low.

Our spirits, before our meeting with the Church, were similarly low. With the help of a good scotch, Larry can easily forget the importance of a meeting and breeze right through it, but sober Larry never forgets for a second that agency jobs may be riding on the outcome of a particular presentation. He gets so anxious he never knows what to do with himself in the last half hour before a meeting begins. Today he was spending it making me as nervous as he was.

I'd taken the precaution of getting Patton to duct tape all the bottles of scotch in the agency shut. In possession of one of these sealed bottles, Larry was admonishing me, wielding the bottle as if it were Excalibur, using it to punctuate what he was saying.

"Don't get sucked in by the man-of-god stuff. These people are ruthless."

"Okay," I said.

"I mean it. The Catholic Church is the oldest, and one of the most successful, corporations in the world. They didn't get that way by being a bunch of pussies. Don't forget, two Borgias were popes. Nasty, nasty family. They murdered everybody they met."

"Okay."

"Go for the throat. Show no mercy. Tell them what they

need to know without any touchy-feely shit. Cold. Hard. Factual. Tough. Don't present like a girl."

"Right."

Larry pointed the blunt end of his bottle at me. "These are the guys who invented the Crusades—a way to rape, pillage, and massacre and still be regarded as a hero—and they got Torquemada in to run the Spanish Inquisition."

"Okay."

"You realize the future of the agency is riding on the outcome of this presentation."

"Thank you for reminding me."

"Everything's ready?"

"Everything."

"What's the time?"

"Twenty minutes to go."

"Twenty minutes? Oh, fuck."

✝

A corporation is an inherently male world. The corporate rituals that all my male colleagues seem to innately understand—even when they don't understand anything else—are things I've had to learn.

When you have a meeting with a client, and they are going to bring six warm bodies, you must also produce six people, or failing that at least five, possibly seven. If they are only bringing two people, you cannot bring six. You must scale down your numbers to approximate theirs. You cannot let the other side greatly outnumber you, nor can you greatly outnumber them.

Even if I try to think like a man, I can think of only one reason to explain this standard practice: If war breaks out in a meeting, the even numbers ensure a fair fight, provided no one is packing a weapon—which, if I continue to think like a man, is very possible.

The matching-numbers ritual was observed in this case, although everyone on the client's side was a priest or bishop or cardinal, and—despite Larry's warnings—people quite unlikely to become violent. As we only needed four people for our side, we had to find two extraneous warm bodies to drag into the room.

We'd had one body lined up since Father Bernadi told us there'd be five representatives of the Church, including himself, attending the meeting. Julie Ryan is always available to fill a seat at a moment's notice. Her job title is long and important sounding enough for clients to believe she has a purpose even if she has no visible function in the meeting.

The second body we scrounged for at the eleventh hour, after one of the receptionists reported six, not five, men of the cloth sitting in the waiting area. Noah—once we'd borrowed a tailored shirt from an obligingly dapper management supervisor, wrestled it over his embellished T-shirt, on which tiny rhinestones were clustered in letters to read PIMPIN' LIKE JESUS, tamed the more energetic sprouts of hair resulting from his most recent nap, and made him promise to not speak unless directly spoken to—was ready to go.

Larry had gotten over his premeeting jitters, and I'd gotten over my own nervousness that I'd fall into my usual trap of saying something rude in front of a man of God. That fear dissipated when I found myself faced with several men of God at the same time. In a group they seemed quaint rather than terrifying. I managed to present the research findings and recommendations without invoking any words that could, with so many priestly ears tuned in, send me straight to hell.

It was only when I presented the strategy we'd use to develop a campaign and was greeted by blank stares all around—except from Father Bernadi, who understands everything but is not a good person for me to focus on in a meeting for fear of going weak at the knees—that it crossed my mind I may have been in hell already, in the Catholic section, of course.

"That's interesting," Father Lauren said. He was seated next to Father Bernadi and was the only other man of God whose name I remembered from the mass introductions at the beginning of the meeting.

In client-speak, "that's interesting" means one of three things:

A) I don't understand a thing you just said.
B) I hate it, hate it, hate it.
C) I don't understand a thing you just said and I hate it, hate it, hate it.

"That's interesting" wasn't the reaction I was hoping for. But then again, Father Lauren was a priest and had never been the client of an advertising agency before, so he probably didn't know any client-speak and might be telling the truth.

"But . . . er . . . but . . . I'm just not sure it's right for us." Father Lauren said.

I was wrong. Client-speak is a language everyone is born with. It just lies dormant until the moment you hire an advertising agency.

"The approach is not as modern as I expected," said the fatter of the two bishops. "To be honest, we were expecting something along the lines of the other faith-based marketing you showed us. This is completely different."

"It's different," I said, "because the Catholic Church is different. If we go hip and modern, or sophisticated and witty, it will end up working against you. Your Church is none of those things."

"It doesn't seem very inviting."

"Neither does Catholicism. 'Open Hearts, Minds, Doors' works for the Methodists, but not for you. Look, it's our job to get them in the door. After that it's up to you guys and your guy upstairs. But there's no point in getting them in the door at any cost. We can't promise them a modern, forward-thinking religion when Catholicism isn't one. We are taking a hard-line approach because Catholicism is a hard-line religion."

"Couldn't we soften the image a little?'

"Not unless you soften the religion. The marketing message we put out there has to match the consumer's Catholic experience. We could say anything to get people interested, but if they find the Church isn't congruent with its advertising, they won't come back. Worse, they'll think they've been had—they'll never trust you again. We have to build a brand consistent with the product."

"I understand your point; however, we then look like the heavies of Christianity."

"You are the heavies—though the Evangelicals seem to be giving you a run for your money. Look, I understand that you're afraid of polarizing the market. But you have to. Rather than trying to cover up the fact that you're an old-fashioned, hard-line religion, we'll make it your strength and build your brand around it. You're never going to get to some people no matter how attractive your ads are. You can't be all things to everybody.

"As our research shows, there are plenty of people out there who want to be told what to do and think. They are your market. Would-be Buddhists and Scientologists aren't. If you want to sell the Church, this is the way to go. If you want to be seen as nice guys, hire a PR company."

"We did."

"Did it work?"

"No."

"There you go."

"It's not a true calling to faith," the bishop said. "You are going to tell people that they should go to church just in case there's a God, who will send them to hell if they don't. That's not really what faith is about."

"No," I said, "it's not, but neither is it about hiring an advertising agency."

Larry threw me a sharp, pleased look that told me I was kicking bishop butt in a manner he approved of.

The bishop with the butt in question chuckled, causing his pink and fluid chins to cascade over his collar in an oddly mesmerizing way.

"Do you believe in God?"

The bishop had a sense of humor. "Do you believe that's relevant?" I said.

He and his chins laughed again. "Let's just say I'm curious."

"Okay," I said. "If you mean a grumpy, bearded old man who watches me when I go to the toilet, then no, I don't believe in God. But if you mean a nonemotional creative source and balancing force, then I'm willing to consider the possibility. Unfortunately, the thing that comes closest to explaining my idea of God is the original Star Wars trilogy, which does nothing to up the believability factor."

The fatter bishop nodded; his chins kept it up long after he stopped. On the agency side of the table, I could see the others exchanging looks, wondering if I'd said something to offend.

I decided to take the bishop by the balls. "Look at it logically. It's a good thing I don't believe what you believe. The most valuable thing we can give you is our objectivity. We can sell the Church because we can separate ourselves from it in a way you can't."

"It is, after all, why we're here," Father Bernadi said. And if he wasn't a priest, and we weren't at a crucial point in a meeting that could decide whether I had a job next year, and there weren't other priests watching, I could've kissed him.

"I suppose it is," the fatter bishop said. "You've certainly given us a great deal to think about." A harrumphing noise came from the other, matching, round bishop, indicating agreement.

"And we have the research to back it up," Larry said.

The fatter bishop tapped the booklet in front of him. It contained all of the information we'd presented today. "The numbers are certainly impressive."

Somehow that, in secret priest code, signaled the end of the meeting. The cardinal, who had not said more than a couple of words the whole afternoon, now stood and thanked us and said his good-byes. The priest who was his assistant, who indeed seemed to exist for no other reason, stood also and mimicked his boss.

By client standards they hadn't asked many questions at all. I wasn't sure if that was a good sign or a bad sign.

I began gathering my visual aids as the others—with the exception of Julie, who was reapplying her lipstick—were shaking hands and thumping backs and doing all the things that men do when a group of them manages to get together without starting a war.

I was exhausted. I'd just outlined a plan to sell the Catholic Church as insurance against eternal damnation—in other words, a plan to scare the hell into people. I felt as if I'd spent a couple of hours handing out cigarettes to eight-year-olds, which some agencies probably do, in theory if not in practice.

It was then I noticed that the priests were halfway to the door but the bishops were standing their ground near me. There was fierce whispering back and forth between the two.

"There is one more thing," said the multichinned bishop. "We thought that you might . . ."

"Yes?" I said.

"Well, we thought—it's just that we heard that you could get good tickets to things—to things that are hard to get good tickets to—and we thought, if it wasn't too much trouble . . ."

"What would you like to see?"

The bishops exchanged looks, both shy to speak up, each hoping the other would take the matter out of their hands. I began to have serious doubts about what it was they wanted tickets for. The slightly less rotund bishop with the chipmunk cheeks finally confessed. To my surprise, the priests wanted to go too—as did Larry, but that came as no surprise to me at all.

From: Sydney Welles <sydneywelles@yahoo.com>
To: God c/o Gandalf@middleearth.com
Cc: elrond@rivendell.com
Date: Thursday, October 20, 2005 7:09 PM PDT

Subject: Books & Burgers

Dear God,

If I had to back a religious group to win I wouldn't back the Catholics. No, I'd have to take into account the contribution made to society, which brings it down to two groups.

1. The Gideons, for the farthest-reaching book distribution system I've ever encountered

2. The In-N-Out Burger Christians, for obvious reasons, which are more apparent when you're hungry.

Syd ☺

Down on the Venice boardwalk you can see a man, wearing only a Speedo and a coat of olive oil, walk on broken glass. In Santa Monica, on Third Street Promenade, against the backdrop of homogenized retail outlets and homogeneous homeless people, you can hear a thirteen-year-old in a tuxedo sing like Louis Armstrong and tap-dance like, well, like no one I've ever seen before. In Malibu, wild dolphins will entertain you when you eat lunch in oceanfront restaurants.

Although it's far from being a pretty city, there are amazing sights to be seen in Los Angeles. But no sight here, however amazing, is as significant as seeing a star. For Angelenos, celebrity spotting is a competitive and at times full-contact sport. There's a constant celebrity safari going on. A-list stars are the biggest game, but anyone remotely famous counts.

Anything you see a celebrity doing is remarkable. Anything at all, whether it's walking, talking, eating, or standing. Humdrum activities become extraordinary when executed by someone famous. So extraordinary, people will pay for the privilege of watching.

Charities know and exploit this. Whenever a fundraiser is held, a collection of celebrities is rounded up and displayed like prize pigs. Here, choosing a charity to support is not about finding a cause that resonates with your soul. No, it's about deciding which celebrities you'd like to hang with.

In the terraced back garden of the Brentwood home of a former senator, Anna was doing an exceptional job of not turning her head while her eyes darted around the room in a way that made me fear for her contact lenses.

"You're doing the LA thing," I said.

"What?"

"Pretending to listen to me while scanning the room for someone better to talk to."

"Well, say something interesting then," she said. "Is that Richard Gere?"

"Where?"

"Behind you."

"I'm not going to look," I said.

"Oh, why not?"

I normally avoid charity events. I'm one of the few nobodies in Los Angeles who regards the celebrities here as a kind of pestilence. There are high infestations of the famous in certain areas of this city, making it practically impossible to do anything without the head-turning, eye-popping, intelligence-reducing presence of a star nearby. It's not the stars themselves but the gaping, blubbering twits they leave in their wake that I find annoying.

But occasionally, when an invitation to an event for a truly worthwhile cause comes through from the media department, I accept and find myself participating in the city's favorite pastime.

"Celebrities at cocktail parties are like those dementor things from the Harry Potter books—they suck the souls out of people."

Anna looked at me blankly.

"Celebrities suck too," I said.

"You don't like Richard Gere?"

"That's not what I mean. It has nothing to do with Richard Gere. It's just that a famous person at a party creates a natural vacuum sucking up everyone's attention and most of their good sense."

She frowned. "He's not very tall, is he?"

"See?" I said. "You're caught in the vortex. You're staring at some actor, trying to look as if you're not staring at him, all the while ignoring your very best friend in the world, who got you tickets to this stupid thing in the first place. Now I ask you, is that right?"

She was too busy rubbernecking to answer me.

At least it meant we were supporting a very fashionable cause. An unfashionable cause, no matter how worthy, will yield only character actors, minor politicians, or people from reality television shows.

Some people think disasters present the biggest opportunity to see stars, but this is not the case. A large tragedy, natural or otherwise, does flush out equally large numbers of the famous; but tragedies of that scale tend to cause telethons, and telethons allow celebrities to appease their publicists in the safety of a television studio.

Supporting the cause or disease du jour is the best bet for a nobody with enough disposable income to rub shoulders with a Somebody.

Anna poked me in the arm. "That's Meryl Streep, over there, about to leave."

I turned to look. The paparazzi stationed at the entrance to the garden had recovered from the zombielike state they'd exhibited when we walked past them, now excitedly shoving each other, cameras up, flashes popping. "Yes, it is."

"She's not very tall either."

"No one is very tall compared to you, and actors are, generally speaking, shorter than most."

"Ooh! There's, um, you know—the one that plays the gay guy on that, what's the name of that—why is the food so small?" The last part was addressed to Vince, who'd returned from his tour of the restaurant-run stalls with three plates that were far from full.

"They're samples," he said. "Not entrees."

"We're going to have to sample a lot of samples to even get close to getting our money's worth," Anna said.

"You may not be expressing the true spirit of charity there," I said.

"And what?" Anna waved her arm to encompass the crowd, dressed in their designer best to gawk at celebrities— whose presence drove all thoughts of the terminally ill children they were here to help from their minds. "This is the true spirit of charity?"

"Point taken."

"Did you invite Jake?" Vince asked before Anna could warn him not to.

"Did I invite Jake? Well, yes, as a matter of fact I did extend the invitation to him. But he won't be attending. No, the poor boy will be too exhausted. He had a busy week in New York, visiting his ex-girlfriend. In fact, he was so busy he didn't get a chance to call me. Not once. So I doubt very much he'll find the time to show up tonight. Why do men do that? Say they'll call and then not call? Why not just say they won't call and make it easier for everyone?"

"Maybe he was busy."

"That's right, stick up for your fellow man. Why do you guys always do that?"

"Why do men have to do the calling?" Vince said. "Why couldn't you call him?"

"Under the circumstances, I chose not to. Anyway, it's not as if I'm going to miss him. I may have waited by the phone like an idiot all week, but let's face it, men who only appreciate women manufactured by Mattel are not worth missing."

"What makes you so sure he won't turn up?"

"Look," I said, "women just know these things, okay? We're infallible like that. Tell you what, if he does show, I'll take back everything bad I've ever said about your gender and be a perfect geisha the rest of the weekend. It's not going to happen. Why are you asking, anyway?"

"He just walked in."

"Oh." I turned. Jake was at the greeting desk, waiting while they searched for his name on the list. "What's he doing here?"

"You invited him," Vince said, helpfully.

"You should stop talking now," Anna said. "Really."

One of the hazards of having an amazon for a friend is that they're easy to pick out in a crowd. Anna's red head, half a foot above everyone else's, functioned as a beacon for Jake to make his way over.

An auctioneer's voice boomed across the garden just as Jake reached us. The voice, on loan from Christie's, herded us onto the paved terrace at the bottom of the garden. There we were encouraged to form a tight mob by charity committee members patrolling the area like sheepdogs.

The former senator whose current terrace we were on stepped up to the microphone, welcoming us with a few sexist remarks. It must've been acceptable to do this back in the century he was a senator; he seemed to think it funny. At his side his wife smiled fiercely, giving us the impression she'd never had an opinion in her life.

Before long the auctioneer once again had control of the microphone and began the night's auctions, making it impossible for us to speak to one another without shouting.

Jake, the main person I wanted to shout at, showed no contrition for not calling me from New York, instead displaying a

232

great deal of interest in my dress. When the first item for auction—a walk-on role in a movie plus tickets to its premiere—sold for a couple of grand, he leaned over, close to my ear, saying:

"That's a different look for you."

"What are you saying?"

"Nothing. Except that you usually wear more fabric."

"You don't like it?"

"I didn't say that."

"But you're implying that this dress is kind of a slut dress."

"What do you mean, 'kind of'?"

It's kind of hard to be mad at Jake when he's in a suit and a flirtatious mood.

"You be quiet," I said. The auction had started again.

After several spa packages, dinner packages, and fine wine collections had gone under the hammer, and Jake had flirted some more with my dress, the evening was over. Now that there was no further way to extract money from us, we were no longer welcome. So much so they turned out the lights to get us to leave.

Anna and I waited in front of the house while Vince and Jake retrieved their cars from the valet parking service.

"You sure told him off for not calling," Anna said.

"I'll speak firmly to him later."

"Sure you will. You went all giggly and girly the moment he arrived."

"I did not." I said. "Did I?"

She was right. I didn't speak to Jake, firmly or otherwise. I didn't have the heart to. He collapsed in his favorite armchair as soon as we got home. The poor boy was exhausted after his trip, and as long as I didn't dwell on possible reasons why he was exhausted, I was still in a charitable mood.

On impulse, I reached up under my dress, pulled down my panties, and stepped out of them. Jake seemed to gain a little energy at that point, sitting up straighter in his chair.

"Don't worry," I said after hitching up the skirt of my dress a few inches to be able to sit comfortably astride his lap. "You won't have to do a thing."

It was around the same time that he said he'd missed me, told me how happy he was to be home, and took the Lord's name in vain a couple of times.

I was happy too. Maybe I'd hit upon the secret to relationships. As long as you're willing to check your brain at the door and ignore inconvenient facts—things like Jake not calling me from New York, and that I still suspected he was hiding something from me—you can believe whatever you want to, and you can be happy. It was just like religion. I had doubts, though, about how long this kind of happiness could last. My guess was not long.

Anyway, even from a secular point of view, you're not supposed to ask men why they haven't called you. What you're supposed to do is retain mystery. If you don't ask, men wonder why you don't ask, and this makes you mysterious to them. And that makes them call you.

Dear God,

I've just spent an entire Saturday afternoon at the Staples Center with a marketing priest, a lawyer priest, a couple of business bishops, and a sober boss. They all wanted to watch men beat each other up on ice, and some hero in the media department produced six last-minute tickets to the Kings game so that they could.

The game was good publicity for you. The clerical collars all in a row-- especially the outrageously photogenic Father Bernadi--attracted the cameras. You got a lot of cutaway shots and a lot of cheers. I daresay the Catholic clergy has not enjoyed such popularity for a long time.

While I find spectator sports incredibly dull, and think I should get heaven points for having to spend my afternoon this way, it occurred to me that perhaps you should forgo conventional advertising and concentrate on the lucrative area of sports sponsorship. Think about it. It's a lot less work for me and you get to hang out with all the star players.

Sydney xox

P.S. Why does LA have two ice hockey teams when it has no naturally occurring ice?

Fisher Bennet McMahon & May
4848 Abott Way Los Angeles CA 90066 USA 310-807-3000 t 310-807-5000 f

Charles Turner
Los Angeles Times
202 W. 1st St.
Los Angeles, CA 90012

October 24, 2005

Dear Charles,

Thank you for your letter. As much as I appreciated getting it, especially after I stood you up, I have to ask: What has gotten into you? Did you fall into a vat of Prozac? I don't remember you ever being quite this flirtatious. But, trite as it may sound, I'm happy that you're happy, even if I can't see the reason for it.

The answers to your questions, in the order you asked them, are:

1. Eighteen.
2. No, never on a plane. But, if it counts, once on a rooftop while a plane flew overhead.
3. It was purple lace.
4. No, I can't run away to Prague. Not right now.
5. Yes, I think so. Why do you ask?

Yours,
Sydney

Larry informed me at 5:30 P.M. Friday that he had a media interview scheduled for 6 P.M. The subject of the interview was the religious research study our agency was known to be conducting. Larry wanted me to take his place in the interview because he had better things to do.

He often has me stand in for him when he can't be bothered. I wasn't concerned. Sure, it was a newspaper interview, and print journalists love to print you out of context—love to edit any glimmer of reason or intelligence out of your words, making you sound like a fanatic or an idiot or both. Sure, I didn't have any time to prepare, so there was a good chance I'd come off as a moron without any journalistic help, but I wasn't worried.

Larry has made a habit of landing me in it at the last minute and most of the situations are much more dire. Like the time he sent me to give a short speech in his place to "a bunch of marketing students." I'd walked into the ballroom of the Regent Beverly Wilshire and found myself speaking in front of fifty MBA graduates from one of the most prestigious graduate schools in the country and over four hundred CEOs, COOs, CFOs, CSOs, CMOs, and any other C types that exist of the largest corporations in the country. In comparison, I didn't find the prospect of one newspaper journalist that daunting—a gross misjudgment on my part.

It wasn't until I was turning onto Ocean Boulevard, two minutes away from the meeting place, that I realized I didn't know how I was supposed to recognize the journalist. I placed a distress call to Patton, who promised to wrest the information from Larry's personal assistant. Sixty seconds later Patton called back. A table had been booked under the name of the journalist, and that name, he told me—without preparing me for the shock at all—was Charles Turner.

Patton started to tell me which paper he was from but I told him thanks, it was okay, I was familiar with his column. By that point I was already in front of the restaurant. The valet parking attendant was holding my door open and there was nothing for me to do but get out of the car. A not-so-discreet cough from the valet guy made me aware I was failing to do so.

Curiosity, not courage, finally nudged me into the restaurant. I told the hostess there was a reservation under Turner. She agreed that there was, and informed me "my party" was waiting for me. I followed her to the table, finding myself getting more apprehensive with each step. All my fantasy versions of this meeting, every hope I'd ever harbored for the relationship, all the mind portraits I'd painted of Charles, were fighting for dominance like Internet porn pop-up ads, overwhelming the meager portion of my brain still functioning.

When she turned, smiled, and I saw Charles for the first time in person, I can honestly say he wasn't what I'd expected. He was so far from what I expected I had to hold onto the back of a chair to ensure I didn't make any sudden dropping moves toward the floor.

My only consolation was that Charles looked almost as shocked as I felt. He'd started to get up upon my arrival and was now frozen halfway to his feet, doing a valid impression of a goldfish.

Meeting Charles would've been a pleasant experience in different circumstances. He was attractive in the way currently considered to be the thing. Blue-eyed and dark-haired, in need of both a haircut and a shave, he looked as if he went about the world doing great justice to blue jeans.

Annoyingly, he recovered himself before I did, and with litheness inappropriate for the gravity of the situation, stood and was at my side of the table in one fluent move.

"Hey," he said, and, after kissing me on my left temple, he loosened the death grip I had on my chair, guided me into it, and returned to his seat. At least there he looked uncomfortable. He rubbed his chin with his knuckles. It's a habit of Jake's. He does it when he's not quite sure what to say.

The busy blur of a drinks waiter came into focus by our table, no doubt directed to us by the hostess after she witnessed the shock on my face. I had just enough presence of mind to order a vodka gimlet on the rocks. Jake ordered another scotch and water. Judging from the way he was draining it, the drink he already had didn't have long to live.

"This is a . . . nice surprise," he said.

I don't think he meant it.

We stared at each other in silence for several minutes until my own loss for words resolved itself in one very appropriate one.

"Asshole."

The drink-laden waiter froze on "asshole," then thawed out just enough to deliver our order before quickly melting away.

I embraced my gimlet and made it disappear.

"Asshole." Vodka had done nothing to change my mind.

"You don't really mean that."

I considered this theory. "Yes, I do."

"You weren't meant to find out like this."

"Was I meant to find out at all?"

"Yes, of course."

We stared at each other. It was evident neither of us knew

what to say. It's when I have nothing to say that I usually speak up.

"So, you moonlight as a newspaper columnist?"

"I started in print. You know that."

"When were you planning on letting me know?"

"I've been trying to tell you for a while now."

"Can't have been trying too hard." I checked my glass. It hadn't refilled itself.

"You'd have found out if you'd gotten into my file drawer that night."

"How—oh, your column?"

He nodded. "My column. Your letters."

"You knew it was me from the start?"

"That first night."

"That night in the bar? I'm not the only Sydney in Los Angeles."

"The pen. The one you threw at me. It had your agency's name on it. You always write to me from work. And I knew you'd be there."

"That's right. I told you—I mean, Charles—that I'd be at that bar that night."

"You did."

"So, you came to—you came there for me—it wasn't just the pen in the head?"

"Yes," he said. "But the pen helped."

I didn't meet Jake by chance. For a moment I wondered what this did to my theory that life is just a series of random coincidences, and therefore essentially meaningless. Luckily the moment passed.

"That makes sense," I said. "Everything makes sense. Here I thought I'd finally found someone who understood me, but that was only because I'd already explained myself to him in full, in writing."

"I'm not the only one who's been keeping Charles a secret."

"What's that supposed to mean?"

"Just that neither of us was blameless. Look," Jake said, "this doesn't have to be bad. Let's not blow it out of proportion."

"I think it's already blown."

I stood up. So far I'd held it together. I felt the need to put an end to the conversation before the situation changed.

"Please sit down," Jake said.

"Thank you, but I should get going. It's been fun and I'd love to stay and have you fuck with my mind some more, but it's getting late. I have places to go."

I left the table in what, at first, promised to be one of the better exits of my romantic career. It was sweeping. It was dramatic. It was only marred by one thing.

Due to its commendably clean state, I didn't notice that the clear glass door of the restaurant was shut. Walking into it with a resounding thud and having Jake, and a couple of waiters, rush to my aid was not just one of those moments that transcend embarrassment to reach a degree of humiliation previously unknown; it also ruined the whole effect of me walking out on Jake without so much as a backward glance. Leaving him a broken man in my glorious wake was now also out of the question.

After the group of concerned waiters offered me a glass of water, ice wrapped in a napkin, and for some reason I couldn't understand a slice of chocolate mud cake, all of which I refused, they dispersed as quickly as they had gathered. I found myself on the side of the door I'd been aiming for when I collided with it. Jake had made it through too, unharmed. While his concern for me and my possible head injury seemed genuine, even in my dazed and confused state I was aware he was having trouble keeping a smirk off his face.

"This isn't funny," I said. I lied. I could see it was exceedingly amusing for anyone who wasn't me.

"No, it's not." To his credit, Jake managed to keep a straight face. "I'm going to take care of the bill. You'll be okay here for a minute?"

I nodded, then waited until his back was turned to hand the valet guy my ticket. My dramatic exit had failed dramatically. Sneaking off was the next best thing. But the way the day was going, I wasn't really surprised when Jake came back just as I was getting into my car.

"Are you okay?" he asked, leaning on the open driver's side door.

"Fine."

"Do you want me to follow you home?"

"No."

"Are you sure you're okay?"

"Yes."

He continued to lean on the door.

"I'm going to need that door to get home. You see, it's attached to my car."

I pulled on the door handle. He didn't give it up.

"I'm fine. Honest." I did my best to sound reassuringly sane, not at all like someone who'd just received a severe blow to the head.

Jake didn't look convinced, but he stopped the tug-of-war with my car door and stood back to watch me drive off. To my credit, although I was still reeling from both physical and emotional blows, I managed not to hit anything else on the way home. All I wanted to do upon reaching that sanctuary was curl up in a ball and never venture out among people again.

What I did do was get dressed and go to a party.

From what I can recall, I had a reasonable time at Julie's birthday party.

I remember putting on a lot of glittery makeup to compensate for the way I felt. I remember putting on a mildly sequined top to balance all the makeup.

I remember the bar was on Fairfax in Hollywood and that it was called a girl's name. I remember a friendly bartender who was setting me up well in the way of vodka and encouraging me to dance on the bar. Whether I danced or not is something, thankfully, I don't remember.

I remember meeting a rocket scientist and a jet-propulsion engineer, both employed by NASA, arm-wrestling with one of them, and getting them both to inhale helium from birthday balloons before singing "Yellow Submarine." I've always believed the secret to mixing well socially lies in the skill of bringing people down to your own intellectual level.

I remember giving a phone number to a guy called Ted. Or was it Todd? He spent an hour trying to chat me up. I thought he deserved it for tenacity.

I remember ending up back at Julie's house and continuing to be well set up for vodka. I remember Julie handing me Brad Pitt on a leash and telling me I could have him to keep me company for the weekend. That way if I'd sustained a concussion from my collision with the restaurant door, and went to sleep without any idea of waking up, Brad Pitt could run around barking and save me. He had yet to perform one useful task in fourteen doggy years, had yet to obey a simple command, but I remember we felt illogically optimistic about his latent savior skills. He needed only a life-and-death situation to nudge his inner Lassie into being.

I remember having to bribe the cabdriver to take us after Brad Pitt tried to eat one of the tires. I remember that after I'd spoken sternly to him for munching on the Michelins, Brad Pitt and I had a good talk on the way home. Well, I talked and gave him a snapshot of my troubles, and he licked my hand a couple of times in a supportive way, in between taking great chomps out of the seat.

By the time we reached my place we were of one mind, having decided to sleep straight through the next day, giving it a miss altogether. Today, after all, hadn't turned out that great. Brad Pitt seemed to think it unlikely that we'd be allowed to sleep uninterrupted. I put his pessimism down to him being a dog and not his own master and dismissed it. I remember looking forward to having my bed all to myself and told Brad Pitt I wasn't going to budge from it for at least twelve hours. That was the plan we finally agreed on.

I didn't know, at the time, that what they say about the best laid plans of mice and men also holds true for those of women and dogs.

Dear God,

Science doesn't lessen you. It makes you so much greater. What science shows us, when it shows us the infinite universe, the microscopic detail of life, or the precise patterns in nature, is that creation is so infinite and so complex that we can only ever be aware of a minute fraction of it.

But if we admit we can only ever comprehend a teeny, tiny part of the universe, we then also have to admit that there is no way any of us can fully understand its creator. A person who can tell you what God is thinking is as likely as an ant that can describe how a car works. Anybody who claims to be able to speak for God is either lying or delusional.

This must be why religions denounce science. If they acknowledged science and incorporated it into their beliefs, they'd have to admit that any being capable of creating the universe is beyond their comprehension. Then they'd have to give up speaking for you, and organized religion would become far too hard to organize.

It all makes sense now.

Syd x

My life to date has been a barren one. I find babies as aesthetically pleasing as the next woman, but I've survived thirty years on earth without succumbing to the need to grow one in my belly.

My less fortunate friends with child have all but disappeared from my life, living as they now do in Diaperland. So the only regular interaction I have with anyone under voting age—with the exception of the devil's spawn across the street—is with Audrey and Lexie, Anna's step-twins-to-be.

I adore the girls. There's a pleasing symmetry to their twinness; miniature, matching human beings have a charm all their own. Mostly, though, I like them because they are unspoiled, good-natured, humane kids in spite of being born horrifically rich.

All that being so, it still came as a jarring shock to me to open my eyes and find them standing by the side of my bed at six thirty in the morning. At first I thought I was seeing double, that there was only one small, pigtailed girl wearing a pink, one-piece pajama suit, feet attached, standing in front of me.

I tried to face the girls with what dignity I could muster. They were, after all, of an impressionable age. Not yet ready to discover I wasn't always the sophisticated woman they knew and looked up to, if for no other reason than that they're really short. I must've succeeded in gaining my composure as the twins regarded me for several seconds in what I'd like to assume was respectful silence. Lexie was the first to break it.

"Who hit you?"

"What?" I said.

"Who hit you?" She considerately raised her voice twenty or thirty decibels so I could hear her better.

"It wasn't a 'who.' It was a 'what.' A bottle of Absolut . . . or maybe it was Grey Goose. I can tell you which when I see how much money is left in my purse. Why do you ask?"

"You have black eyes. Like the panda in the zoo."

I ran my little finger under my left eye and found it gained a substantial black smudge.

"That? Don't worry about that. It's the slutty eye makeup I had on last night. It'll come off."

Audrey seemed to doubt my claim but the question she asked was, "Can we get into bed with you?"

"Depends. Is there anyone else in the bed?"

"Just him." She pointed past me to the foot of the bed.

Brad Pitt had snuck onto the bed during the brief time I'd been asleep even though we'd discussed the designated sleeping areas for dogs and human beings at some length before retiring. A large, ugly dog was already in my bed. Adding two gorgeous little girls to the mix wouldn't make much difference. I told them to get in.

The most direct route must've been over the top of me, because that was the path trodden. I had to clutch the edges of the mattress as the bed began to tilt and heave. The girls—and Brad Pitt, who awoke to join the fun—bounced, squealed, and barked. Their joy reached a crescendo of brain-mincing yelps all around and caused the room to sway in a way I found distracting. After what seemed like several long hours, the other occupants of my bed calmed down, the world leveled out, and my nausea eased slightly.

"What's 'slutty'?" Lexie said.

I tried to come off as a stern authority figure while also toying with the idea of vomiting. "Where did you hear that word?"

"From you."

"Really? Oh. Okay. Well. Um. You know the way you two just jumped into bed with me?"

"Uh-huh."

"Well, in different circumstances, jumping into bed with someone like that would be considered slutty. Do you understand what I mean?"

"No."

"I'm very glad to hear it. Where's your wicked stepmother?"

Both girls glanced toward the kitchen. A loud smashing sound came from that direction. I sat up in bed.

"Anna?"

"Sorry, sorry. But it was ugly anyway."

Anna's voice was followed by the rest of her, and once I saw her, with two steaming mugs holding what all my barely working senses told me was freshly brewed coffee, I forgave her for entering and breaking. She placed the mugs on the chest of drawers, pulled a pint-sized bottle of scotch from the pocket of her green Chinese silk dressing gown, and showed me the label.

"Want some?"

"Will I need it?"

"Very likely." She doused the coffee and handed me a cup. I took it gratefully. A sip or two and I felt better. Not like my old familiar self. That was impossible because there was still at least half a bottle of vodka diluting my blood, but at least now I felt like someone I was vaguely acquainted with.

The girls had settled into bed and immediately fallen asleep in the way only five-year-olds can. Anna, after shucking off her fluffy, stiletto mules, had settled herself at the end of the bed and was absently drumming her fingers on Brad Pitt's flat head.

"Nice shoes," I said. I didn't think anyone actually wore shoes like that outside of 1940s movies, and then only in mysterious places called boudoirs.

"You look like shit. What did you do to yourself last night?"

"Serious damage, obviously. Why are you here?"

"I don't think I can go through with this wedding."

It is my duty as chief bridesmaid—and only bridesmaid over the age of six—to remain calm in the face of bridal wedding nerves, even before seven in the morning, the day before the wedding. "Oh, really. Why is that?"

"I shouldn't have gone strapless. My arms look too fat in the dress. I can't wear it."

"Trust me, if you lost any more weight off your arms, you'd look like the Venus de Milo."

"I left Vince."

My white sheets nearly acquired a striking café noir stain. "But . . . the wedding . . . it's tomorrow. You'll lose your deposit. You can't have left him. Not now."

"Why not now?"

I placed my coffee carefully on the bedside cabinet. "What about the girls?"

"What about them?"

"You can't just take off with them like that," I said.

"Why not? I'm keeping them as my share of the settlement."

"This isn't a joint property issue. And it's . . . it's not fair to Vince."

"I know. I know. The fair thing to do would be to get one each, but could you separate them? They're a matched set."

"Wait. Wait. Don't you have to carry them around in your uterus, or raise them from seed, or something of that magnitude, before they'll grant you custody? How are you going to take care of them? Are you getting Louise in the settlement too?"

"She wouldn't come," Anna said. "Didn't think it was a good idea. Strange, she's normally quite sensible. It doesn't matter. We'll do without a nanny. Lots of people do, you know, and I'll have plenty of help from my best friend."

I glanced around the room. "You mean me, don't you?"

"Of course I mean you. Who else?" Anna leaned forward, placed her coffee mug on the bedside table, and grabbed me by the shoulders. "You have to promise me something."

"Okay, what?"

"If anything happens to me, you'll take care of the girls."

"But they have Vince—"

"No, I mean, should anything happen to the both of us, you have to take the girls. Promise me."

"Me? You want me to take the girls? What about Vince's parents?"

"They're too old. Promise you will."

"Yes, okay, I promise. Of course I will. Of course."

Anna calmed down a little—enough that I thought it was safe to ask, "What's really wrong here?"

"It's all so final, this marriage business. And the thing is, it's not just me and Vince. What about the girls? What happens to them if we fuck it up? They've already lost one mother."

"So what are you doing? You leave now, you'll definitely fuck it up."

"How can I know for sure that this is the right thing to do? The best thing for everyone?"

"You can't know for sure. No one can—have a little faith. It'll all work out."

"You're telling me to have faith? Christ, now I know I'm in trouble."

"It's just nerves. Getting married is a big deal."

"Whatever. Look, we'll stay here until we get on our feet. The house seems a lot smaller than the last time I was here . . . but it'll be fun. I'm almost sure of it. We could become one of those nonnuclear families that conservative politicians get so upset about. Though I suppose Jake might not like it either."

"Well, actually, Jake and I, we kind of broke up."

"That's great. See, it's all working out already." Anna got up, gave Brad Pitt's left ear a gentle yank, and went to see who was at the door. For some reason my doorbell was ringing at twenty to seven on Saturday morning.

"Don't worry," I said, "they'll get back together. This is just a prewedding episode. That's probably your daddy trying to break my doorbell now." I was saying it more to reassure myself than anyone else. The twins were asleep.

I decided to join them and was rearranging myself in the space left to me when Anna came back into the room with Jake Reed, aka Charles Turner, in tow. I hid under the covers, hoping he'd go away. No such luck. He unearthed me by folding back the comforter.

"You look like shit," he said.

"Charming. No wonder she broke up with you," Anna said.

"She broke up with me?" Jake was concerned. "When?"

One of the twins turned over and said, "Shit, shit, shit, shit," in a sleepy voice.

"I think you forgot to tell him something," Anna said.

"Yeah, you did," he said.

They were ganging up on me.

"I can't be expected to let everyone know everything right away. It must have slipped my mind—I might be concussed. How come you let him in? You're supposed to be my best friend."

"He had a key."

"Does everybody have a key to my house?" I pulled the comforter back over my head as the doorbell rang again. I peeked out at the alarm clock. It told me seven o'clock was still fifteen minutes away. I had a feeling it was going to be a long day.

"Who'd be calling so early on a Saturday?" Anna was on her way to the door again.

"I have no idea," I said. "All the people I know who'd do a rotten thing like that are already here."

It occurred to me that if Anna left the room I'd be more or less alone with Jake; the short people in my bed provided no protection. I sat up. "Wait, don't go . . . whoever it is probably has a key too."

Anna was gone. The doorbell continued to sound, rather more violently than necessary, I thought.

Jake had seated himself in the chair under the window.

"Please, make yourself at home," I said.

He leaned back in the chair, propping his feet up on the foot of the bed. He didn't seem to be at all aware of the awkwardness of the situation—of him being in my bedroom now we were no longer together—and had somehow acquired my cup of coffee and was taking a sip.

"What's in this?"

"Scotch. If you want something else you have to get it yourself."

"I'm not here for the coffee."

"What are you here for?"

"What do you think I'm here for?"

"This isn't a good time. I'm very busy. As you can see, I have a lot on this morning."

"You don't look as if you have that much on at all."

I followed his gaze down to my nightgown. A couple of buttons had come undone and it wasn't doing a good job protecting my modesty. Unable to think of anything to say, I strategically withdrew under the covers to do the buttons up.

Raised voices came from the front door region of the house.

"Vince must be here," I said to my comforter.

"Sounds like it."

The argument escalated. Judging from the stomping going on, the conflict went free-range, taking in most of the rest of the house and ending up in the kitchen, where it was enhanced by the sound effects of cabinet doors being opened and slammed shut. I wondered what it was they were looking for.

"Tell them they're going to wake the twins," I said.

"The twins aren't in any danger of waking."

I propped myself up on my elbows. Jake was right. The girls were profoundly asleep. The battle being waged in my kitchen needed to reach an all-out nuclear assault before it'd disturb them.

"I guess they have a few things to sort out before the wedding," Jake said.

"I guess so."

"Are we going to talk about it?"

"Vince and Anna?'

"You know what I mean."

Exhaustion made me honest. "I do," I said, "but I've had

about two minutes' sleep and I promise you, you don't want to talk to me right now. I am not a reasonable human being. Could we please sleep on it?"

"We'll talk later?"

"Yes, sleep first, talk later. An excellent plan. Thank you and good night or morning or whatever it is." I closed my eyes.

Drowsiness came in an instant; the world receded into the ether. In a kitchen, in a galaxy far, far away, an argument lost intensity and became quiet. Closer, somewhere in this solar system, someone dropped shoes on the floor and got into bed beside me. I tried to tell him no, no vacancy, bed full of small, identical, pink space invaders with feet built into their garments, no possible room. Especially not for him as he was actually two people in one, making a total of five people and one dog in the bed.

Jake felt warm and comfortable when he wrapped himself around me, so I let the matter rest for a second and sleep got to me first, well before I could warn him about Brad Pitt's proclivity for nibbling on exposed toes.

Dear God,

With its confession-and-absolution-system, Catholicism, as a product, reminds me most of a cleaning product--laundry detergent comes first to mind. Go out and sin. Confess. Repent. Be absolved. Repeat process.

Can you imagine the ads if we sold the church like detergent?

While we see before and after shots of a sullen, taciturn kid transforming into a beamish, bouncing boy, much to the joy of his stereotypical Soccer Mom and Business Dad, a female voice-over says: "We thought our son Henry was beyond all help. At times we were sure he was possessed by the devil. Then a friend recommended Catholicism. We tried it and it started working right away. After a year, it got all of the sin out. We still can't believe it. The results are truly miraculous. Now Henry is a good boy. He's an altar boy and the priest's favorite. We're so proud of him." Insert the appropriate before and after pictures and finish with the deep male voice-over they use for all commercials of the kind: "The Catholic Church: removes the most stubborn sins."

Maybe all religion is a kind of soul soap. Perhaps that's why they say cleanliness is next to godliness. Some people do a little light cleaning once a week, while others wait for a lifetime of muck to accumulate before undergoing a dramatic cleansing. The latter tend to be the most annoying.

Me, I think that life leaves stains. Some wash out but others are there to stay, no matter how long you soak.

Sydney x

I awoke to the sound of an ambulance siren, disturbingly loud and close, before it abruptly stopped, leaving me wondering if I'd dreamt it. The room was cool and quiet. I was alone. The clock by my bed showed noon. No one rang my doorbell. No one hogged my sheets. No one smashed my plates. My head no longer felt like a small grenade had gone off inside it. Gratitude for my complete reversal of fortune propelled me out of bed into the shower.

Moisture in the tub indicated someone had been there before me. My hot water system is continuous, and provided they hadn't used all the clean towels, I didn't care if an entire basketball team had dropped by to shower, which, considering the events of the early morning, was likely.

I stood under the water until my fingers and toes were pruney and I'd run out of shower activities to perform. It then took half a bottle or so of eye-makeup remover to remove most of the black under my eyes. Some of the black, it turned out, was natural.

My reflection, resembling something vaguely human once more, reminded me I was human, and that for all human beings except models and actors, food is necessary for survival. The kitchen, then, was my next port of call, and what I found there made me glad I'd bothered to get partially dressed, albeit in an old Bert & Ernie T-shirt and equally vintage underpants announcing, incorrectly, it was Tuesday.

Brad Pitt was asleep in a strip of sunlight on the floor in his usual position of repose. His big, baggy head rested between his front legs, stretched out straight in front of him. His back legs were stretched out straight behind him. He was sleeping like Superman in full flight, but he wasn't even close to being the main event in my kitchen.

Seated at the small table was a godlike creature wearing a towel in the most casual of arrangements around his waist. The vision was bending sunlight to his will. It glinted off bronzed skin, highlighted damp, tousled hair, and added a dangerously sexy gleam to his eyes.

In other words, it was Jake sitting there looking hot.

A newspaper was open on the table in front of him, but his attention was fixed on a spot of vacant wall. A spot that, in spite of appearances, was so interesting it took him several moments to notice I was in the room. I managed to sidle over to the fridge, opening the door to discover it had been filled with an array of omelet fillings, all of them known favorites of Anna's, before I gained his attention.

Upon divining my presence, he did display definite signs of being pleased to find me within arm's length, instantly inviting me to sit on his lap. In light of my having broken up with him, I felt obligated to refuse. My lack of compliance with his preferred seating plan caused Jake to go all alpha male on me. I ended up on his lap anyway. He offered to show me what was under his towel and continued the dominant male behavior until I gave up wrestling him and agreed to look under it.

Not long after that, we came to a mutual decision to have sex up against the fridge. Other than that slight transgression and the one that followed about half an hour afterward on one of my kitchen chairs—which, by the way, are a lot stronger than they look—I was in complete command of the situation and unrelenting in my decision that things were over between us.

Jake, for some reason, seemed to think he could convince me otherwise. He had the nerve to say, "I don't see the problem."

"That would be because you're using boy logic."

"Well, I am a boy."

"I can see that. There is, in fact, such a thing as too much evidence. Put your towel back on."

"I'll get dressed—unless . . ."

"I don't think so," I said. Though his suggestion was not without merit, having sex with him for the third time in the same afternoon might give him the impression I wasn't really over him.

I followed him into the bedroom where he pulled on socks, boxers, jeans, and a long-sleeved T-shirt, in that order. I took the opportunity to gain a light sweater and a pair of jeans of my own.

"Why do you use a pseudonym for your column?"

Jake settled himself on the bed. "I like the freedom it gives me to say whatever I want without having to answer to too many people."

"Why Charles?"

"Jake didn't sound like a writer's name."

"Chuck does?"

"Think Chuck Dickens." Jake patted the space beside him. "Come here. Promise I won't seduce you. Scout's honor," he said.

"You were never a scout." I sat anyway, figuring I could quickly dampen any ardor he felt by asking the right questions.

"It's my middle name," Jake said.

"Charles?"

"Old family name. Someone in every generation gets stuck with it. I'm lucky my parents took pity on me and didn't give it to me as a first name."

"Very lucky. I had doubts about dating someone named Chuck. It's not a name I can imagine myself even uttering during sex—although it does rhyme with . . . um, what were we talking about?"

"Todd wants to ask you out."

"Who is Todd?"

"That's the same question I was going to ask you. He called my place late last night wanting to speak to you."

"To me?"

"Yep."

"Are you sure?"

"You're the only Sydney I know. Besides, you fit the description he gave."

"Todd?"

"That's what he claimed."

"Why did he call you?"

"That I can't tell you."

"Oh?" I said. And then, "Oh."

"I take it the penny has dropped."

"He's this guy I met at Julie's party . . ."

"Go on."

"I had to give him a phone number for trying so hard to pick me up. And, well, I didn't want to give him mine."

"So you gave him mine?"

"Okay, when you take it out of context like that it sounds bad. But you see, when you give a guy a number to get rid of him, it has to be one you know in case they ask you to repeat it. I guess your number was top of mind. That he called and annoyed you late at night is really just a happy coincidence."

"Poor guy. Must be tough, paling in comparison to me. I'll be nicer to him next time he calls." Jake stretched out on my bed, grabbing a couple of pillows to prop up his big head.

"Please don't encourage him."

"Are you going to tell me why you think we've broken up?"

"You lied to me," I said.

"I didn't exactly lie. I withheld information."

"It's the same thing. Why didn't you tell me about Charles?"

"I could ask you the same question. And another. Why didn't you tell Charles about me?"

I could see the point he was making but I wasn't ready to admit it. "I asked first."

"I did try to tell you. I would've told you if your behavior hadn't been so erratic."

"You're saying it's my fault you didn't tell me?"

"I didn't want to scare you off."

"I don't scare all that easily."

"Come on. We had an amazing thirty-six-hour first date, which we agreed at the time was something special. You were as happy about it as I was and yet you disappeared for two weeks. If I'd told you I was Charles, you'd have been so thrilled that I'd probably never have seen you again."

I hate it when people have reasonable answers for everything.

"What's the big deal? You like Charles. You like me. Now you have both of us in one neat package. You should be twice as happy."

"You're using boy logic again."

"I don't get it, Syd." Jake sat back up on the bed. "We seem to be getting along just fine."

"Getting along has never been our problem. Our problem is . . ." What was the problem? I was having trouble defining it.

Jake didn't seem to have the same trouble. "This isn't about Charles at all, is it?"

As soon as he said that, I felt very exposed.

"You know, not every woman's goal is to end up some guy's handmaiden for the next fifty years. Some of us want more out of life."

"We're not living in the dark ages. You can have a relationship and a life."

"It's not the same. Men have an unfair advantage. You're allowed to make more mistakes. You can still start a family at age fifty."

"This isn't a gender issue."

"Fine for you to say when your gender doesn't have a use-by date."

"None of that matters with us."

"If it works out," I said.

"Are you so sure this won't work out?"

"Why are you so optimistic? You fell out of love with Kim."

"I don't think I ever was in love with Kim."

"You dated the girl for two years. It proves my point exactly. What were you doing? Killing time until the girl you're supposed to marry graduates high school?"

I thought I was going hear his "not every guy is an asshole" speech, but instead Jake answered the question. "I was with Kim because I wanted to be with someone and I guess I thought, maybe, that was all there was."

"Okay."

"You have to remember, I hadn't yet met you."

Well, that just made me feel worse. Tears, of their own accord, started to roll down my cheeks. I tried to blink them away, but that only seemed to increase the flow. I used the sleeves of my sweater, pulled over my fists, to stem the tide.

I could see Jake was making an effort to be patient. "Why can't we just see where this goes?"

"I don't want to see," I said. I'm sure it sounded as petulant to his ears as it did to mine.

"Why not?"

"I just don't believe in happily ever after."

"I'm beginning to think you don't believe in anything at all."

Now he was angry, and my sleeves were soggy enough without having to take that statement into consideration. True, I didn't believe in what Jake seemed to believe in, or what most other people believed in, but there had to be something I believed in. If I could only think what it was. I changed the subject.

"Anyway, how do I know for sure you never saw Kim in New York?"

"I guess you can't know for sure. But you could try having a little faith in me."

"Faith? I should believe whatever you say because believing it makes my life neater and easier? That's what you want me to do?"

"I think the work you've been doing has made you very cynical."

"I'll take cynical over stupid any day."

"Sometimes," Jake said, "people believe in something or somebody because the belief itself, regardless of whether it's true or not, makes their lives better."

"Not me. I'm sorry. You've put your faith in the wrong person."

"I don't think so."

"Trust me, there's a twenty-two-year-old out there waiting for you who'll believe anything you want her to believe. When you find her, you'll thank me for this."

"You really have issues, don't you?"

"If you've only just realized that now, you're in serious trouble. Look, I'm sorry, but this is . . . I can't pretend that I believe in something when I don't."

"Then why start this in the first place?"

"I didn't think it'd get this far. I thought that, because of Charles . . ."

"You'd always have a way out."

"Yes," I said.

Jake stared at me. He stared for a full minute, almost without blinking, but whatever it was he was trying to see eluded him.

"Are you sure this is what you want?"

I wasn't sure, but I said I was.

"So that's it?" Jake stood and looked out the window. He didn't appear to see anything of interest, but he kept at it for a while before he picked up his shoes and slipped them on, not bothering to tie the laces.

"I wish I knew why you won't let yourself be happy," he said.

Happy? Christ, I wasn't trying for happy—just for manageable.

At the bedroom door he paused, looking back. I thought he was going to say something more, but he was silent. I wondered if I could stop him from going if I said the right thing. I was sorely tempted to try. Only I had no idea what to say.

"So, I guess this means I'll be going stag to the wedding."

"I'll call and give them my apologies," he said.

Brad Pitt eagerly followed Jake to the front door, then returned to glare at me reproachfully when it slammed in his face. That's why I don't own a dog. They have no discernment whatsoever when it comes to whose side they should be on in a fight.

"Trust me, it'll be easier this way," I said. "It was already getting too hard and it was definitely taking up too much time. I want my old, uncomplicated life back."

Brad Pitt did not look convinced.

"Oh, what do you know? You're a dog; you love everybody. It's really very pathetic."

I had a funny empty feeling inside me. It turned out to be hunger, but even so I was aware I'd lost a lot more than an argument. I'd hated the paranoid, insecure person I'd become while I was with Jake. But knowing that I was self-reliant and capable of leading a relatively enviable life not dependent on any other person wasn't the consolation it used to be.

There was nothing to do about it, nothing to do but try to hold it together. All the same, all I wanted to do was to keep crying into my sleeves. What I needed was outside intervention. The only thing that can save you from drowning in the murky self-pity of your own tragedy is someone else's greater tragedy.

From: Sydney Welles <sydneywelles@yahoo.com>
To: God c/o specialfxdepartment@universalpictures.com
Date: Saturday, October 29, 2005 5:33 PM PDT
Subject: Heaven & Other Unrealistic Endings

Dear God,

I like a happy ending as much as the next Hollywood studio exec, but I suspect that when a film ends on a soaring, impossibly happy note, nobody in the audience is crying from happiness. No, they're genuinely crying, because they know nothing like that will ever happen in real life.

For most people, happily ever after is shelved, alongside Santa, the Easter Bunny, and the Tooth Fairy, well before adolescence. We soon learn there's no such thing. Yet as soon as people stop believing, they become part of the great conspiracy. They lie to little kids, elaborately, at considerable expense and trouble, to keep these myths going.

Why is it that adults feel better if children believe in fairy tales and bogeypersons and happy endings? Why is it that no matter how much gritty reality people have endured, no matter how dire the circumstances of their lives, no matter what mistakes they've made, they still want to believe that life works out in the end, just like a fairy tale? After all, isn't heaven the ultimate fairy tale ending? It's the only story of its kind to survive the end of childhood. The only one that becomes more popular the older people get.

How can we still believe in heaven when all the other happy endings we were promised turned out to be lies? Are we the most gullible race in existence? Or just the most tenacious? Or both?

Sydney

When the doorbell rang two hours after Jake left, I only fleetingly indulged the thought that it was Jake ringing it. Really, he was the last person I expected, or rather, the next to last. The people on my doorstep were the least expected of all—Cupid and Cupid's mother, the incongruously named Sunny.

From what Cupid has told me of his maternal grandparents, I've gathered that his mother was the offspring of real hippies from the sixties who gave their five children natural names: Sky, Sunny, Sandy, Meadow, and River. Sunny had disappointed her parents by embracing capitalism, but had continued their tradition of choosing children's names that guaranteed the kids who bore them were bullied at school.

Sunny was not herself. Her normally not-a-hair-out-of-place coiffure was seriously awry, her mascara worn two inches below the area usually recommended for the application of that product, her shoes and purse mismatched. Though her shoes, if you weren't too fussy, matched the small, ugly, leather suitcase she carried in her right hand.

More than her disheveled appearance and Cupid's disquietingly waiflike demeanor, it was the little suitcase that disturbed me—the suitcase and the bulging *Spiderman II* backpack on Cupid's back.

Deathly pale under her fake tan, Sunny began to speak rapidly, breathlessly, and slightly hysterically—I only managed to catch every other word. I made a little sense of what she was saying. Something of a serious medical nature had happened to her husband. It required her to spend the next few days at Cedars-Sinai. Cupid's old nanny had the flu and his babysitter wasn't allowed to stay out all night. Sunny's brother was over-seas and her younger sisters were irresponsible—free-range nymphomaniacs attracted to men with questionable grooming habits—and very likely to leave the kid somewhere and forget about him. Her husband had no brothers and sisters, and being an only, late child, his mother was too old to look after Cupid. Certain friends she'd normally turn to were nowhere to be found. And the mother's group she belonged to was composed of a bunch of calorie-deficient cows. I was wondering why she was sharing all of this information with me until I clearly heard her say, "The thing is, he said he wanted to stay with you."

"With me?" I looked at Cupid. He looked at his mother's shoes. It was hard not to stare at them. They were a truly hideous mustard leather.

"My parents will pick him up first thing in the morning. They're driving through the night to get here. They can't get here any sooner." Sunny shook her head. "It's an ideological problem: economic inequality. Until we reach a time where everybody in the world can afford to travel by plane, they re-fuse to fly."

"I see," I said.

"Do you think we'll be able to make this happen?"

"I'd like to think so, but realistically I don't think that we will ever reach that kind of economic equality until we can manage to curb corporate greed and—"

"No, I meant is it okay for Cupid to stay with you tonight? Or if you prefer, you can stay at our place with him."

Cupid had transferred his attention to my shoes, pink fluffy slippers with a cheeky monkey's head embroidered on the front of each. Even so, they were not at all deserving of the scowl he was treating them to.

"Yes, of course he can stay. I'd be happy to have him.

Please, come in." Someone had said that out loud. It had sounded a lot like my voice.

Brad Pitt, who'd been standing quietly behind me all this time, barked his welcome. Sunny flinched when she noticed the dog but visibly steeled herself, prodding Cupid through the open doorway before following him in.

Ten minutes later, Sunny was gone and Cupid and I were seated at my kitchen table engaged in a staring contest.

"Do you have PlayStation 2?"

I shook my head. "Not even PlayStation 1."

"X-Box?"

"I don't think so, but I can't be sure. I don't know what it is."

"Nintendo 64?"

"No. And none of the other sixty-three either."

"Sixty-three what?"

"I have no idea."

"I brought my GameBoy. Do you want to play?"

"Maybe later. Have you had dinner?"

He shook his head.

I got up, pulled open the fridge door, and stared at its contents, hoping they'd add up in my mind to something easy that'd appeal to the appetite of a sad seven-year-old boy. I wondered how close that appetite would be to that of cheerful five-year-old twin girls with a live-in cook. I spied a hunk of cheese that only needed to be melted in a pan with a knob of butter, seasoned, and mixed with a little milk to become a sauce.

"How about gorgonzola pasta and arugula salad?"

"What's that?"

"It's a mild blue cheese—wait, no, you won't like it. I didn't like blue cheese when I was your age. Too stinky."

Cupid perked up. "My dad eats stinky cheese." His face returned to its forlorn expression. "Maybe I'll like it too— like him. Do you think I'll like it?"

"No," I said.

"What is ar-roog-goo-lah?"

"Oh, arugula salad. You won't like that either, come to think of it. It's kind of bitter."

"I don't like salad."

"Neither did I when I was your age. Hated the stuff. What do you like?"

He sighed. "All the things I like, I'm not allowed to have."

"Is that so? Well, tonight is different. Tonight you are only allowed to eat what you like."

Cupid regarded me with suspicion. "Anything? No broccoli? You won't tell."

"I won't tell."

"Promise, cross your heart, hope to die?"

"Yes. All of the above."

He was not convinced of my good intentions, but he said, "I want a cheeseburger, but not a junior one. I want a grown-up one."

"Okay."

"With big fries."

"Okay."

"And a strawberry milkshake. The biggest one."

"Okay."

"Really?"

"Really."

"What will happen if I don't finish my food?"

"Nothing at all. If you don't, Brad Pitt will. Do you want to eat out or bring it back here?"

He thought it over. "Here. Do you have any PG movies?"

"I do, or we could go to the video store if you like."

"Can we go in your Mini?"

"Yes."

"Can I help drive?"

"No."

✝

Long after Cupid's appetite for junk had been sated and we'd watched two movies that fulfilled his mental junk requirements—they both provided more evidence for my theory that almost all mainstream Hollywood films are made for seven-year-old boys—I heard a muffled noise coming from my second room, where Cupid should have been asleep on the day bed. I listened for a few minutes; the low noise continued steadily.

By the light in the hallway, which Cupid had insisted I leave on in case I was scared, I could see his golden head was facedown on his pillow, into which he was sobbing as if all the PlayStations in the world had stopped working. Comfort was required and as there was only me or Brad Pitt—who'd been standing sentinel by Cupid's bed all night—around to give it, I turned on the lamp and sat on the side of the bed next to Cupid's prostrate form. Brad Pitt, in his Superman position on the floor, considerately became a footrest for me.

I reached out and softly touched the mop of curls on the pillow. "Well," I said, "look who's had too much sugar."

He lifted his head and glared at me defiantly through tears. "I feel sick."

"Okay. Where do you feel sick?"

He pointed vaguely in the direction of his stomach and chest.

"Kind of a general middle-part sick, is it?"

He made a snuffling sound in agreement.

"I've heard it's going around. Does it hurt?"

"It feels funny in here." Sitting up, he pointed to the space between his chest and stomach. "Maybe it's a heart attack like my dad's."

"Trust me, you're in the low-risk category for heart disease. Maybe your tummy is a little unsettled from all that food."

He nodded miserably. I was compelled, by the mysterious magnetic force sad little children have surrounding them, to put my arm around him.

"Your dad is being taken care of by some of the best doctors in the world. Everything is going to be okay. You'll see in the morning."

A flood of fresh tears and snot broke through. I placed the tissues from the small side cabinet on the bed beside him, hoping he was old enough to blow his nose on his own. He ignored the Kleenex, using his sleeve and my sheets instead.

"Your TV isn't very big," he said.

"No, it's not. But I'll let you in on a little secret. Bigger is not always better. When it comes to television, the bigger the screen, the less interesting the life of the person who owns it. You'll work this out as you get older."

Cupid sniffed. "Your dog is ugly."

"He's not my dog. But you're right, he's very ugly."

"You don't have any toys."

"I know. It sucks. But I'm going to get some, and you can help me choose them. Are you tired?"

"No," he said.

Then he yawned three times in a row, laid his head on my shoulder, and cried himself to sleep.

✝

Morning Star—I suspect that wasn't the name on her birth certificate, as her husband, Frank, had called her Maureen a couple of times—stared at me, or rather at the air around me, with such concentration I wondered if she'd slipped into a trance.

"Lovely," she said. "Frank, come take a look at this."

Frank, who in the short time I'd known him did everything he was told to, came to have a look.

"Very nice," he said after a minute or two.

"What is?"

"Your aura, honey," Morning Star said. "You have a very powerful aura."

I looked around, seeing nothing at all where they both had stared. "I do? What color is it?"

"Why, it's golden, of course."

"Of course."

Frank had returned to carrying out a previous order he'd been given—to gather up Cupid's belongings—and was helping Cupid to put his bag on his back. "Are we all ready to go?"

"All set," Morning Star said, holding out her hand for Cupid to take.

His grandparents had no idea what Cupid was talking about most of the time, but it was clear they adored their only grandchild and that Cupid, equally perplexed by them, adored them in return, although he did his best to hide his affection in front of me.

The morning had begun well, with a call from Sunny to tell Cupid his father was in stable condition and the doctors were optimistic about a full recovery. Shortly afterward, Sunny's parents had arrived in, of all things, a brand-new Lexus. I later discovered Sunny leased it for her parents because she didn't want them driving Cupid around in their beat-up old van when he visited.

While his grandparents refreshed themselves, Cupid and I went for a walk along the beach to watch the passing parade of the weird, wonderful, and terrifying on the Venice boardwalk. Cupid had his photo taken with the aliens sitting on the beach and his head patted for free by the guitar-playing, roller-skating, turbaned man who's been rolling up and down the boardwalk for as long as anyone can remember. After watching a man with no shirt on—and not much in the way of pants either—walk on his hands on the sand, we took his idea and improved on it. Veering off the path, taking off our shoes, squishing our toes in the sand, we made footprints all the way down to the Santa Monica pier, where we rode the Ferris wheel.

Upon our return, we made an early lunch of lentil patties and bean sprouts at the nearest vegan restaurant I knew of. Or at least Frank and Morning Star did. Cupid and I merely pretended to, having taken the precaution of bolting down hot dogs and chicken nuggets while we were on the pier.

Now, as we stood by the Lexus in which his grandparents were already seated, Cupid was shuffling his feet in an embarrassed way in front of me.

"Where is your rabbit?"

"I don't know, I haven't seen him for weeks now. I think he's run away. So a road trip, huh? Should be lots of fun, especially with those guys."

"They sing all the way. They don't even turn on the radio," Cupid said. He didn't seem unhappy at the prospect, even though he had a television screen and DVD player in the back of the SUV his mother drove.

"Do I get a good-bye kiss?"

"Yuck! No. No way." He shook his head violently, making vomiting noises, his tongue hanging out in disgust, in case I missed the gist of what he was saying.

"All right then, so I'll see you in a week or so."

Cupid and I solemnly shook hands.

He paused just before getting into the car. Putting his knapsack on the ground, he rummaged around in it and produced a complicated piece of red and gray plastic about the size of both my fists together. He handed it to me.

"You can keep this until you get some toys of your own," he said. "It's my fifth favorite toy."

I blinked back sudden tears. "Thank you. I'm honored."

"You have to take care of it."

"I will. I promise. What is it?"

"It's a Transformer—don't you know anything?"

"Apparently not."

As the car drove away, I glanced at my watch and then down at Brad Pitt, who was stolidly enduring the departure of the little human being who had pulled his tail and won his fickle canine devotion, to the point that he'd foolishly ignored the only person in the house capable of using the can opener.

I nudged him with my foot. "I have to get ready," I said. "I have bridesmaid duties all afternoon and a wedding to attend at the end of the day. At least I hope I do. I better call and check."

From: Sydney Welles <sydneywelles@yahoo.com>
To: God c/o info@weather.com
Date: Sunday, October 30, 2005 1:02 PM PDT
Subject: Give me a sign

Hi God,

If you think that breaking up with Jake was the wrong thing to do, could you give me a sign? Only don't make it rain. Anna would never forgive me--the wedding ceremony is a sunset special, on the beach. Thanks.

Syd x

"One Love," the original Marley version, was playing but my progress down the aisle was much slower than the beat dictated; a pace requested by the nervous bride. I was easily outpaced. Lexie and Audrey skipped ahead of me down the sand in a wild zigzag pattern, pelting everyone within shot with blossoms.

As far as bridesmaids go, I didn't fit the part. My dress did not make me look twice my size and age. Instead of shoes impossible to walk down the aisle in, I had jewelled flip-flops on my feet. I'd even escaped big bridesmaid hair. A large orchid had been tucked behind my left ear by a West Hollywood hairstylist, but otherwise my hair was allowed to do what it liked. I held a bouquet of more of the orchids—Cattleya orchids, according to the overpriced, overbearing Beverly Hills florist who made it up.

Brad Pitt was my date for the evening. To cut a long story short, I told Anna I'd rather date a dog than call Jake, beg his forgiveness, and ask him to reconsider attending the wedding— I wasn't ready to admit I was wrong yet. An unfortunate choice of words, because she knew I was dogsitting Brad Pitt for the weekend and asked me to bring him along to amuse the kids. He was holding court with a group of them now.

The twins wore dresses in the same fabric and color as mine but with skirts poufy enough to satisfy little-girl notions of high fashion. They wore their orchids in top knots and were barefoot, having abandoned their miniature versions of my slippers once they found their feet preferred the feel of cool sand to that of expensive, custom-made leather.

Vince and his business partner and best man, Michael, were watching our progress down the aisle. They were dressed in white linen suits, mirrored sunglasses, and candy-colored shirts, and they were smoking cigars. It was a good facsimile of the Miami gangster look. Vince must've been allowed to choose the outfits himself.

I was over three quarters of the way down the aisle when I was brought up short by what I thought was a shriek from the tent where I'd left Anna. It could also have been the wind. The twins had already reached Vince and Michael and were attempting to scale them. I was unsure what to do.

A smart-ass in the crowd said, "I think they're waiting for you up there." I cranked my face back into a smile and dragged myself the rest of the way to the floral archway, set up in the middle of the small Malibu beach where the others had arranged themselves in the usual wedding formation.

There we waited for Anna to appear. And waited. And waited. Two minutes passed with no sign of a bride. I started to get worried. The song ended, and after a short silence and some furtive whispering in the crowd, it began to play again from the start. Still no bride.

I caught Vince's eye and inclined my head toward the tent, silently asking if he wanted me to go back and get her. He was considering the option when we heard, "Sorry, sorry. Damned hem got caught on a tent peg. We had to pin it. Thanks for waiting. It's not like you can start without me anyway."

Anna appeared at the bottom of the aisle. Her wedding gown was a strapless sheath in the shade of emerald green that looks stunning on women with creamy skin and red, red hair—both of which Anna has—but is avoided by everyone else outside of a leprechaun colony for good reason. A white orchid was tucked behind her left ear, a stray from the cluster she was carrying. There was no doubt that Anna made a beautiful bride, but she was glowing in a way she had not been when I left the tent. Her serenity, as she sweetly smiled her way down the aisle, made me suspicious.

As she reached us, I leaned in to whisper: "What is it?"

"Gin," she said.

The marriage celebrant stepped up and began the ceremony.

✝

The reception, like the ceremony, took place on the beach, in the huge marquee set up for the purpose. Once my official duties were over and the photographer could not coax any more light from the setting sun or smiles from the bridal party, the rest of the evening passed in a blur. I diligently performed my unofficial bridesmaid's duty. I flirted with everybody—man, woman, or dog—within striking range, and only checked my cell phone for nonexistent messages from Jake every two or three minutes. He'd left one during the ceremony when my cell was turned off, but that was only to point out my hypocrisy in being maid of honor at a ceremony I didn't believe in. I couldn't tell from his tone whether he was angry or teasing.

However, it wasn't as if I spent the whole night dwelling on the Jake situation. I managed to forget about him for the time I had to get up and give my speech. About four minutes in total.

Besides, other people kept bringing him up. At one point in the evening, I had an interesting conversation about him with Anna's cousin, Brigid, a financial wizard and complete slut. She cornered me halfway through dinner by the champagne bar.

"Anna said you're seeing Jake Reed," she said.

"Not anymore. Why, do you know him?"

Brigid nodded. "Not half as well as I'd like to."

"Really?"

"Why'd you guys break up?"

"Just a guess, but I'd say it probably had something to do with him being gay."

"No." She rolled her eyes. "No—so typical. It figures. No one cute is straight anymore."

"Isn't it always the way?"

"Funny. He didn't register on the old gaydar. I'm usually infallible."

"He's not fully out of the closet. Still dates girls, you know, for appearances."

"Oh, God, one of those—"

"Tell me about it. A real waste of time. I mean, you could invest years in someone like that . . ."

"You poor thing."

"Excuse me, I have to go see what Brad Pitt is up to." He was sniffing the main tent pole to see if it was worthy of his pee.

Brigid scanned the room excitedly. "Brad Pitt's here? Where?"

I pointed him out.

"That's a dog," she said.

"Yes."

Much later, after the twins had gone home to bed, I caught the bouquet in spite of myself. I'd separated myself from the little horde of squealing single women and gone to sit in an out-of-the-way spot at the bar to watch the scramble and tackle. A wedding really isn't the best place to go directly after you've broken up with your boyfriend. I'd been sitting by myself for just long enough to recognize that although two people I loved had just gotten married, I was miserable—when the bouquet sailed through the air in a high, graceful arc and landed in my lap. It's not widely known, but Anna played basketball in college. She's still a good shot, even backward while wearing a strapless dress.

We saw Vince and Anna off, inserting them into the Town Car that was taking them to a hotel on the beach in Santa Monica, where they were to spend one night before flying to Spain. By this stage the band members had reached their ballad phase, and a man who looked vaguely familiar to me walked up and introduced himself.

"I'm Tony," he said, "and baby, I think I'm in love."

He struck me as the kind of guy who wears sunglasses at the gym so he can stare at women's body parts without anyone knowing what he's up to, or so he's stupid enough to believe.

"Tony," I said. "Who do you think you're in love with?"

"You, babe." He winked at me, made his right hand into a gun, and shot me.

"Have we met?"

"Hey, that was supposed to be my line." He shot me again, making a clicking noise with his mouth as he pulled the trigger.

I remembered him. He was the guy from the toilet bar going around shooting all his friends, the one Anna had threatened to introduce me to the night I met Jake.

"It's not possible we've met before," he said, finger cocked and ready to fire once more. "I'd remember you."

"Is that some kind of affliction?"

He glanced around, confused. "What?"

"That thing you do when you pretend to shoot people with your hand. Is it some kind of disorder?"

"Whaddya mean? It's my thing."

"Trust me. You'd be much more popular if you stopped doing it."

"I'm popular now."

"Okay. Look, why don't you go shoot someone else. This isn't a great night for me."

He winked and made the clicking noise. "Don't be too sure about that, babe. Your luck is about to change."

"Please don't talk to me anymore."

"Right," he said uncertainly before regaining his seemingly indestructible confidence. "I get it." He pulled his hands out of imaginary holsters on his hips and let both barrels off, point-blank, in my face. "You want to dance?"

"With you? No, not if my life depended on it."

"Hey, come on. I think we, you and I, the two of us, could be good together."

"It's late and you're desperately trying to score before you leave the party."

"You want I give you a ride home?"

"I really think you should go and bother someone else," I said.

Brigid, with another of Anna's red-headed cousins, caught us on her way out, a bottle of champagne the worse for wear.

"Hey, you need a ride? We got a cab waiting," she said.

"That'd be great," I said.

"Hey, babe, you got a ride."

"You be quiet, Tony."

"Well, come on then," Brigid said. Then she passed out.

By the time we'd laid her facedown on the backseat of the cab and her cousin was installed in the front seat, there was no room left in the cab for me.

"Your friend has great tits," Tony said, using his hands to emphasize his words.

"Thank you."

"I gotta tell you, I don't like it when women drink that much. A drunk woman is just not sexy."

"Oh, you mean in the way a drunk man is?"

He seemed confused.

"You said something about a ride," I said.

"Stay right where you are babe, I'll get the Corvette."

"You're kidding, right?"

"About what?"

What the hell, it was late, I needed a ride, and I wasn't planning on getting anything more. "Fine. Get the Corvette."

I was pleased to see Tony's face fall when he saw Brad Pitt waiting with me. He clearly didn't want the dog in his car, but also didn't want to ruin what he thought were his chances with me. In the end his libido won out and Brad Pitt was ensconced on my lap, where, I was proud to see, he drooled liberally all over the leather upholstery whenever he had a chance.

The conversation was a little stilted on the way home because I answered Tony only when he didn't say something that offended me in some way. But because of the lack of traffic, the trip passed quickly enough.

"So," I said as we pulled up outside my house. "Thanks for the ride."

"No problem, baby. You gonna invite me in?"

"Don't be ridiculous."

"It's only a quarter to twelve. The night is young and so are we."

"I'm much older than I look. And I'm really tired."

"You sure about that? You sure you want to let me get away? It's a big, lonely world out there."

Obviously, Tony was God's way of telling me what He

thought of my breaking up with Jake. I knew I deserved it, but I think I'd have preferred a natural disaster.

"I'm not sure about anything anymore," I said. "But I'm willing to take my chances on this. Good night. And thank you."

Tony reached into his inside jacket pocket and produced a small bottle of breath spray. He squirted it a couple of times into his mouth.

Brad Pitt saw it coming before I did and started barking loudly in alarm. I was struggling with the dog and the car door so it took a few moments more before I realized Tony was swooping in for a good night kiss, rather than leaning in to help me with the door. I moved my head, but not quite swiftly enough. The kiss landed on the corner of my mouth.

Then the earth moved, but not in a good way. It registered four point six on the Richter scale and distracted Tony from his task long enough for me to make a dignified escape. Thank God.

Dear God,

I've come to a conclusion that I think holds true for all religious beliefs (and most everything else in life):

The more convinced you are that you're right, the more likely it is that you're wrong.

Faith, it seems, needs a little doubt mixed in to remain healthy.

Perhaps this is why you remain a mystery. If people will kill in your name and on your behalf when your existence can't even be proven, imagine the wholesale slaughter that'd occur if you came out of the celestial closet.

Speak soon,

Sydney x

Brad Pitt had sniffed and rejected twenty-two potential peeing places and was in the process of dismissing the twenty-third.

I was regretting volunteering to take him for his walk while Julie was in a meeting. "Come on, boy, does it really matter where you pee?"

Brad Pitt looked at me in a way that told me how little I understood the business of pissing, how little I understood most things that were important in life.

"Well, you'd better decide soon. I have to get back to work."

We both knew that was a lie. Bishop Fullerton—he of the many chins—had called Larry this morning to tell him we'd been awarded the Church account. And I'd been sampling beer all afternoon—I wasn't much in the mood for work. Not that I was drinking on purpose. No, that was work—research for our beer client. A bar crawl of the worst sports bars on the Westside, which for some reason were the only bars with the beers we required on tap.

Besides, I could get away with taking it easy for a while. The Church account was in the bag, and I was the goose that laid that particular golden egg.

As Brad Pitt investigated a mailbox, a small bush, and a rear tire, I wondered why I wasn't happy with my success. I suspect the problem was that, golden egg or not, it made me a goose.

By this time we'd reached a church down the street from the agency. A sign in front of it said JESUS SAVES and underneath, in smaller type, told us that Tuesday-evening bingo would commence at six, with a grand prize of two hundred dollars, which I assume was the amount Jesus had saved.

There was still an hour before bingo, but we had company. The large square front lawn of the church was split equally in two by a path. Two little old ladies occupied one side of the lawn. They were the kind of comfortable old ladies with old-fashioned breasts like large loaves of unbaked bread, who filled out the rest of their flower-print dresses in the same doughlike manner, balancing rose-covered straw hats, brims the size of Australia, on their heads. In addition to these considerable feats they were gossiping at the speed of sound and setting up a table for cake and the makings of coffee at almost as great a rate.

Brad Pitt sniffed the air with joy. He took off at a gallop, a bulldog's version of a gallop, involving a torrent of drool. The leash jerked out of my hand, and, barking as though he'd discovered the promised land, Brad Pitt ran up the path. The church, it seemed, met with his approval as a urinal. I ran after him, catching up with him at the double front doors of the main building.

"Oh, God, why here? Do you have to pee on holy ground in front of the ladies' bingo committee?"

He lined himself up to christen the church steps. The ladies stopped arranging cupcakes on paper plates to point and shake their continent-sized headgear in disapproval. I picked up the end of the leash, giving it a tug.

"Don't pee on the church. Don't pee on the church. Please don't pee on the church."

To my amazement, Brad Pitt complied. He walked away from the stairs with great dignity, once again taking the leash out of my hands, and made his way to the flowerbeds at the side of the building, where he lifted a leg to piss on God's roses.

I threw an apologetic look at the little old ladies. They looked as if they'd like very much to take me behind the church and beat me up.

Praying for Brad Pitt to hurry up, I couldn't help but notice a man emerging from the church dragging a rectangular folding table behind him. When he had the table outside, he sent it clattering down to the bottom of the stairs with a shove. He followed slowly, step by step, and picked it up again before he became aware of me.

The man grinned at me as if he'd never have another chance to grin again. "What a day, huh? What a day?"

"It's some day, all right," I said.

"Makes you happy you're alive, don't it?"

I made a noise to indicate I didn't disagree with this statement in principle.

The man looked to be about a hundred and twenty-five years old and shuffled along, dragging the table, at the rate of twenty inches a minute. He was wheezing heavily and his face had turned the same shade as my nail polish, Starlet Scarlet. I estimated he had approximately thirty seconds to live.

I glanced at Brad Pitt, still watering the roses in what was shaping up to be a marathon pee. He was doing fine without my help. I couldn't say the same about the old man.

My heavy-lifting skills being less rusty than my resuscitation skills, I bent my knees and picked up the other end of the table as it inched by. The load lighter, the old man picked up the pace by a couple of yards per minute. Eventually we made it to the shade of a large tree in front of the church, as far away from the cake stall as you could be and still be on the lawn. Under the tree, several boxes were piled. I winced, imagining how long it must have taken for him to move them there.

When he turned around, the old man was surprised, but not unhappily so, to find me on the other end of the table. I helped to set the table up. We spread an old fitted sheet over it. He had carried it concealed inside the beige, zip-front jacket all men over seventy wear. The sheet was decorated with faded Winnie the Poohs dipping their paws into jars of honey, causing envy in an equal number of worn-out Piglets looking on. Although the breeze was moving slower than traffic on the freeway where the 10 feeds the 405 South, at the man's request I duct-taped the sheet to the table legs while he kept up a continual stream of bright conversation.

Brad Pitt, having finished sprinkling the roses, came over to see what I was doing on my hands and knees, and sniffed interestedly at the table legs, seeming quite put out that he had no urine left. He tried to eat some duct tape until a slight lift in the breeze alerted him that there was a vast amount of sugar and flour nearby. Immediately he trotted back to the church stairs and climbed to the top to survey the lay of the land.

"Have you seen it?" The old man was referring to a current film.

"No. Not yet."

"You'll love it."

"You seem to see a lot of films."

"I go to the movies all the time. On Tuesdays I go with my movie buddy, on Thursdays by myself, and on Sundays with my girlfriend. Thrillers and action on Tuesday, independent on Thursday, and whatever she wants on Sunday." He winked at me.

"Your girlfriend?"

He beamed pinkly and proudly. "Had the same one for sixty-five years."

"That's nice," I said, surprised to find I meant it.

"What about you? You got a fella?"

"No."

"Why not? Nice young girl like you? I bet there are a lot of young men keen on you? If I wasn't already spoken for, I'd take you out myself."

"I wouldn't be able to keep up with you," I said.

"Well, I keep in shape. I keep in shape."

This guy was definitely the survivor of something—of a stroke, cancer, a heart attack. He had that second-chance-at-life, every-day-is-a-bonus cheerfulness that I normally find annoying. Today I found it soothing.

I studied the beaming old man before me. Did he just decide one day that he was going to be happy for what was left of his life? Was it that easy? Were the rest of us just complicating everything? Missing the point?

He was unloading boxes, producing the usual garage-sale fare that provides proof beyond doubt that, no matter how we try to dress it up with more meaning, life is merely a series of bad purchasing decisions. Yet he was happy.

He fished out a nearly new teddy bear from a box. He sighed, losing a good deal of his aggressively chipper manner, though he was still brimming with joy compared to a normal person.

"Some little boy or girl . . . they probably begged their parents to buy this for them, probably gave them hell until they did . . . and now they don't want it anymore . . . now you can buy it for a quarter." He sat the bear carefully on the table so its feet dangled over the edge.

Out of the eye corner I was keeping on Brad Pitt, I saw he had abandoned his command position atop the stairs and was now making a wide circle around the ladies and cakes. The ladies, spilling over the edges of their folding beach chairs beside their table, were taking a break, as yet unaware of the advancing canine threat. It was time to get going. In five minutes I'd have to buy every cake the stall held.

Picking up an ornate teacup and saucer, the old man examined them closely before putting them down on the end of the table where the better junk was going.

"You know what the matter is with the world today?"

I have several hundred theories but I kept them to myself. "No, what?"

He spread his hands, indicating the flotsam and jetsam of people's lives that he was arranging on the table.

"Nobody values anything anymore. They buy, buy, buy, but it's just for the sake of buying. What do you expect? These days everything is for sale."

The guy had a point. And it was the same point I'd made with months of research. You can sell anything. But what did that prove exactly?

"I'm sorry," I said. "I missed what you said."

"I said: The best things in life are free, not because they aren't worth anything, but because you can't buy them with money."

I felt a sudden chill. I put my hands in my pockets to wrap my jacket around me. My right hand closed around a folded piece of paper. I pulled it out. It was a dollar bill. I unfolded it and looked into the solemn face of George Washington. The first president gave me an idea.

"Can I take the bear off your hands for a dollar?"

The grin to end all grins reappeared on the old man's face,

just before the first of the little old lady shrieks reached my ears. "Sure," he said. "You need a receipt?"

✟

Father Bernadi was an instant favorite of the local Ladies' Social Club. They regarded him as a hero without need of any special effort on his part. In the course of his usual late-afternoon stroll he merely reached out, grabbed Brad Pitt's leash, and became one.

True, he checked the dog just as Brad Pitt had been preparing to launch himself at the table holding cake and coffee for the evening's bingo enthusiasts, but I think it would be fair to say that had I been the one to get there first, had I been the leash grabber, the disaster averter, it wouldn't have resulted in quite so many dewy-eyed, gushing thanks, and certainly not as much free cake, if any.

A newly minted Congressional Medal of Honor winner could not have been made more of, even if he'd single-handedly subdued a misbehaving Middle Eastern nation and handed these ladies title deeds for oil wells liberated in their names.

I arrived on the scene with the same heroic intentions just a few seconds after the priest and received nothing but glowering looks, and those only when eyes could be spared from Father Bernadi who, after soothing the savage beast, also managed to convince Our Ladies of Cake to embrace the menace. It was settled within minutes. Beaming and blushing, the ladies were to watch Brad Pitt while the priest explored the church.

As his guest in his expedition, something that Father Bernadi quickly assured the women I would be, I was officially noticed and treated to smiles and floppy nods of their hats. Those same smiles, passable as friendly when pasted on the face of a respectable senior citizen in the light of day, would've sent me scurrying in the other direction if I'd encountered them in a dark alley. I knew to not push my luck. I stood silently by while Father Bernadi finished playing priest in shining armor.

After he politely refused four more offers of cake, I followed the priest into the church. There was something immediately familiar about the cool, dark, hush of the place. It occurred to me that all places of worship shared a similar stillness, no matter what the religion or denomination. God, it seems, is the universe's head librarian, shushing everyone who enters one of his houses.

Our peace lasted several seconds before it was shattered. An organist, unseen by us, began hammering out a series of pompous, wrathful chords, which I assumed formed a battering song of praise to the glory of God.

I stood in the aisle, flinching in time with the music, while the priest made a round of the room. I joined him when he'd chosen a pew to sit on.

"Not very catchy, is it?" I had to practically yell to make myself heard.

"Nice bear," Father Bernadi said. He didn't raise his voice, but somehow I heard him through the dissonant sounds made by the invisible organist.

I'd forgotten the teddy bear I was carrying in a headlock under my left arm. I sat it on the bench between us.

"I promised my neighbor's kid I'd get some toys. He was probably expecting something more sophisticated, but it'll give him something for his battle toys to maul and decapitate."

"A sacrificial bear?"

"Should you be in this church? Isn't it sort of like being unfaithful?"

"The ecumenical movement used to be quite strong in the Catholic Church. I am a practical rather than academic theologian. Ecumenicalism is easier for everyone. I stand by the one light, many lamps ideal."

"Except that what you're doing now isn't exactly going to foster a very ecumenical attitude, is it?"

Father Bernadi's undivided attention, when bestowed on me as it was then, makes me feel the need to explain myself, and I always become more loquacious than I plan to be.

"Well, once you start advertising," I said, "all the others will jump on the bandwagon and it's going to be a free-for-all. All of you out there claiming to be the One True Faith: It's hardly going to promote unity among the churches, is it?"

"Our mandate is to save only one Church."

"And in doing that you could seriously damage religion as a whole." My voice was beginning to get hoarse from yelling.

Father Bernadi waited for me to go on. I waited for the organist to finish a very loud passage in a particularly nasty hymn.

"It's like you said at that midlife crisis bar that night," I said. "Everyone is acquiring more and more stuff, yet they're more dissatisfied than ever. And things are getting worse.

"Our culture is becoming shallower. There's a kind of mindless greed in the choices we make. Nobody wants standard-issue American dream anymore. They want American dream Plus, Plus, Plus—bigger, better, more. Nothing they get will ever be enough.

"And people are willing to sacrifice everything else in their lives to make these purchases, even though anything we purchase is something that we'll replace as soon as they make a better model. That's the irony, we sacrifice things that can't be replaced—our time and personal relationships—for things that are easily replaceable, things we'll actually want to replace."

"You seem to be very lucid on this subject today," Father Bernadi said.

"The thing is, if you sell religion the way you sell everything else, it becomes a commodity. Faith becomes upgradeable and therefore disposable. Is that what you really want?"

"I'm curious. Why does it matter to you if religion becomes a commodity? You are not religious."

"You're right," I said. "I don't believe what you believe and I don't think I ever will. But it should matter to you. Consuming is about getting the goods, having the goods, then getting more, better goods. It is never about doing good. It's at odds with the spiritual values you believe in.

"Don't you see? If you advertise, people will rationalize their choice of religion the way they rationalize any purchase: What's in it for me? Correct me if I'm wrong, but I don't think this was quite the message Jesus was trying to pass on."

The hideous hymnal chords had stopped abruptly—apparently proving too much even for the organist—leaving me shouting over the silence in their wake. In the temporary void, I again felt the empty calm common to all places of worship. It was the emptiness not the calm I noted this time. Whatever people find in here must be whatever it is they bring in with them.

After a moment, a cheering rendition of Mancini's "Baby Elephant Walk" started up. The unexpectedness of the tune made me laugh out loud.

"You seem to be upset," Father Bernadi said.

"I'm not ups—" But I was upset. I shouldn't drink anything during the day; it makes me far too emotional. I shifted in my seat, wondering why they don't install comfortable seating in churches. Does God have something against upholstery? Are cushions the work of the devil? It was impossible to get cozy on the hard wooden pew. My new teddy bear, for one, looked decidedly unhappy. It was in the process of sliding off the bench. I reached out to straighten it up while the priest waited patiently for an answer. Around us the church was filling up fast with the happy noise of immature, ambulant elephants.

"I don't know," I said. "I guess . . . I guess that I don't think what we're doing is right."

Father Bernadi seemed to consider this for a moment. "Why is that?"

The priest was the gentlest interrogator I'd ever encountered, but the question made me a little angry. I poked at my bear, forcing it to sit up straighter.

"Because . . . because there has to be something that can't be bought or sold," I said.

The expression on Father Bernadi's face was enigmatic. He produced a real cloth handkerchief from a secret storage place on his immaculately tailored person and handed it to me. I stared stupidly at it until I realized he must've given it to me for a reason. I made a quick swipe across the moistness leaking onto my cheeks. The tears were a surprise. I hadn't had enough beer to be this emotional.

Having vented my feelings, I felt foolish. It was not an unreasonable feeling to entertain when you realize you've been preaching to a priest in a church. I looked to my teddy bear for a little solidarity. It stared straight ahead, pretending not to know me.

"What do I know?" I said. "I don't know anything." I gave the bear a prod in the head, more sharply than I'd intended. It flopped toward Father Bernadi. "I've only ever been to church to see what the bride wore."

The priest picked up my bear and placed it on the other side of him, safely out of my range. "A person's faith is not determined by where they sit for two hours a week," he said. "It is determined by what is most important to them. If that is money or power, I assure you they will never reach true understanding no matter how long they sit in church."

I remembered something I'd heard once about hospitals being full of sick people and churches being full of sinners. I decided this was not the time to bring that up.

"There are people who are capable only of believing what they were brought up to believe," Father Bernadi said. "You are not one of those people. There are also people who refuse to believe in anything. You think you are one of these people, but you are not."

"What do you mean?"

"There are people who believe only what they find agrees with their own reason and common sense, what they understand in their hearts. This, I think, is the only way for beliefs to be wise, for them to last. It is, of course, the hardest way, the bravest way, because sometimes you will be alone in what you believe—but it is also the best way. This is the way you are."

The organist switched from "Baby Elephant Walk" to the "Peter Gunn" theme, though this wasn't immediately obvious. We both stopped to listen until it dawned on us exactly what the organist was trying to play.

"You are a lot closer to understanding than you think," Father Bernadi said.

"I don't understand a thing."

"That is all you can understand," he said, looking more Sphinx-like than ever.

Dear God,

Please accept my resignation.

In spite of my general agnosticism, Dadaist tendencies, depression-induced bouts of mild nihilism, and general cynicism, I'm pretty sure that no one should be able to buy salvation in three easy payments of $49.99.

I no longer wish to work for you. I don't even know if I have been working for you. After all, you don't organize religions, people do. And they'll keep organizing them. Religions aren't static things. As the world changes, as people continue to change, religions will change too. Anyone who says otherwise is trying to sell something. I should know.

I don't know if it's an afterlife or another life, heaven or hell, nirvana or nothing that awaits us. I don't think anyone knows for sure.

As far as I can see only one thing is for certain: We all die. While I don't know if there's life after death, I do know there's life before death. And the only logical reason to be alive is to live. And that seems to be something I haven't been doing.

I've been working, forgetting all the other things that make up life, the things I'm supposed to be doing as well—eating, drinking, spending time with people I like, dancing, singing (but not so that anyone can hear), laughing, playing, and, at some stage, making something out of popsicle sticks. That's all going to change now.

Yours faithfully,

Sydney Welles

To cope with the stress and disappointment love and religion had introduced into my life, I'd taken to sitting on my front porch at the end of the day. A reckless choice of porches, as it leaves me in full view of Cupid's second-story bedroom window. More often than not—since he came back from his stay with his grandparents and his father came home from the hospital—Cupid comes to join me on the porch. We've settled into a kind of routine. What passes for civil conversation with Cupid always starts the same way.

"Why can't I have a beer?"

"Because."

"Because why?"

"Because if you do you'll stay the height you are now forever and your hair won't go curly anymore."

"Is that true?"

"I don't know. But I can't give you beer. You wouldn't like it anyway."

"How do you know?"

"I didn't like beer when I first tasted it. I still don't really."

"Why does everyone drink it?"

"It's just something you have to do when you're grown up. You're too short to understand. You can have juice or flavored milk. Those are your choices."

"I have no choices."

Cupid soon gives in to the inevitable and disappears into my house, returning with a nonalcoholic drink from the fridge, a straw from the top drawer, and a scrounged snack from the pantry. I frisk him to make sure he didn't get a beer after all, and we settle in for a chat until his mother wails for him to come inside. Most days, he unfailingly introduces a topic of conversation in some way painful for me.

"What happened to your boyfriend? Why doesn't he park his car here anymore?"

"He's . . . actually, I'm not exactly sure where he is."

"What'd you do?"

"What makes you think I did anything?"

Cupid raised a cynical and weary eyebrow. He'd seen it all before, it seemed, several times. "Cheese puff?" he said, holding out the bag.

"Where did you get those? I didn't know I had any."

"Behind the cans of tomatoes on the top shelf."

"How did you reach the top shelf—no, never mind, don't tell me. What I don't know your parents can't sue me for."

"What did you do?"

"I didn't do anything. He pretended to be someone he wasn't. No, actually, he pretended not to be someone he was—oh, never mind—the point is, it was his fault, okay?"

Cupid's face took on its dubious, one-eyebrow-lifted, Jedi master Yoda expression again.

"Okay, okay. It was my fault. It had nothing to do with who he was or wasn't. I just got scared."

"I get scared sometimes when I wake up in the middle of the night and I think there's something there in the dark."

"That would be scary."

"But I can turn on my lamp and see nothing's there."

"That's very brave and clever of you, but my situation is slightly more complicated than that." Or was it? "Anyway, what's the point of investing everything in one person? What if it doesn't work? What do you do then?"

"You have a do-over," he said. He inserted several cheese

puffs into his mouth, holding them all in his left cheek, where the collection formed a large irregular hump.

"How old are you?"

He filled his other cheek with cheese puffs before answering my question. His mouth was too full to speak, but he held up eight fingers when he spoke, making me afraid I'd end up with cheese puffs all over my porch, as it only left him with two fingers to hold onto the bag.

"I was being rhetorical." And he was lying. He was seven.

Cupid placed the bag next to his soda on the floor, raised his hands to his face, and squashed his cheeks flat, opening his mouth afterward to display the orange goo within.

"Gross," I said. That was the reaction he was after. I was rewarded with a very cheesy grin.

"Still gross."

"Are you going to get a new boyfriend?"

"No, I'm not going to get a new boyfriend—" Cupid's concern for my romantic welfare suddenly struck me as aberrant. Concern for anyone or anything is not normally a part of the demonic child's oeuvre.

"Why are you so worried about me?"

"I don't care. But Mommy does."

"Okay, why is your mother concerned about me?"

"She said that if you mess this one up, you'll never get married and move away. And we'll never get a nice family living across the street to fix up the house."

"I see."

"But she said it's okay for you to be my friend."

"She did?"

Cupid nodded. He was starting to refill his mouth.

"So we're friends."

"Yeah," he said. "But you're not my girlfriend or anything."

"Got it."

Cupid scanned my small front yard, paying particular attention to the bushes. "Did your rabbit come back yet?"

"No. I guess he's left me too. I'm not having much luck with bunnies or boyfriends."

"He'll come back." Cupid said. "Cheese puff?"

I resisted the temptation to ask Cupid whether he was referring to Jake or Harry Rex.

"A cheese puff isn't going to help me. Stop looking like a smug little Buddha over there. You don't have the answers either."

He came to sit beside me on the old wooden porch swing. It creaked in welcome. Cupid sipped on his straw, staring intently at the orange staining the sky as the sun committed suicide on jagged rooftops.

"They're in the back of the book," he said.

"What are in the back of the book?"

"The answers. You're not supposed to look at them. Not until you've tried to figure it out yourself first."

Below the rooftop horizon, the sun's power dimmed. Darkness would soon swaddle us, but in the intermission between day and night all glowed amber, and all was tranquil. The peace would be broken soon enough. By Cupid's mother telling him, and the rest of the street, it was time for his bath.

"Your schoolyard philosophy is surprisingly profound," I said, "but sometimes life just goes to sh—crap. Things are more complicated when you're grown up. There's no book with answers in the back. And questions don't have one right answer. They have lots of answers or no answer at all. Or else the right answer is staring you in the face, but it's of no use until you can figure out what question to ask."

Cupid sucked the last moisture from the orange soda can, making a horrendous noise.

"You can say 'shit.' I won't tell."

"Why am I having this conversation with you? You're seven. How could you possibly understand what I want out of life?"

He closed one eye to peer into his soda can, to make absolutely sure it was empty. "All I want is someone to sit with at lunchtime—no matter what. Even if Mommy makes me wear those stupid, orange-stripey pants."

Maybe he did understand. "Yeah," I said. "Me, too."

Cupid was clearly a genius.

"And I want to be sixteen."

Or maybe he was just a boy.

"No, you don't. Virtually all sixteen-year-old boys are idiots. I remember. That's when hormones take over and you can no longer use your brain to do anything but think about sex, and it doesn't stop until you're . . . actually, I don't think it ever stops. Enjoy being a preteen while you still can."

Cupid placed the can on the floor and picked up the cheese puffs. He picked out a smallish one and stuffed it up his right nostril. Then, with surprising precision, blocked his left nostril with a finger and blew the cheese puff back into the bag.

"Cheese puff?" he said, shoving the open bag within inches of my nose.

His eyes rounded, innocently enough, but I thought I caught the hint of a challenge in their blue porcelain perfection. It also could have been just a reflection from the last throes of the dying light. I wondered if he was trying to tell me something important. Then I wondered why I imagined a seven-year-old had anything important to say to me. Before I had an answer, the sun snuffed out, and Cupid's mother began bellowing for him to come inside.

From: Sydney Welles <s.welles@fbmm.com>
To: God c/o info@godmademedoit.net
Date: Thursday, November 17, 2005 9:25 AM PDT
Subject: Of Priests and Men

Dear God,

I spoke to Father Bernadi about resigning and he was, as to be expected, very understanding about the whole thing, going so far as to agree with me that perhaps advertising may not be the answer to the Church's problems.

It seems to be just more bureaucratic handling of the situation. When what really needs to happen is an internal change in the Church. I, for one, think you have to ease up the attitude on divorce, contraception, gays, and women if you want to attract the masses. I also think you ought to allow Catholic priests to marry.

There are forty-eight thousand Catholic priests in the country. Trust me, forty-eight thousand men who believe in marriage and who've had practice at not screwing around would be a welcome addition to the dating world for single women everywhere.

Syd x

My exit interview with Larry had been a remarkably civilized affair, conducted in his office over three rounds of gin and tonic divided unequally between us. I had half one gin and tonic. Larry had five and a half. He no longer needed to be sober now the Church account was secured.

"So you're not pregnant?"

"No," I said.

"Dying?"

"Only at the same rate as everyone else."

"So that stuff about taking six months off to work out what you want from life is true, then?"

"It's true."

"Well, good luck. You'll need it."

"Thank you for taking it all so well," I said.

"Nothing to thank me for. This is a very stupid business with no redeeming qualities other than a few good laughs and sex with nice people. But the laughs are getting fewer and farther between. As for the sex—you don't even get to see anybody naked these days. I saw everybody naked back when streaking at parties was the thing to do. Whatever happened to streaking?

"Nobody drinks martinis at lunch or throws parties in their hot tubs or has sex on the boardroom table anymore—or if they do, they do it with a person they're allowed to have sex with, not someone completely inappropriate—what's the point?

"It's all been downhill since the end of the eighties. Why stick around if it's no fun? None of this is important. Not in the grand scheme of things. In the grand scheme there's only one thing that matters. If I could remember what it was, I'd tell you."

"Why do you stick around?"

"Me? This is my life. I didn't expect to live this long and now I'm too old to change. You're not. Go fucking forth; find yourself. Find a new career if you have to. Have a life. Have babies—but don't bring the shitty little things in to see me. Come in for lunch anytime without them. And come back to work anytime you want. The door will always be open, any office in the network, anywhere in the world, as long as my liver holds out."

"Thank you. I appreciate that."

"Gives you something to fall back on if you wake up one morning and discover leaving here was the greatest mistake of your life."

"Thanks, I'll keep it in mind. Well, good luck with the Catholics."

"Don't worry, if the Catholics don't pan out, the Mormons are ready and waiting."

"You're kidding?"

"Nope. Not kidding. It makes more sense for them to advertise than anyone else. No chance of advertising trivializing that religious experience. They did that themselves. They're a religion founded on a book someone found and claimed was the lost book of Abraham or some such biblical personage, which—since they can now read hieroglyphics—is apparently only some ancient laundry list. It's a religion based on a meaningless text, and yet it's the fastest growing religion in the country. You can't get better than that. They've had a publicity department since the thirties. They have an unpaid army of door-to-door salesmen. They're all on Prozac, and they're all-American. Best of all, everybody ends up a Mormon."

"What do you mean?"

"They convert you once you're dead. They convert everyone. Popes, presidents, prostitutes, everyone."

"Are they allowed to do that?"

"Whether they are or not, they do it. That has to be the supreme irony of life. We think we have free will and independent thought, but the one inescapable truth of life is we're all going to be Mormons sooner or later."

✝

Noah was waiting for me in the parking lot on my way out. In a way more awkward than usual, he handed me a parcel. Inside was a black, girl-shaped T-shirt in my size. It said: FRIENDS DON'T LET FRIENDS HAVE MULLETS.

"It's sentimental, but . . ."

"Thank you," I said. I gave him a hug.

"In theory," he said, "you're still my boss, so that was sexual harassment."

"So sue me. You're coming to the party?"

"Are you kidding? Larry said the agency is going to pay. Of course I'm coming. Everybody is coming. It's free."

"You're a true friend."

"Leave before I have you thrown out by security."

"I'll miss you too," I said.

"Hey, you'll never guess who Julie is seeing, as of last Friday night."

"Okay, who?"

"Patton."

"No," I said. "No."

"Afraid so. And it looks like true love."

"What does true love look like?"

Noah shrugged. "I don't know; it's one of those things. You know it when you see it."

"I guess I'll have to see it, then. You going to stay on?"

"For a few months. There's that new assistant they've hired for Julie—I feel I should stick around long enough to get to know her. Then I think it may be time to go back to academia. Finish my dissertation—well, first, start my dissertation—and give my mother the opportunity to say, 'My son, the professor,' at least once before she falls off the mortal coil. It's your fault. You've inspired me. If you can leave a good job with no idea what you're going to be next—except poor—I can leave a mediocre job to live off my trust fund."

"I don't know what to say," I said.

I drove home from what was to be, for the time being at least, my last day on the job. I was still amazed at how easy it was to walk away. Somehow that made it easier to think of going back as a possibility—one of many possibilities. Ironically, I'd quit my job, and instead of my world coming to an end, my life was full of possibilities that weren't there before. I could do anything—except perhaps get my head around Julie and Patton.

Pondering the possibility of true love between them, I missed the turn I was supposed to make off Washington Place. I found myself having to pick my way home, slowly, through a maze of backstreets.

On one of these streets I saw him, and, of course, when I saw him I couldn't help but pull over and get out of the car.

There he was, after all this time. And he looked exactly the same as when I'd seen him last. As sorry a creature as I'd ever laid eyes on.

My Harry Rex.

He was sitting on the well-kept lawn of a blue weatherboard house. And he was in love—completely besotted. Noah was right; you do know it when you see it, although in this case it was obviously unrequited.

She was the kind of bunny they put in the pet store window along with the puppies and kittens to lure you in. Petite and honey-colored, with large melted-chocolate eyes and soft, soft fur, she was quite possibly the most beautiful rabbit I'd ever seen.

Her cage was formed simply. A sheet of chicken coop wire about four feet high had been curved around and joined in a circle and placed on the grass. The top of the cage was left open. Though separated from her by the wire, Harry Rex's passion did not seem to be dampened by the impossibility of physical contact.

He ignored me. Ignored my pleading with him. Ignored my promises of a nice, new bunny hutch, squeaky toys, and as many pieces of toast as he could eat. I did not get a flicker of his attention until I found a chocolate bar in my purse.

Harry Rex turned when he heard the rustling of the wrapper. I broke off a piece and placed it on the ground in front of him, then took a couple of steps backward. I figured he could be lured into the car by chocolate. After all, the same principle had worked on E.T., who was a far more sophisticated life-form.

Harry Rex hopped over to the piece of chocolate, sniffed it, and looked at me before picking it up in his mouth. He turned and hopped back to the cage, where he pushed it through the chicken wire. He did exactly the same with the rest of the chocolate bar, piece by piece, giving it all up for love. The object of that love, it must be said, scarfed down the candy as fast as he could bring it to her, doing so without any delicacy.

Once he was sure there was no more chocolate to be had, Harry Rex went back to ignoring me, mesmerized once again by the chocolate hog in the cage. I could see there was no way I could convince him to come with me willingly. He was giving up the promise of a cushy life to live on the outside of this girl rabbit's cage, when it was clear she wasn't the least bit interested in him.

Love sure does make you stupid.

"I'll come back and visit you," I said. "I'll bring more chocolate." I figured I could at least help him win over his girlfriend. "Maybe some M&Ms?"

Harry Rex didn't even blink.

"Okay, I'm going now," I said. "Bye."

I turned back to take a final look at them. For a creature pining away from unrequited love, Harry Rex seemed remarkably content.

I sat in the car and watched them for a while. Somewhere nearby, someone was playing the Beatles. They had gone from being back in the USSR to proclaiming that all you need is love. Popular music is full of rotten romantic advice.

As I continued to watch Harry Rex and his lady bunny friend, a new thought occurred to me. Maybe my rabbit wasn't quite right in his rabbit head, but if a beat-up old street bunny could believe in it, maybe love was grand after all.

Dear God,

Jesus said, "Love each other, as I loved you." He did not say, "Call now. Sign up today. Believe in me and only me and pay the fees in full, or you won't get into the good heaven." That was some other guy on TV.

I'm with Jesus on this one. I'm beginning to believe that love is as good a reason for living as we'll ever find. Love, unconditional, brotherly, or otherwise, is the one thing every major religion preaches--once you get past their advertised differences and unique selling points.

Love conquers all, love makes the world go round, love is in the air, love is all around us and love is all you need.

Love is the answer.

Only problem is nobody knows what the question is.

Love,

Syd

Charles Turner
22 Indiana Avenue, #1
Venice, CA 90291

November 25, 2005

Dear Charles,

In spite of the obvious drawbacks of your personality, I like you a great deal. For a while there, I even imagined myself in love with you. Of course, I'm not in love with you and never was.

You can't be in love with someone you've never met. That only works in Hollywood romantic comedies, and then only very badly. In real life, love is more than just a meeting of minds; other body parts have to meet too.

However, I am in love. When I realized it—or rather, admitted it to myself—it scared me a little. Scared the crap out of me, actually. I behaved badly and may have messed things up beyond repair. But I've been trying to get my shit together and all I can do is hope that he will give me another chance.

I have my doubts, but Anna assures me that everything will be fine. She called me from her honeymoon in Spain to tell me this. She says men are stupid like that, and all I have to do is show up wearing something short or tight, and tell him he was right about everything whether he was or not. Then again, this is a woman who thinks any relationship issue can be solved with a well-timed blow job. Actually, Anna could be right about that one.

What do you think my chances are?

Yours, Sydney

P.S. By the way, if things don't work out with Jake, I'll give you a call.

Once I'd mailed the last letter I'd ever write to Charles, I called my parents and, after managing to calm them down—it wasn't my designated day for calling, so they assumed the sky had fallen—I proceeded to bring them up to date on my life. Needless to say, there were still parts I left out for their own good, but the whole exercise was far less painful than I'd anticipated.

My mother was a little upset to find out I was no longer dating Matt—she watches his soap—but was interested in Anna's nuptials and in both Charles and Jake. She thought they were two different people and nothing I told her could convince her otherwise. That's my mother: you can't give her too much information—or too much wine—all at once and expect her to keep facts straight.

My father didn't balk at my newly unemployed state. He had no career advice to offer—he still has no idea what exactly it is I do when I am employed—but he went so far as to say that I must know what I was doing, and only asked if I needed money once. He had a lot to say, however, on the subject of God and religion—so much that I had to distract him with the promise of a visit at the end of the month to be able to get off the phone.

Both my parents asked me if I'd spoken to my sister. I said I had, so I had to call her too. Buoyed by the relative success of those calls, I made a few more calls and as a result found myself, several days later, arriving home early one evening laden with enough food to throw a dinner party for six. There was good reason for that. The next evening I was throwing a dinner party for six. Now I have time to talk to people again,

I find that I still have a lot of friends. I'll need to throw several more dinners just to feed them all.

I'd also bought some cheesy snacks and fruit juice for Cupid. I was a little disappointed not to find him awaiting me on my porch. His company at the end of the day was something, I realized with mild horror, I now looked forward to. Afraid that I'd miss him if I took the groceries inside, I left them at my feet on the porch while I scanned the street for him.

I didn't have to wait long. Though technically it was Jake, not Cupid, who showed up first. His car pulled up in front of my house. The passenger door opened and Cupid hopped out.

The only thing not astonishing about the situation was that Cupid, once he spotted me, gave me the finger before scurrying across to his side of the street.

Jake got out of the car and after briefly glancing at me—standing on my porch with my mouth hanging attractively open—turned to Cupid, who'd stationed himself on the curb in front of his gate. Cupid waved at me from there, indicating he had to go inside.

Jake said something to Cupid I didn't catch. Cupid nodded.

"Okay," Jake said. He turned back to me. I was still standing on the porch, still wondering at the little scene that had been enacted before me, but at least now I'd managed to close my mouth.

As Jake started toward me, my heartbeat became erratic, my throat tightened, my breath got shorter, and my limbs felt paralyzed. If this was love, it was very similar to the onset of a panic attack. What if he'd received my letter and had come to tell me he didn't share my feelings? What if he'd received my letter and had come to tell me he did share my feelings? What if he hadn't received my letter? What if I really was having a panic attack?

Not being able to look him in the eye, I focused on his feet.

As he climbed over the garden gate—it was still stuck—I noticed his socks didn't match. This, for some reason, made me feel better. I forced myself to take deep breaths. I was going to be cool, calm, collected. I wasn't going to ask about the letter. I'd wait for him to introduce the subject. I was not going to ask. I was not going to ask.

"Did you get my letter?" I wasn't certain whether or not I'd said that out loud.

Jake was smiling but he was smiling the kind of smile that has its hands hidden deep in its pockets. I couldn't tell if it was friend or foe, but I tentatively returned it.

"I had an interesting meeting with my financial advisor today."

That wasn't quite what I'd expected him to say.

"You have a financial advisor? Oh, stupid question. You obviously do, as you met with him today."

"Her. I met with her today."

Little warning bells went off in my head. I had no idea why. "The meeting went well?"

He nodded. "Except that she's under the impression I'm gay."

The world is an unconscionably small place that is good to Jake and wicked to me.

"She is? That's interesting. You know, I wasn't going to say anything, but now that you've brought it up, I may as well just come out with it. It's that shirt you're wearing. It's kind of, well, lilac. Don't get me wrong. I like it. But people jump to conclusions so easily. Personally, I think it's great that you're confident enough in your masculinity to wear a shirt that color. Really great . . . really . . ."

"Brigid mentioned she had a very reliable source. You, in fact."

"Oh." Shit.

"Why are you telling everyone I'm gay?"

I was stupid. I was jealous. I was a bridesmaid. Chief bridesmaid, a C-level job—the pressure got to me.

"I'm not telling everyone you're gay. I only told Brigid. It must have been Brigid who told everyone else. No discretion at all, that girl. Are you sure you want her taking care of your money?"

"She offered to set me up with someone. She said she's told him all about me and he's really looking forward to meeting me."

"Of course he is. Any guy would be lucky to get you."

"Thanks."

"Do you know what I think? I think a healthy disregard for gender stereotypes is extremely sexy in a man."

"Do you?"

"I was only trying to protect you. Anna's got this whole raft of cousins, all predatory redheads. At the hen's night, no penis within a half-mile radius was safe. And you'd just broken up with someone: me. You were vulnerable—"

"I think you were jealous."

"Was not."

"There's a grown-up answer."

I tried to think of a grown-up answer.

"Don't worry about it," Jake said. "Brigid also asked me if it'd be a good idea to introduce you to someone—one of her ex-boyfriends. There's one—out of several hundred—she thinks you'll like. I said to be sure to tell him you had syphilis."

"You what?"

He smiled modestly. "Let's call it even."

"Syphilis is so nineteenth century."

"It's making a comeback." Jake stepped up onto the porch and examined the contents of the three grocery bags sitting on it before he settled himself on the porch swing.

I knew then that everything was going to be fine. I sat beside him.

"There's something I have to tell you," he said.

Then again, maybe I was wrong about everything being fine. I braced myself. "Okay."

"A couple of weeks ago, I accepted a new assignment."

"Okay." So far, this was not so bad.

"It requires me to relocate to Manhattan for a year."

"Oh." It was bad.

Jake's eyes told me that what he was going to say next was difficult for him to put into words. I hoped he wasn't going to tell me he and New York City's other recent acquisition were getting back together.

"I don't suppose there's any way you'd come?"

"You mean to visit?"

"No, I mean come with me."

"Come to New York with you? For the whole twelve months?"

"That's the general idea."

"You want me to quit my job, leave my home, my friends, my life, the right to turn right on a red light, and this excellent climate, solely so you have company while you do your job on the other side of the country?"

"Yes," he said.

"If things don't work out?"

"They'll work out."

"You're asking me to give up my life for you."

"It's a big decision, I know. You don't have to decide anything right this—"

"I'd love to go," I said. "Thank you."

Jake seemed a little thrown by my answer. But when it sank in, he had a smile for me, a smile worth moving across the country for—not literally, of course.

"Are you saying yes?"

I was surprised at how easy it was to say, "Yes."

Jake seemed to consider me from all angles. "In that case, it's up to you whether we go or stay."

"I don't understand."

"If you'll move for me, I'll stay for you, if that's what you want."

"You will? Really?" Maybe this relationship business wasn't as hard as I thought it was. "That's very equal of you. But I think I'd like to go."

Jake reached out with his foot and tapped one of the grocery bags.

"If you're going to cook me dinner, shouldn't you invite me in?"

"You're pretty confident for a guy wearing odd socks. Are you sure you want to come in? I have syphilis."

Judging by the way he kissed me, he was sure.

"What was that about?" I pointed at Cupid, who was still standing across the street, watching us. "Why was Freddy Krueger Junior in your car?"

"I found him wandering around outside my house when I got home. He was lost. He recognized me as your friend and asked me to bring him home. It was as good an excuse as any to see you, after I got that letter begging me to take you back."

"I didn't actually beg—Cupid was lost?"

"Yes."

"He knows his way around this neighborhood better than anyone."

Jake shrugged. "Must've gotten disoriented—it's getting dark. He's only what? Six? Good little kid."

"Is it possible we're talking about the same child?"

I stood, unlocked my front door, and pushed it open. Jake picked up two of the grocery bags and walked inside as if it were a perfectly natural thing for him to do.

Across the street, Cupid stooped to pick up something. There wasn't a lot of light left, but I could see it was a small animal he was holding, a small animal with rabbit-shaped ears. Cupid and the critter he carried seemed to be on good terms. He was petting it, and I could hear he was talking to it, but not what he was saying.

"Are you going to stand out there all night?"

I picked up the remaining bag and turned to the house.

"I'm coming," I said, but I paused to look back across the street and wave good night to Cupid. He and his bunny-shaped bundle were gone, his tall front gate closed.

I'd have to give him the fifty bucks we'd agreed on tomorrow.

Dear God,

I've finally figured out that we are never going to figure it out.

Arguing over why we're here is a waste of time. If you had intended us to solve the mystery of existence, you'd have made us a lot smarter.

Hey, the only reason I even know what the Greatest Mystery of Existence is is because Larry told me. Of course, once he did tell me, it made perfect sense.

He found out ten years ago while having dinner in Paris. Larry described his meal as a healthy portion of a cud-chewing mammal that, conveniently for the chef, had met its end by drowning in a rich cream sauce.

At the next table was an old man, also dining alone, who was both Portuguese and a marine biologist. He always ordered the stuffed cabbage, every time he dined at this bistro, every time he found himself in Paris. He had just turned seventy-five when Larry met him and could tell Larry which of the bistro's waitresses he'd tried to sleep with forty years ago.

Larry, when deep in his cups, sometimes wonders out loud if the marine biologist is still alive. Still studying a strange and wonderful fish covered in taste buds, which stands on the bottom of the ocean on three fins, tripodlike, finding its way around in the complete darkness by tasting the water. Still traveling the world and telling anyone who would listen, over red wine and stuffed cabbage, what was ruining the world: large corporations with no value for nature or human life. And still regretful there was so much yet to be discovered, so much he did not know, both twenty thousand leagues under the sea and on dry land.

It wasn't until dinner was over, when their respective bills had arrived and Larry asked him how much would be appropriate to leave as a tip, that the old Portuguese marine biologist told Larry what Larry told me.

"The greatest mystery of existence," he'd said as he adjusted his glasses to examine his bill, "is how much to tip where."

It's true. If you can figure that out, the rest of life is easy.

Sydney Welles

P.S. See you in about 47 years, if it's true the average life expectancy for a person living in the U.S. is 77.1 years, and if you exist, and if I'm good.

Acknowledgments

Thank you to Adele Lang and Tim Hallinan for helping me to start; Linda Hobrock for getting me through; and Kim Witherspoon, David Forrer, and Lindsay Sagnette for a very happy ending. Many thanks, too, to Araminta Whitley, for giving me Kim and David and to Rebecca Watson for giving me Araminta. And I'm also grateful to Andreas Smetana for being the world's best photographer, the Ladies Libation League (Culver City Chapter) for the cocktails, and Corey Mitchell for denying me the literary experience of starving in a garret.

A Note on the Author

Susi Rajah trained as an art director and worked in advertising until she was fed up enough to attempt a novel. She is the coauthor of two serious nonfiction books, one of which is *How to Spot a Bastard by His Star Sign*. Susi wrote this novel in Los Angeles but has since moved to New York City, where she lives with her first husband. She likes people who buy her cocktails, plane tickets, and Manhattan real estate.

A Note on the Author